GOOD MAN
gone

PETER MCPHIE

PUBLISHER: COLONSAY CORPORATION
CONTACT: www.petermcphie.com
Good Man Gone/Peter McPhie—1st edition
ISBN 978-0-9952877-2-3 (Paperback)
ISBN 978-0-9952877-3-0 (e-book)
VISIT www.petermcphie.com

For Helga

CHAPTER 1

NOW

It's not every day that a good man sets a killing in motion. But sometimes in a life there are desperate times and those times can be answered only with desperate measures.

So it was with Chester Carter.

Thirty-four, of middling looks, six feet and strong, Chester had always been a shy man. He had never been a rebel, had always believed in order and rules in even everyday things like not trying to get ahead of someone in a line. So until recently, the idea of a killing was as far from his mind as the planet Pluto.

But things had profoundly changed him inside, emboldened him in a way that would greatly surprise others; it most certainly surprised him. He thought that maybe he was always like that but that life had just never called upon him. Maybe you don't know yourself until it does and puts you to the test.

Chester knew, as anyone would, that if you're going to set a killing in motion, it's much better if no one knows it's you who's behind it. That was why he sent a small sealed packet by cab to the Hotel Albert to 'Mr. Clyne, personal and confidential', which contained $500 in twenties and a note that Chester had revised eight times that said, 'I need you to put me in touch with a guy who can do the end-of-the-line thing to one person. The guy can't be from Columbus, better north. The job's not around here either. You have to vouch for the guy, no blowback. I don't need a name, just a phone number. The $500 is good faith. I will telephone you in two days. Ken.'

Clyne, who wore many gold rings on fat fingers, lived at the Hotel Albert, an establishment once majestic, now seedy and unrepentant. In the underworld of Columbus and locales beyond, Clyne knew people. If you needed to acquire something illegal, or needed something really done to someone, Clyne was the go-to. But only the go-to. Never the do. Never those fat fingers dirty. He just knew the people you needed to know.

Two days after he sent the packet, Chester entered a phone booth and called the hotel and got Clyne's 'assistant', who said to send another $1,500, which Chester did. He was given another number to call, this one long distance.

A young woman answered and said, "The man you need wants $2,000 to talk. You deliver it in Detroit to Chantelle. She runs Huey's Big Laundromat. Put the money in an envelope and put on it, 'from Ken'".

"Then what?"

"Chantelle gives you an envelope."

The next day, wearing a low hat and wide dark sunglasses, Chester walked by the Laundromat twice. The first time, he saw a formidable-looking Asian woman whom he took to be Chantelle standing behind a counter looking ill-tempered and making change. The second time, she was banging on a dryer to make it go.

He found a cab two blocks over. He gave the cabbie a packet with instructions to give it to Chantelle and to bring back the envelope she would give him.

The envelope Chester got back contained only a small piece of paper with a penciled phone number. When Chester called it, the voice he heard was gravelly, maybe conditioned by a pack a day.

"So, it's Ken, is it?" the voice said.

"Yes, it's Ken," Chester said.

"I'm Roly. What is it you want exactly?"

Chester felt his nerves lashing him like a whip, having never talked to a cold killer for hire. "A hit," he said.

"That's pretty rough talk, Ken. Let's just call it an arrangement." Roly's voice was calm. "So, tell me about it."

"It's a woman from Ohio. But she'll be at a cottage in Ontario," Chester said.

Roly didn't answer quickly. "Like where in Ontario? It's a big place."

"A couple of hours north of Toronto. So about six hours from Detroit, depending on traffic."

"Is this your wife?"

Gee, Chester thought, does the wife thing happen that often that Roly could jump to that conclusion so fast? But Chester had reasons not to want to give it away, and had prepared. "No. A friend's friend."

"Some friend."

Chester forced himself to sound relaxed. "Well you know how it is. Love off the rails."

"Sometimes I know how it is. Mostly I don't want to know how it is." Roly paused. "You're the one talking to me, to keep suspicion away from the friend."

"That's it exactly. We're working together." Chester felt a knot bunching in his throat. "So, here's the thing, you have to use a tie, a silk-tie. No gun."

"*Strangulation?* What the hell for?"

Chester had expected this part wouldn't go well. "It just has to be that way, that's all. Non-negotiable. But think, no gun noise, no bullet, no blood, less forensic evidence. Cleaner."

"Ken," Roly's voice was loud, and he said 'Ken' in a way that said he was mighty put out by being told obvious things when *he* was the professional. "I know a thing or two. I watch television, too. And what's with silk? Less fibers?"

"That's it exactly."

Roly was quiet for a time. "Nobody said anything about strangulation." His voice was calm again, business-like. "There was no stipulation. That really changes things."

"What do you mean?" Chester said, as if he didn't know.

"What do *you* mean?" Roly was loud again. "Strangulation is ten times different from a scoped rifle at two hundred yards. Puts you damn close to the scene."

"Are you saying it's off? Or changes the price?"

"It sure as hell changes the price."

There was a long silence and Chester wondered whether he was expected to say something. But then Roly said, "Tell me more."

"So, she's twenty-nine, and very attractive..." Chester's voice trailed off.

Roly waited a moment for more information, but it didn't come. "You're not setting me up with a date. I already assumed she wasn't somebody's grandmother. Tell me something actually useful. Like is she big? Strong? Fast? Knows martial arts? I'm only working with a fucking silk-tie remember."

"No martial arts. Five-five, a hundred and twenty, pretty good fitness. But not stronger than you would expect."

"People are always a lot stronger than you would expect when they're being strangled to death. But I already know to expect that. Tell me about the cottage set up."

"The neighbors, since it's all cottages, aren't there most times."

"Most times? I've been around the block enough times to know that just when I'm doing it, neighbors will show up." He was chafing, edge in his voice. "Let's just pretend they *are* there. We're talking strangulation in a cottage, probably open windows, thin walls, neighbors, people likely on the lake."

"The neighbors aren't that close. And even if they are there, they can't see the cottage."

"But can they see the property? I have to cross the property to get to the cottage. I don't come in from the sky like Santa Claus."

Chester felt Roly's impatience. But the guy was thorough, which was good. But it might also be bad, if things didn't go right. He began to feel nervous about dealing with Roly. Maybe he was in over his head. But he said, "Ya, you're right. Neighbors can't see the cottage but can see a good bit of the property."

"Like I said." Roly seemed to be lighting a cigarette, a flick of a rasp on a lighter, a snap of metal, a sudden suck of air. "I assume the woman will be alone? I don't need a whole tie rack?"

"She'll be alone."

"Where is the property exactly? I'll want to check it out first."

"I can't tell you yet. You only find out the day before the job.

That's the way I want it. Take it or leave it. Non-negotiable."

Chester had expected the real resistance would happen right here. Roly was quiet for what seemed a long time. He heard Roly finally exhale, a long, drawn out exhale, like a full cloud of smoke filled with considerations.

"I've got to protect myself," Chester said.

"Like I don't? It's a two-way street," Roly said. "You know the price is climbing."

"I understand. But I can tell you things. You can get at the property by canoe on the side away from the neighbors. Nobody will hear you."

"Oh, that's *good*." The sarcasm was dripping. "I make my getaway in a canoe. Look, I'm from Detroit, not Minnesota. I've never been near a canoe. I want 450 horses at my disposal, not a fucking paddle."

"But the road to the cottage is miles long, a slow, narrow, gravel road, only traveled by quiet cottagers. A muscle car would stand out like neon lights."

"See. That's why I want to case the place first. See what's going to work. And not a fucking canoe."

"There's fishing boats you could rent. I think your best bet is by water. In and out like nothing unusual."

Roly was inhaling again, working the tobacco, a whistle through the teeth. "Look, I make those decisions based on what I see, or I don't do it. Take it or leave it. Non-negotiable."

Again, Chester had anticipated the objection. "What about this? I tell you the lake, but not the specific cottage. You can scout the area out, take a week beforehand."

Chester had another reason for wanting Roly in that area for many days before the hit. It might seem to the police less like a directed hit and more like a random attack, him staying in motels for days and such.

"How big is the lake?" Roly asked.

"I don't know, maybe three miles long, a mile wide. Lots of coves and inlets."

"What's an inlet?"

"Where the shore is dented in. Where you can't be seen as easy."

"How many cottages?"

"I don't know, maybe a hundred and fifty."

Roly thought for a while. "I'm not going to be hung out to dry. If I don't like the set up when I get to see it, I don't do it."

Down to brass tacks. "So what's the price?" Chester asked.

"Fifty."

"Whoa. A lot of money. No can do."

"Strangulation of someone you've never seen, in their cottage, with no real chance to case it, where there's likely neighbors, where your getaway is a boat on an open fucking lake in tourist season? Inlets or not. Check out the black book. Keep it apples to apples."

Chester was still thinking when Roly said, "I'd go forty-five if you get me a picture of her and tell me exactly what cottage we're talking about three days ahead of time."

"No." Chester was firm. "The day before or not at all."

"You're keeping your cards close. You've got your reasons. I just wonder what they are."

Chester certainly did have his reasons and certainly didn't want to share them. "If my friend decides he wants to call it off anytime up to a day before, he doesn't want anything of this to trace back to him. Or to me. It's the way it has to be."

"You'll pay the fifty then?"

"I'll pay the fifty."

Roly took a long drag and a long exhale. "When's this got to happen?"

"The week starting the 8th of July. Three weeks from now."

"So, what's this lake called?"

"Ring Lake."

"Ring? Like a bell?"

"Ya. Or like a wedding." A pause, then Chester said, "It's in what they call 'cottage country', lots and lots of lakes, two hours north of Toronto."

"So, I want another $8,000, paid like before through Chantelle at the laundry. Puts you ten grand in with me. Shows me you're serious. Covers expenses to reconnoiter the area beforehand. Maybe buys me some canoe lessons."

Chester almost smiled. He was warming to Roly, but that was not a good thing, not in the least, not with what was coming.

CHAPTER 2

BEFORE

The Chester who was setting a killing in motion was a whole lot different from the Chester of six years earlier.

Six years earlier Chester sat down at a table at the outdoor patio of a home-style restaurant outside of Columbus for just a coffee and a piece of pie. But he bit into a lot more than that.

He always noticed the waitresses, but not like a wolf or anything. He had always been shy, particularly around women, and more particularly around attractive women, although at six feet and strong and of average looks, there was no ready explanation for his shyness, even to himself. He just was, and most times, with women, it paralyzed him, and he knew that was not a particularly attractive feature.

But the waitresses there were always friendly to him, and he to them, in a shy sort of way. He always tipped extra.

He knew all the waitresses. But he had never seen *her* before. She walked by him to serve a customer chicken fingers and fries with gravy two tables over. She was so beautiful he wondered afterwards how he had even noticed what food she was carrying.

He worried she might be the one serving him. She would come over and he would freeze up. She would give him the once-over glance then dismiss him in her mind as she took his order. He hoped one of the other waitresses who already knew him would come by instead and he would enjoy a word of friendly conversation.

What was she doing in this place? She could be a model or a receptionist in a high-class hotel or any number of better things than a waitress at a home-style diner.

She walked over to him. "Hi," she said. "It's a real warm one today."

She was looking at him, smiling, in no hurry, making conversation, not going straight to the order. Her voice was liquid honey and it caused a sensation in him he couldn't describe to himself even later. He couldn't say 'coffee and cherry pie' because that was too many words and because she was looking at him, her eyes soft and smiling.

'Coffee,' he said.

She hadn't even asked for his order.

"Thank you. I'll be right back," she said so pleasantly and with a natural smile.

He didn't want the moment to go, the moment when he was all she was looking at, in no hurry to do anything else, as if she enjoyed it. It touched him like a magic-spell and he was now in a trance, his whole being stilled. He didn't want to move a single muscle lest the feeling disappear.

She was back with his coffee. His senses were alive, his eyes following the cup and saucer placed so delicately by her sculptured hand, a tinkle of the spoon on the saucer, the coffee lapping in the cup when her beautiful hand released the saucer to the table. He was reluctant to look up at her face because she might not look at him the same as she did before and it would all be over.

His eyes looked only at his coffee.

Her voice spoke. "I saw you're driving that really heavy looking truck. Specialty Tools Works."

His mind whirled. She was making conversation again.

She sat down. At the table. His table. "Do you mind?" she asked.

He knew that even his new haircut couldn't have achieved this in a million plus years.

He looked up at her. She was smiling at him. She said again, "Do you mind? I'm on break now." She was not only beautiful, but polite.

He knew she would be used to hearing suave or gushing responses from men because men would walk for hours over hot sand to have the chance to sit this close to her for even a minute.

His voice crawled out from where it was hiding deep in his throat and he knew it would sound in need of an oil and lube. "Would be fine."

"Thank you. I hope I'm not bothering you. Do you come here much?"

He urged a syllable. "Yes."

Chester was then twenty-eight. He had dated women before but had always been awkward. He had found that once he was re-laxed, he could get on well. But something always got in the way of his dating and it always came to an end. He hadn't dated any-one for a long time and was way out of practice. And here with her, he was so far out of his league, it wasn't even the same game.

"So, Specialty Tools Works. What's that?"

He felt a surge of confidence. She wanted to know about something that he knew everything about, and that she knew nothing about, just like a customer. Even though he wasn't a company salesmen but just an installer, he could launch into a patter he had down so cold he could be in the middle of a four-way car crash and the words would just keep coming.

He cleared his throat. "The premier tool company that offers its customers only the best in custom manufacturing equipment with deep cost-savings." His tongue, lips, and vocal apparatus were running entirely on automatic. "The guarantees that come with every custom piece beat every competitor hands down. And all product is made right here in Ohio."

He was only at the preliminary stage, but looking at her eyes looking at his, he blanked.

"Quite the salesman," she said smiling at him, and reached her hand across to shake. He lifted his right hand and she took it and shook. "My name's Candace."

Her hand was warm, luxurious putty.

After moments of watching him, waiting for his response but getting none, she said, "What's yours?"

"Ches."

"Oh. Never heard that one before."

"It's not like Knight to Queen's Bishop three." This was automatic, too, the only clever line he knew, an icebreaker, which he always used with women.

A pretty wrinkle appeared on her brow as she studied him. "Okay, Ches not Knight to Queen's Bishop three. What's it short for?"

Not only beautiful and polite, but smart, remembering the words just like that.

"Chester."

Her smile widened, as he knew it would. She couldn't help it. Her lips - warm full red petals - were parted to show her perfect teeth. What would those lips feel like? He knew they would overload his fuse panel.

He knew she was amused at his name. People always were. Luckily he was still on automatic and said what he always said. "I know. My mom liked westerns."

She was still smiling, looking steady at him even as her hand reached into her purse and worked there a moment. Then it withdrew a cigarette. "Do you smoke?"

He shook his head. "No."

She got up. Was she going to leave?

She flicked her lighter. It didn't catch. She flicked it again, then again, and brought the flame to the cigarette. He watched her face, so beautiful and relaxed. That's what he really noticed - she was so very relaxed.

She walked to the next table, took a gentle drag, and placed the cigarette in the ashtray,

the cigarette giving off a blue curling plume in abject sorrow at being parted from her warm, full lips.

Beautiful, polite, smart. And thoughtful.

She sat back down at his table. "So, your mom liked westerns."

"Ya. Can't be helped now."

"But yes it can. I wasn't always Candace."

"No?"

"No." Her face slowly transformed like she was remembering an old sorrow, her eyes turning to look into the distance, thinking on something way back. Her voice was quiet. "Got it legally changed." After a few moments her eyes came back to his, a sorrow, her voice still quiet. "Philomena. As in patron saint of babies, infants, the young. Martyred at thirteen." He saw one of her hands lightly rub the other several moments. "My mother thought much further back than westerns."

She got up and went to her cigarette at the next table. Chester watched her take a pull, saw sadness playing on her face as she did.

Here she was talking to him just like they were friends, nothing put-on. He found himself relaxing. They had a bond. They were each born of like-minded parents who saddled their child with a stuck-in-the-past name, not able to recognize that a baby by its very newness, with its whole life ahead, should have a now name.

She sat down again and her voice was wistful. "They took me from my mom. They said she wasn't in touch with reality. I was a foster child at six."

She was a fragile flower, talking like she knew she could trust him with anything. They were having a real conversation. And the thing was, he was getting even more relaxed.

"For heaven's sake," he said. "Just like my mom, too. Not *always* out of touch with reality, but…frequent interruptions in service."

She burst into a laugh which animated her whole face. He really liked her laugh. It sounded genuine, her eyes sparkling, her cheek bones so beautiful.

He was encouraged now and just kept going. "I was shipped out to an uncle when I was ten. Lived with him until I was eighteen. He had no wife. I had no sister, or brother. It was just the two of us. Didn't get the least bit of experience with a girl or woman at close range."

"Did better than me. I had five sets of foster parents before I was sixteen." But her face fell serious again. "The dads, so called, tended to paw at me."

Her eyes were sad, something old tugging her very deep, Chester thought. Her voice was confessional. "From the time I was about twelve I was waiting for a prince to come along and rescue me."

After a few moments, he said, sympathetically, "And?"

She paused, her voice quiet, "They were in very short supply."

She got up like she suddenly remembered she had a cigarette going. She leaned way over and picked it up, took a deep draw, set it down and turned back to him.

Her demeanor changed, like she had pulled herself out of it, her voice like it was at the beginning - energetic, happy. "When your truck pulled up, I thought, gee, that looks like a Wells Fargo truck, expensive and heavy looking, the big double wheels at the back to handle real weight. Different color, of course, and I saw the writing. It's funny, I remember when I first saw a Wells Fargo truck when I was a kid and was told what it was, and I thought, paper money doesn't weigh that much, and surely they don't carry that much coin. Then I realized all that heaviness and steel is for protection against machine guns and bombs, not because the money's so heavy."

She looked fully at him now. "So, what nice things are in your expensive looking heavy-duty truck?"

Chester was feeling more and more comfortable because she kept asking about things that he knew so well. And because they had a bond. "Very, very expensive custom equipment. Tools, machines you can't buy off a shelf anywhere. Just from us. One tool can cost twenty thousand. A machine, fifty, sixty. And the truck's *full* of them."

She was clearly impressed, as he guessed she would be. She leaned in a little closer to him but was not even aware she was doing it he figured.

"So expensive. So why do people buy so many of them?"

"Because they pay for themselves in three years."

"How do they do that?"

She showed a lot of natural intelligence in her questions, he noticed. But mostly he noticed her extraordinary good looks which she knew how to show off to best advantage.

"They cut labor costs. Boost productivity. Let's say you have two shifts, a guy doing a task each shift. He gets paid eight hours, but with coffee breaks, and with him shooting the shi... breeze on average of five minutes an hour, you get less than seven hours of productivity."

"I see. But a machine doesn't take breaks," she said, "or shoot the shi...breeze."

They both laughed.

"And the same machine can work three shifts a day, seven days a week."

"And it gets no holiday pay either," she said.

She sure was quick, he thought.

"And no sick days. No tummy aches," she added.

"Not if you grease them proper."

"And no bereavement days."

He looked at her, serious. "Not unless... the *sister* machine dies!" He laughed and slapped the table like he was killing a bug.

Her eyes sparkled. "Got to go to the funeral service! At the scrap yard!"

They both bellowed and this time she slapped the table.

She really was a smart one. What was she doing working here and now talking so close with him with her undivided attention?

He knew they could get along like crazy.

But he also knew she was too good for him.

And then she said it. "I see you're not married. Unless… you're one of those guys who slips off the ring."

He knew then and there that some married guy had stung her. "No. Not married. Not even a girlfriend. And that's the truth."

She looked down. "I didn't mean to be so personal."

He figured she had blurted it because, caught up in the joyous moment, she just had to know.

CHAPTER 3

BEFORE

Three days after Chester met Candace, he returned to the restaurant as prearranged to pick her up after her shift to take her on a date. They were going on a picnic in the park down by the water's edge because she had said she liked to 'sit in the park and watch people and nature. And people's nature.'

Before picking her up, he had grabbed some wings and fries for their picnic and had a cooler with a couple of cold ones. As he pulled into the parking lot, she came out of the restaurant in a yellow blouse and khaki shorts and sandals, and for Chester, as he watched her through the windshield, time stood still. He felt like by some crazy mistake he had won a date with a Miss Universe contestant in a charity raffle that he hadn't even bought a ticket for. His nerves kicked in but he breathed deeply, telling himself she said she really wanted to see him. He hoped his favorite golf shirt and shorts hadn't slipped out of fashion when he wasn't looking.

On the grass overlooking the water, he spread a blanket and they sat themselves down and he set the food out and she said, "So, how old are you, Chester?"

"Twenty-eight. How about you?"

"Twenty-three."

Chester thought it was nice the way she got things out of the way, direct like, like when she got into his just-waxed and chamoised Camaro at the restaurant parking lot and she asked, 'This paid for?', which it was, a hundred percent. He knew she was reacting to the higher trim package with leather upholstery because he didn't think she would have guessed that under the hood was the 335-horsepower 3.6-liter V6 with 284 pound-feet of torque.

Seagulls circled overhead squawking at their fries. He handed her a beer in an insulated holder and took one for himself and touched his holder to her holder. "Cheers," he said.

"Cheers," she said and gave him a beautiful smile, and to Chester, the beer tasted like champagne. They each put a chicken wing on their paper plate. "So what do you do exactly for Specialty Tools Works?"

"Well I'm not a salesman like maybe you thought. I install their custom-made equipment in the factories of their customers. I do Ohio and Michigan, plus Ontario."

"That must take a lot of talent, every piece being different, being custom-made." She bit into the wing, delicately, he noticed, dabbing a paper napkin at the edges of her mouth.

He had to remember to use a napkin too. He also had to remember not to brag. "Well you have to know a few things," he said.

She laughed. "Well where'd you learn those few things?"

"I trained as a mechanic first, thinking I'd probably do trucks, but someone told me to go for tool and die, so I did. Took course after course nights and weekends for three years. Got hired by Specialty Tools Works and worked in their shop for a year. But a higher up spotted me and said he wanted me trained for installs."

"Spotted you? Why you?"

"Well... I don't like to brag."

"Go ahead."

"He said I stood out."

"Well, well. Stood out. So you must do okay on the income front."

"Okay enough."

Chester wasn't stupid. He knew where that question was aimed, but he liked it, liked that she was direct, straight-forward, practical like. He was actually paid very well and it was one thing he was proud of. He didn't have to wonder if it would be useful to him for her to know how well. But he thought it would be bragging to come out and tell her an actual figure. So he just said, "Actually, I make good money."

He knew she could see he was bursting to say something more, and he saw that she was bursting to know something more. "I'll bet it's more than I think," she teased, leaning into him.

"Who knows?" he laughed.

"Well you do, for one."

"Well no, I don't know what you think."

"Fifty," she fired, sort of playful, sort of teasing. And sort of earnest.

He only smiled.

"Sixty." She said it like a punch.

He laughed.

She fired again. "Seventy."

He laughed again.

"Seventy-five."

She bandied higher and higher numbers at him in staccato, now only in earnest, and so fast she quickly passed the mark but she made him laugh so much he couldn't stop her until she reached twice his actual salary, including bonuses, and he said, "maybe a little high there."

She was laughing now, too, but a little differently, and she didn't take her eyes from his even while she took a long slow swig from her beer and reached her hand blindly for another fry.

He just couldn't hold back now. "And," he said, "things may be on the move there."

"There where?"

"On the income front."

Her eyes watched him and took on fresh sparkle and she swallowed the fry. "Meaning?"

"They said they've got their eye on me."

"Meaning?"

"Well...I don't like to brag."

"Go ahead."

"They say I'm the best. They've got their eye on me."

"Meaning?"

"Promotion. Regional install manager."

"Meaning?"

"Twelve States, plus Ontario."

"Well, well." Her eyes changed from sparkle to a deep glow and she looked at him while she slid a chicken wing slowly across her lips and licked it like it really tasted good. He figured he didn't even have to tell her that regional install manager meant a big jump in salary.

They ate more and talked less, like she suddenly had a bigger appetite, polishing off the wings and fries in short order.

"So, Chester-soon-to-be-regional-install-manager, where do you live?"

"At my house."

She broke out laughing. "Well isn't that a coincidence. You live at your house."

He laughed now, too. "I guess that was stupid."

"No, I guess that wasn't fair," she said. "Guess you thought I meant *in what* do you live? Sorry. Anyway, I guess you meant you *own* your house."

"Yes, I do."

"Well, well."

"Well, me and the bank. I have a mortgage. They're about 80%."

"Sure. And you live alone?"

"Ya."

"Well."

He opened his wallet to take out a picture like it was a picture of a dear child.

"Just a sec," she said. "Gotta have one." She took out a cigarette and her lighter and got up and moved away a few feet.

He looked at the picture of his house a moment, taken from the curb showing the deep front yard, long before you got right up to the house, or in it, the house being best enjoyed from the curb.

He reached up and handed her the picture. She studied it, very quiet, taking small draws on her cigarette. He watched her face and her eyes change, and it reminded him of that faraway, sad look she had in the restaurant when she told him about her mother and her real name. Maybe the picture reminded her of their house way back because her face wasn't as light-spirited now.

After a bit, she handed him back the picture.

"Where do *you* live?" he said.

"Nowhere that I would care to have a picture of."

"Oh."

He tried to think of something to lighten things up. "You know, Candace, to be honest, I was so struck by you having shown interest in me at the restaurant that I thought it had to be a practical joke, such a beautiful woman sitting down at my table."

She watched him with interest.

He continued. "As a sensible explanation, a practical joke seemed the most likely. I even wanted to tell you then and there that I knew it was a practical joke so I didn't look completely stupid. I wondered how the guys from the shop had rigged that one, one for the ages. But I didn't see anyone around who might be in on it. To say something about it being a practical joke when it wasn't, I would look even stupider. So I said nothing. Luckily."

She reached and took his hand. "Don't be down on yourself, Chester." Her eyes and her voice were soft. "I saw a pleasant looking man sitting there. I saw a warm smile and a smile tells you a lot about a person. I saw a nice man. And then we talked, and I knew I was completely right."

*

Chester decided that their second date had to be a couple of notches up from beer and wings and seagulls crapping around them in the park. He settled on wine and steak in a restaurant with white linen and soft candles and quiet music that made you think of riding a gondola in Venice.

Candace wore a satin dress, and when she walked into the restaurant, Chester noticed every man's head swiveled like he had just seen a flying saucer. Chester wore his best suit, the dark one he wore to funerals. She said he looked elegant. No one had ever told him that.

During dinner they re-ordered wine twice, and then, un-solicited and unexpected for Chester, Candace began to talk non-stop about her relationships. As she downed her wine, he learned that the guys had all been 'opportunistic'.

"Guys with fast money?" he asked.

"And fast cars," she said, annoyed at the memories.

Chester felt a sudden pain. "My Camaro isn't as fast as it might seem. Slower 0-60 than you'd think."

She seemed not to care how fast his Camaro was. She just grabbed at her wine glass and said, "And fast words, and fast eyes, and fast hands," and took another gulp.

The last guy, Bernhard, was a husband she didn't know was a husband. "He finally revealed he was married and that his wife was a high-heeled, bad-ass attorney with a lightning temper who said that if he didn't smarten up and drop me pronto, she would gut him like a fish."

Chester waited a few moments, holding his breath. "And?"

"Well you don't see him anywhere around here, do you?"

"No."

"Four months of torrid love and," she snapped her finger, "over."

"When was that... over?"

"Three weeks ago this coming Friday. 4:30 P.M. Just in time for the weekend."

Chester wasn't quick with words at the best of times, and this wasn't close to the best of times. "Oh."

It was probably the first time she was dumped, Chester thought. Who else but a guy married to a lightning-tempered attorney about to gut him like a fish would dump Candace? He figured that in every other case, Candace would have done the dumping.

"Do you think he really loved you?" he said.

"No."

"No?"

"No."

"Oh." Chester paused to consider his phrasing, but it came out the usual way. "Did you really love *him*?"

"I doubt it."

"But you said 'torrid *love*'."

"Well torrid something. There was sure torrid something."

"Oh." Chester felt the urgent need to swallow half a glass of wine, and did. "But you don't know?"

"Don't know. Probably just in love with the idea."

"What idea?"

"Being in love."

"You don't know if you were in love?"

She looked at him. "You're really persistent there."

Her tone wasn't the least bit mean, Chester saw.

She continued. "When I strip him of all the nice things he gave me - the jewelry, the dresses, the diamonds - I don't know. It's like...I don't know. I mean, *when* are you in love? I'm not good with that one actually. Okay?"

"Okay."

"Like...when you're on the ground and you see a plane in the sky, you know it's in the sky, right?"

"Right." He wondered if wine did this to her all the time.

"But *when* is it in the sky? You tell me. If you're in a plane, and you take off, *when* are you in the sky? See what I mean?"

Chester imagined seeing planes at various altitudes.

"Whether you're on the ground looking up, or in the plane looking down, *when* is the plane in the sky?" she said. "Is it when it's two thousand feet up? Or just five hundred? Cause it's not in the sky when it's ten feet up."

"Just off the ground."

"Right. Or even if you're high up, you could still just be in the *air*, but not in the sky."

Chester understood gradations, mostly in metals, but still he felt he was getting it. "You're thinking you were just in the air with him?"

She shrugged. "I don't know. Or what if it's raining?"

Chester's imagination was now strained. "Raining? Like in the relationship? Or are you talking about the plane and sky thing?"

"Ya, the plane and sky thing. That's what we're *talking* about."

Chester nodded earnestly like it was obvious and he was a dolt.

"And is it different between the day and the night?" she said. Her eyes seemed to say it was. "At night you see the twinkling stars and it's easy. That's the sky."

But that's the stars, Chester thought. Where's the plane? He also wondered about the twinkling jewelry Bernhard gave her those torrid starry nights and he figured it was at those times that she was in the sky.

"Get my point?" she said.

"Think so."

She said she was tired of feeling 'like a flat stone being skimmed across water'. She wanted a guy who, for starters, wasn't married, preferably not even in a romantic relationship, although she had pried one or two loose from those. Her preference now was a guy not on the make but a guy who was well grounded, stable, down to earth, who wanted 'a real relationship, a loving relationship'.

"Me, too," Chester blurted.

Then he remembered what he had in his pocket. In all their talk about Bernhard and torrid love, he had forgotten about it, which, he thought, was no surprise given that what he had was so inconsiderable it could never compete with Bernhard's starry gifts that took her to the sky. He calculated that his gift had so little lift potential it would struggle to get her even along the runway let alone airborne.

But he took the tiny, delicately-wrapped box from his suit pocket anyway. She looked at him in surprise. He handed it to her. She opened the wrapping slowly.

It was a gold-colored Zippo lighter.

"Why thank you," she said.

"I noticed you were having trouble getting the other one to light sometimes," he said. "Look at the bottom."

She turned it over. Inscribed in fine italic script was '*CP*'. She looked at him in half surprise. "Is it what I think it is?"

He nodded. "Our secret."

She looked at it again. "Candace Philomena. That's very nice, Chester. And thoughtful." She looked up from the lighter, looked at him, her face now serious. "What do you feel for me?"

Chester wasn't quick with words of feeling. "Well...I'm nuts for you."

She laughed. But seeing his embarrassment at her laugh, she smiled warmly, which put him more at ease with the question, more at ease with himself. "That doesn't really say it completely. I'm, ...bananas and bonkers, too."

She reached her hand to his and held it gently, her eyes on his. "Chester, you really are a charmer."

*

The courtship was swift and expensive.

It wasn't that Candace demanded extravagances, like high-priced concerts, intimate dining experiences, and get-a-way weekends touring Ohio's wineries and micro-breweries while experiencing the best romantic hide-a-ways featuring in-room Jacuzzis and gas fireplaces. She was merely suggestive, and Chester was highly receptive.

He had always been a careful saver, just as if he had been born with a biological savings' gene that controlled spending as much as another gene controlled eye color. Not that he was stingy, just careful. But now, with Candace in his life, he cared not in the least that his three credit cards were spinning like cherries in a slot machine.

Within two months Candace moved in with him and things started to happen right away, propelled by what she told Chester was 'a woman's touch', which, he soon recognized, had been sorely absent.

Take, for example, 'a good dusting'. Chester only knew that to mean what you got when you were on the losing end of a fistfight. Sure, he would wax and chamois and buff his Camaro till it glowed, naturally, because people were going to see it. But dusting the top of a fridge, or under a bed, or behind furniture? Who was ever going to see there? But when she explained why that wasn't the point, he got it.

And somehow everything fit neatly into his kitchen cupboards if you did it right. No need to have all the coffee cups arrayed in a long line along the back splash.

And the bathroom cabinets, he readily saw they had 'way too much useless stuff in them'. When you really got down to it, his stuff only needed the right-hand side of the very top shelf.

Some second-hand furniture that he had found online two years before – 'big soft armchair, sofa with good springs, historic armoire, ample dresser with matching ample night table, $600 or best offer' (which Chester's was, at $415) - were all gone like a vanishing act in the first week, Candace explaining with tender sympathy 'the reason is beyond simple taste differences, Chester. Trust me on that.'

And there were his clothes which appeared suddenly on the bed in piles to which she pointed and said: 'Garbage or donate?' Luckily she had saved him a lot of time, three garbage bags already full of his clothes on the floor at the foot of the bed.

He quickly came to realize that she was always right in these choices about the house and him and everything else. He liked that she told him how to dress, what to buy for food, what to buy for the house, what to buy for her. In all these things he came to think of Candace as like a very talented auto-body man with a good eye who's transforming a bent and rusted clunker into something that anyone would proudly drive down the street.

Things went along tickety-boo. Happy days carried them forward and Chester was completely over the moon in love. To say there was spring in his step wouldn't capture it; it was more like he was bouncing across a trampoline.

One month after she moved in, Candace became pregnant. She seemed very happy, so Chester was, too.

She mentioned marriage. So Chester proposed.

She mentioned a destination wedding, like the Bahamas, a ceremony on a beach. And while they're already there, they might just as well take the extended ten-night special, all inclusive, and upgrade to the honeymoon package, which only made sense to Chester, too.

Six months after he had first set eyes on her, they were married, and Chester was the proudest man to have ever walked the face of the earth.

CHAPTER 4

NOW

Chester knew that if you're walking around Detroit with $8,000 in cash bulging in your pants' pocket, especially in the neighborhood where Huey's Big Laundromat was located, you should have a gun. And Chester did, a Beretta M9, reputed to be the best semi-automatic handgun there is for self-defense and concealed carry. Accurate and dependable, he knew it was the official side-arm of the U.S. military.

A few years earlier, a fellow installer at the company, a young father of three, had been held up by a gun-toting guy late at night. The guy figured the expensive-looking truck carried expensive stuff. The company installer had put up no resistance, but he was shot dead. Chester and a few others had vowed that no triple-A asshole was ever going to leave their kids fatherless. Several, like Chester, had acquired a Beretta.

Chester was in Detroit because he had to deliver to Roly the further $8,000 through Chantelle at the Laundromat to seal the 'arrangement', and Chester had the money.

But before handing over the money, he had an issue to resolve with Roly and was going to call him. Chester would never, of course, use his own phone to make the call. He had bought three burner phones that morning in Detroit at a retail cell-phone store. He bought with cash. There was no contract required, no record of ownership, nothing that would connect him with the phones or the phone calls. But he didn't want to use the burners yet because he decided to use each one only once and might need all of them at the rental cottage where there weren't any payphones.

He stepped into a phone booth that he had spotted earlier. It was in a quiet corner, no pedestrian traffic anywhere, and had a Plexiglas folding door for privacy. He closed the door and dialed.

"Hi," Roly said.

"Hi, Roly. It's Ken. I've got the $8,000 you wanted to bring you up to ten grand. I'll get it to Chantelle today."

"Good."

"But first I want us to agree on the details on the last forty grand. You said we would talk. I want to talk."

"Sure. Talk."

"I'm not giving you all that money before I know the job's actually done. Non-negotiable. I don't even know who you are, remember."

"I get that. And I don't know who you are, remember."

"So, I'm going to hold back half of the money until after the job's done."

"You mean half the forty."

"No, half the fifty."

"No, Ken. You can hold back half the forty until after the job. That's twenty. And that's max."

Chester had already considered that would be reasonable, especially with his contingency plan. "Well okay then. The hold back is twenty."

"I want that first twenty, which brings me up to thirty, before I do the job."

"I get that, Roly. But I don't want to give you that first twenty until I know you're actually going to show up at the cottage and do the job."

"You were connected to me through Clyne. And I don't go back on Clyne."

"I can't trust that, not for that kind of money. I've got it figured this way – I'll leave that first twenty inside the cottage under the bed in the main bedroom, in cash in a shoe box. You've got my word it'll be there."

"That's not real comforting."

"Well you can check it's there before you do her."

"The thing is I have to go into the cottage, and likely be seen and likely have to silence her, before I even know if the money's there."

"Well what would be the point of me having you go to the cottage if the money's not there? You're not going to do her in that case. It does nothing except make you real upset. And I haven't forgotten you're a hit man."

"But I don't know who you are."

"At that point you're going to know the cottage, and that will get you a long way to knowing who I am. It just doesn't make sense for us, the husband and me, not to have the money there. Look at it from our side. We're still taking a chance. With the money in the cottage you could just waltz in and grab the twenty from under the bed and not do the job."

It was important to Chester that Roly continue to think there was a husband involved here, separate from Chester, because he worried Roly might otherwise come early, looking just to rob the cottage of the $20,000.

Chester continued. "I'm bringing the money at lunchtime on the day and putting it under the bed. When you come, you could screw us by taking the money and just explain to the wife that there's been some mistake, you thought it was someone else's cottage, you're sorry for the intrusion. That's where the trust comes in from us. See? Or, if she gave you some grief, you could just knock her out, take the money, still not do her, and leave."

Roly was silent. Then he said, "Wife? What's this about 'the wife'? You told me before it was a friend's 'friend'? You said I was doing a friend's friend."

Chester swallowed. With his nerves going in that first conversation, he knew he had said it was a friend's friend. He hadn't been quite able to say 'wife' at that time. He was thinking hard now how to cover it, but maybe not hard enough. "They're getting married."

"You mean since I talked to you just a few days ago, they decided to get married? And the guy still wants me to do her?"

"I know it's weird. It's…an inheritance thing. He needs to have her actually married to him before you do her. Some legal thing. So they're getting married next week."

"You didn't mention that little fact. You said I was doing a friend's friend, love off the rails. Now they're getting married. She'll be his wife and the job's still on. Like, am I doing her on their honeymoon?"

"No. It's still the same woman. Just her. Everything's the same."

"There's moving parts here, like a moving target."

"Well, it is what it is."

"No, it is what it wasn't."

"Well I'm sorry it's different, but I don't see it makes any difference."

There was silence from Roly, other than it sounded like he was letting out a long thoughtful exhale of smoke. "Anything else you want to tell me? Bridal party going to show when I'm there?"

"No."

Roly said nothing and Chester heard his breathing settling. "So," Chester said, pushing on, "the twenty will be in cash in a shoe box under the bed."

"It better be."

"It will be. Check before doing her if you want."

"I'll do just that." A long pause, then, "The last twenty, after I do the job, how do I know you won't stiff me for that?"

"Well like I said, you're a hit man and I'm not. I don't want to spend the rest of my life hiding under a rock. And also, after you do the job, you're going to know *exactly* who I am. The police and news people are going to be all over this. I'm the guy who's visiting the husband several times in the week at the cottage and golfing with him at the very moment you do her. They're going to ask the husband all about his week, any visitors. I'm going to be identified, that's for sure. I'm part of his alibi, where he was when she was done. The police and news people will ask lots, and it'll be out there for anyone to see who I am, where I live, where I work. It won't take Sherlock Holmes to find me."

There was a pause, a kind of "Mmmm." Roly seemed satisfied. "The last $20,000, I want it three days after the job's done, through Chantelle."

"Okay," Chester said.

"What day's this got to happen?"

"The week of the cottage rental starts Sunday, July 8. So middle to later in that week. Has to appear that the killer knew the woman was there at the cottage, was watching her for days, so it doesn't look like a prearranged hit."

"Ya, for sure."

"Like she was out there visible to people on the lake, sunning on the dock, seen by passing boaters. Like the killer saw some routines over a few days."

"And is she going to be visible like that?"

"You want to believe it. So it has to be later, like Wednesday or Thursday or Friday."

"How will I know when? And when she'll be alone?"

"I'll let you know as we go. Need the weather to cooperate, too."

"Why?"

"The husband and I are going to be away golfing when you do her. If there's bad weather, there's no golfing. No golfing, no hit."

CHAPTER 5

BEFORE

When the baby was born, they chose the name Amara, derived from Spanish and Italian, meaning, 'love, or grace'.

To Chester, in the first months after Amara's birth, Candace seemed on and off. She was disoriented and seemed to him to have a hard time handling both marriage and a baby at the same time, as if being married and having a baby didn't belong together in the same arrangement.

He wondered if it was postpartum depression, not that he knew what it looked like. In the lunchroom at Specialty Tools while the guys were eating, he put the question out. "How was your wife after the baby was born? Like, did she have postpartum depression? Or was she disoriented?"

There were vacant looks in some, eyes moving around aimlessly in the heads of others, trying to remember.

One said, "I kind of thought she was off some days. I

would say, 'how are you, honey?' And she would say, 'Does it matter? You're just going to tell me to buck up.' We didn't get further than that, so I don't know."

Another said, "No, I didn't see anything different. Steady steady. She does her thing, I do mine. Another mouth to feed. We keep plowing on."

Most said 'forget exactly.'

On the way out of the lunch room, one of the older guys, putting his hand on Chester's shoulder, said, "First kid always throws things off for the mother, juggling this and that. And the dad's in a new orbit like a guy in a spacecraft orbiting the earth, going around and around, looking down on something familiar, but it isn't really, seeing everything from a new angle. But things smooth out after a time."

And that seemed to be true. Things smoothed out and Candace settled in and became a good mother. Having Amara as a constant companion, although a little demanding 24/7, seemed to give Candace an anchor, or a focus, which, of course, it really did because it wasn't like you could just forget about Amara for any period of time like she was a piece of furniture and go off and do something carefree. So she really was more like an anchor.

When Amara was one, Candace went back to work, this time as a day-time receptionist at a large tanning salon and spa where her natural beauty said to customers: 'this place has class'.

In that second year, Chester began to experience some un-easiness. He knew that his warm smile and being six feet and strong was only part of what had impressed Candace in the beginning. He knew he had won her over mostly because of the lifestyle he offered her. He could, and did, lift her from a sort of poverty, not just money poverty, but cultural poverty

- now she had Netflix and went to rock concerts. He had raised her up to the next rung.

But at times it seemed that was not enough for her. She had gotten used to that and maybe her gratitude was slipping. She seemed to want the *next* rung, without actually saying it. He believed this because she asked him about his work and about 'climbing the ladder,' speaking of rungs. She knew, of course, he didn't get the promotion they had been expecting from the time he first met her and which would have meant more money. He worried she might think he was a dud.

Again, though, it wasn't that Candace out and out spoke of wanting more things or more money. It was more that, to Chester's mind, and maybe an over-sensitive one, it just lingered in the air.

Because it nagged at him, he thought that getting more money was the answer and he should do that. But he soon realized there weren't many options for him to do that. In fact, there were none. Unless he robbed a bank. But robbing a bank would be plain wrong. On the other hand, he was head-over-heels in love, so wrong didn't hold the same sway. But a bank had cameras and other sophisticated equipment and you could easily get caught or killed and that would defeat the whole point.

So instead of robbing a bank he just continued to put things on credit cards like a regular law-abiding citizen. Like when he surprised Candace with an all-inclusive trip to St. Lucia (next next rung) where they did an excursion which involved sailing around the entire island on a catamaran with forty other people onboard. Midway, they stopped to snorkel off a reef, all passengers supplied with mask, flippers, and snorkel, the reef reputed to be teeming with exotic colorful fish. But as it turned out, for the twenty guys who hit the water, no tiny darting colorful fish or sea creature thing could hold a candle to Candace's luminescent yellow bikini which jammed their orienting systems causing them to snorkel in perpetual confusion around her, bumping into one another, oblivious to the whereabouts of fish.

He knew she enjoyed attention, although she didn't really indulge in getting it in most situations, apart from screaming color choices in bikinis. But who doesn't like a little attention? And Chester didn't mind because she always came back warmed to him.

And moreover, she knew the difference between attention and love.

CHAPTER 6

BEFORE

There were times when Chester got a glimpse into Candace's past, usually through a very small window.

He had once come upon a lined sheet of paper on the dresser on which a poem had been written, followed by a note, all in Candace's hand, a much younger hand. It wasn't addressed to him, or to anyone.

It read:

'All love is sweet
Given or returned.
Common as light is love,
And its familiar voice
Wearies not ever.'
P B Shelley

Under that, it said:

'Sure. So says the poet. Goody for him.

But I know otherwise. Love is not common as light. Or if it is, then I must live only in darkness, because there is no love, so there must be no light.

I am lost. Love has not found me. But darkness has found me.

Light and love are somewhere else.

So I must leave this place, this house, this life. In search of the light.'

Chester asked her about it. She said she had come upon it tucked in an old school notebook of hers. She said that in tenth grade in English class they read that poem. The poet was English, too, a romantic poet the teacher said, meaning he lived in the Romantic period, a period Candace said she knew she didn't live in back then, that was for sure. At that time she was living with her fifth, and last, foster family, in the very last days, and that the dad, like so many others, was a 'predator'.

"Did you leave that house?" Chester asked. "In search of the light?"

"You bet I did. Beat it out of there the day I turned sixteen and nobody could stop me."

Chester remembered she didn't say whether she found the light, although he had asked her. In his heart he hoped that she had found the light, and that it was Chester.

Another time, when Amara was almost three, Chester was out for a walk with Amara after supper and they ran into one of the neighbors, Sue Findlay, walking with her young daughter, Rebecca, who was a friend of Amara. The Findlays were walking their playful golden retriever on a long leash. Being allowed to pet the dog put Amara into a kind of ecstasy. She did it again and again, and then, 'just one more time', eleven times.

When they got home, Chester put Amara to bed, and later Candace arrived home from shopping. He told her about meeting Sue Finlay and their golden retriever. "Amara would just love a dog."

He saw a shadow fall across Candace's face. She said, sternly, "No."

Chester was surprised. "Why not?"

"I don't want a dog. EVER."

Chester was stunned. "Wow," he said. "You're pretty definite."

"More definite than pretty definite," she said. "Definite definite." She walked away into the bedroom and shut the door.

Chester was pretty sure she didn't go there just to go to bed for the night, since it was only 8:05. He corrected himself: he wasn't just pretty sure, but definite definite sure.

After twenty minutes she emerged and came and sat on the couch in the living room where he was looking through a Popular Mechanics magazine. He saw that she had been crying.

"What is it, Candace?"

"Sorry. It just hit me hard."

"What hit you hard?"

"A memory. But I still don't want a dog."

She wasn't looking at him, her eyes down, a big sadness still about her.

"Definite definite?" he said, trying to lighten the mood.

She nodded, not the least lightened.

He waited, watching her. He felt a sadness rising in himself.

"When I was eight," she said, "my foster mother at the time took me to a country market to get a bushel of fresh apples. It was only September, but a cold day. At the market, beside the gravel parking lot, they had wire mesh pens and there were rabbits in them eating lettuce. We watched them for awhile and I didn't want to leave them. The man who owned the market came out and said the rabbits were for sale, only $4.00 each."

Chester folded his magazine and set it down and watched Candace.

"We took one home, a young one," she said. "I had a wire mesh cage set up in the corner of the back yard and every day I would let her out and play with her on the grass. Then I would put her back in and put a carrot and lettuce inside and watch her munch. She was so white, so soft, her pink eyes so big looking at me. So helpless. I was her only friend. Her protector."

Chester found himself swallowing. This was promising to be a sad and tragic story. "What was her name?" he said quietly.

"Flopsy."

Chester nodded. Of course. A girl burdened with a name like Philomena was going to stay with a standard when it was up to her to name any living breathing thing.

"One day before going to school, I put her back in the cage and ran inside to get a carrot for her. I had to get my backpack, too."

Chester saw a tear form in her eye, then drop onto her shirt, but her hands stayed clasped together in her lap.

"I came back outside. The cage door was open and the cage was empty. I looked all around. Then I glimpsed her just slipping underneath our back fence. I ran, but I couldn't climb the fence. Through the fence boards I saw her hopping into the neighbor's yard, further and further along the grass, further and further away from me."

She paused, and Chester held his breath. "Then I saw the neighbor's German shepherd come running from the corner of their house."

Chester felt an almost physical blow. He had once seen a Doberman corner a rabbit by a hedge row. The rabbit couldn't make a move either way and froze, overcome by fright, its body trembling, its eyes big and helpless. The Doberman lunged, grabbing it up in its bared teeth, shaking the soft white bundle violently, tearing it open alive, blood spurting everywhere, the rabbit silent through it all.

"I hadn't closed her door properly. She trusted me. I didn't protect her. I was her only friend."

The experience would leave a big hole in any eight-year-old girl, Chester thought. But for Candace, who knew at eight what it was to be helpless, it would be even bigger. It wouldn't help her to think that life was anything other than savage and cruel.

It struck him, as it had so many times before, how much a thing like that can linger so long, that even big people still struggle with a thing that happened long ago when they were little people, and in profound ways and for reasons that no one else can ever understand. He figured that in Candace's case there were probably as many of those things still lurking about deep in her troubled head as there are stars in the heavens.

He thought about it more, that maybe Candace, a girl who was always shuffled around, a girl who didn't know how long she would have any set of foster parents, always the new girl in the school, maybe she had to work very hard to make a friend, just one friend, a friend she would hold onto tight for dear life, a friend she totally counted on, put all her trust in, like Flopsy had in her. And maybe that friend dropped her and she had no friend. Or maybe that friend who she trusted didn't protect her, let her slip through some door, and little Philomena was set among the wolves.

He could imagine her being betrayed, a girl of good looks that other girls could love to hate, a girl fragile inside, so very easy to mock and tease. They didn't know that to her, her good looks counted for nothing when inside was an ugly life, a never-ending despair. He heard her voice in his head, her words from way back when they first met in that restaurant, 'the dads, so-called, tended to paw at me.'

All she wanted as a little girl was to belong, to belong to one family, to be loved by one family, like other kids were loved by one family, to be secure like other kids were secure in one family. To have a dad who would protect her.

He looked over at her, sitting on the couch, quiet, her eyes down, maybe remembering some other incident, her past world full of incidents, all locked from him, feeling so much more pain from that past than Chester knew he could ever know.

But what he did know, and knew it with his whole aching heart, was that he loved her with a burning.

CHAPTER 7

BEFORE

Chester had wanted another child, even another two. He had told Candace how excited he would be to have more now that Amara was three. At least one more. And Amara would be thrilled to have a baby brother or sister.

But Candace seemed not to want more. She hadn't actually said no to the idea of more the way she had said it about the dog, definite definite. But she hadn't said yes. Or even maybe.

Was it she didn't want another child but felt she was letting him down on that? Or was it she just didn't want another child with him? But maybe with someone else?

Maybe he was just being over-sensitive, but that question had crept into his head, along with the big corollary - was she planning to split and take Amara?

He considered that when she met him she was only 23. He knew people change and mature with the passing years. He worried that maybe the package she wanted in a guy when she was 23 wasn't the package she wanted in a guy when she was 27.

That had preyed on his mind. He knew he couldn't live if that happened.

He had watched two guys at Specialty Tools go through separations - painful, lonely, and devastating for the kids. He told Candace all about it over supper every night for days, always taking his time, building it with a lot of tragic detail, watching her reactions closely, trying to read her mind, if there was anything special to read as she slowly twirled the spaghetti in the spoon. She never asked any questions, just said, 'pass the wine.'

After supper, offhand, he would invite her to remember the good old times together, four years ago, like the day they met, talking at the restaurant about productivity numbers of manufacturing equipment. She was so damn funny. But she didn't seem to recall it, certainly not in Technicolor the way Chester did, although, when he reminded her about machines taking time off for bereavement, her eyes showed some recognition.

He knew that deep down her painful past, full of rejection, was a weight on her, and sometimes it was a lot heavier and squashed her happiness and sent her reeling with a heavy heart. He had seen her depressed, slumped in a chair some times for a whole day, and she wouldn't talk about it. He knew she had seen a psychologist at times in her teens, and later, too, and that she had a form of something called 'dissociative disorder' that caused her to sometimes 'depersonalize', which meant that she was sometimes detached from herself, detached from things around her, too. Reality could blur for a time. The psychologist told her it was a coping mechanism, developed when she was a child when she couldn't face her pain, so detached from herself.

Chester knew she didn't like to talk about it, other than saying 'it is what it is', and that it came from her life 'being turned upside down and inside out over and over' when she was young.

All he could do was continue to shower her with love, with hugs and kisses, with flowers and chocolates. He did everything she asked him to do around the house, and anywhere else. He told her he worshipped her, not in those exact words, but in different words that came to him on the spot, like maybe when her finger lifted and drew her hair behind one ear, he might say, 'your pretty little ear makes me want to kiss you all over'. The words were not always as coherent and direct as that, sometimes stumbling out like mumbo-jumbo, but he was certain she always got the drift.

But, nevertheless, he felt things dipping here and there. She wouldn't look at him the way she did before, or she was quiet too long, or she was absent even when she was present. Not just absent but distant, like casting around for some marker, some bearing in all this, like a ship or a dinghy looking for a lighthouse in a fog. And sometimes, not a lot at first, but just sometimes, and more later, she seemed to ignore him when he talked sometimes, like maybe he wasn't too interesting.

Over time he noticed things just slipped - a notch here, a notch there - like a slipping clutch, like somewhere in this relationship there was a worn pilot bearing, or a warped clutch disc, or maybe it was a warped pressure plate, because pretty clearly the full power of the engine wasn't reaching the transmission.

*

He often found himself observing her in social settings.

Like one winter night when there were six couples at a house party over in the next block. Five of the wives stood talking in the kitchen while Candace sat in the living room, surrounded by all five husbands who jockeyed for position to get closer to her, maybe to have a closer look, maybe to say something that would impress her. Earlier, around a corner, he had overheard one of the husbands say to another, 'Chester's wife's a fetching beauty.'

As the men crowded her, Chester saw a look in her eyes that he had seen before, like light bouncing off diamonds. She didn't speak much when the attention was strong. Prima donna didn't describe her because she didn't strut and hold herself forth in that way, squashing all rivals. She was a quiet beauty, at least around other women. Around men she would open up more, but tonight she seemed quiet.

Her eyes caught Chester's for a moment and he saw a small smile, mysterious, like the Mona Lisa. And like the Mona Lisa, he could never tell what it meant. Was she saying to him, 'even with this swarm of male attention, you'll always be my number one, baby'? Or was she saying, 'this reminds me of when I was sixteen and they were thirteen'? Or was she saying, 'we should get out like this more often?' Or was she saying, 'these guys are a bunch of fumblers?' Or, well, it could be any of a dozen things.

He left the room to get another beer in the dining room. He heard male laughter erupt from the living room. Did someone say something to her they wouldn't say in his presence? Or did she say something to them she wouldn't say in his presence? Maybe a dozen things was conservative.

Men ogled her. But their interest was only her beauty. Chester knew they were too blinded by that to see that the real magic was inside. No other man had ever seen her the way he saw her. No other man *could* ever see her that way, the way she deserved to be seen. He only hoped that she saw things that way, too, that no other man could really see her like Chester did, not just the beauty and the sometimes crackerjack wit, but know and feel her deep lingering sorrows, know the little girl lost inside, accept her wobbles, give her the steady love that slow and steady rain gives to parched earth, give her the hope that a Spring sun gives to a rose bush after it has huddled through winter's blast.

Chester peered out the dining room window as he popped the cap off a beer. From an outdoor floodlight shining in the backyard, he saw that it was snowing, or maybe it was a freezing sleet, icy flakes hitting the window pane, turning to water and creeping down the pane on the outside. The pane was cold on the outside and warm on the inside, but still, there was enough warmth in the pane to turn the threatening sleeting ice to water.

Candace was like the window pane, he thought, one side in the warmth, one side in the cold. His love, and Amara's, too, was what gave her her warm side. Her wretched past, with its swirling icy flakes of rejection and pain pressing her memory, gave her her cold side.

Without him she would be cold on both sides, and the icy flakes, when they hit, would stay ice, building up, thickening, freezing solid, and she wouldn't be able to see a thing. Or feel a thing. Except the cold.

But he would never let that happen. He would always be there for her, loving her with a burning.

CHAPTER 8

BEFORE

It was just after Amara turned five.

One evening near Amara's bedtime, Chester was in the kitchen eating a sandwich and could hear Candace and Amara in the living room.

"The book's called Cinderella," Candace said. "It's a story I read a hundred times when I was a little girl. And it takes place a very long time ago."

"Okay. Where?"

"I don't know. Europe somewhere. But it doesn't matter where because it could be in any country."

"In the United States?"

"No. Because United States didn't have castles and princes."

"Oh." Amara was a little disappointed.

"But that isn't the point. The point isn't where it is, but what it's about. It's about people, and they're the same in every country."

"In the United States?"

"Sure. People are people if you scratch the surface."

Chester had heard of Cinderella, but he had never read it. Similarly, he had heard of Snow White, The Three Little Pigs, and Hansel and Gretel, but had never read them. As a kid, he read comics, lots of comics.

But as he listened to Candace read, he realized that somehow he knew the story. He listened to Candace explaining the hard parts, highlighting the cruelties of the world when you're a poor downtrodden like young Cinderella, her mother gone, despised by the cruel stepsisters and ordered around all the time, having to do all the scum jobs every day like scrubbing the floors and cleaning out the ashes in the fireplaces. And getting zero social time.

"See how it says she had to clean out the cinders from the fireplace?"

"Ya."

"Well, cinders are little dirty black chunks that are left after the wood is burnt in the fire. You see, that's how she got her name, Cinder-Ella. They gave her that name to make fun of her because she was the one who had to do that dirty job. They would say, 'look at dirty little CINDER-Ella." Candace's voice had real edge to it when she said that.

"That was not being nice to say that to her," Amara said.

"No, it wasn't."

"Was her name just Ella before?"

"I've got to think so, but they don't say."

That edge in her voice when she said 'Cinder-ella' - and then Chester got it, saw it clearly. Candace as a little girl had been hurt by others as Cinderella had, so saw herself in Cinderella. She said she had read the book a hundred times. More than any other little girl she knew, she was Cinderella, the real thing, because how many others had lost their mother like Candace had, her only anchor in her tender and young life. And how many others had to live with strangers like Candace had, and how many others were teased mercilessly because they didn't belong to the family, feeling lonely and fearing her tomorrows? Candace and Cinderella – they shared each other's sorrows. Secret best friends.

But for Candace, the story ended there, at the Cinder-ella stage, because for Candace there was no fairy godmother to produce the dress, the slippers, the whole nine yards. That's where their lives diverged. Candace didn't get to be decked out in finery and go to a fancy ball, transported by a horse-drawn carriage. There was no fancy ball, no glass slippers, no prince charming. She just stayed the cinder wench, cold rejection day after day, sitting alone in the chimney corner among the ashes, shifting from family to family, always an outsider. No lifting her out of misery into a bright new tomorrow. Nope. Misery just kept coming.

In his head he heard the words Candace said that day they met at the restaurant. 'From the time I was about twelve, I was waiting for a prince to come along and rescue me...but they were in very short supply.'

Candace and Amara finished the story and he heard Candace say, "Not every little girl has a fairy godmother."

"No?"

"No. Maybe some. But I didn't, or at least not the kind that can do much of anything."

"Then what are they good for?"

"Absolutely nothing. Worse, when you're little, they hold out some dumb hope to you when there isn't any. Not one bit of hope. You're on your own."

"Oh."

Chester figured that probably wasn't the usual way to wrap up that story, but it wasn't his area of expertise.

*

Although Candace had given short shrift to fairy godmothers, she seemed to have a thing for princes. After the Cinderella story night, Chester noticed that at reading time, fairy tales with princes and princesses became a staple, or those with princes and country damsels who were wannabe princesses and who didn't want to be eaten by a dragon.

Although Chester hadn't read fairy tales as a kid, he did watch TV. He knew about damsels in distress. Sometimes they were tied to a railway track. Sometimes they were imprisoned in a dank dungeon, the next meal of a dragon or an ugly ogre. But they were always, to say the least, ill-treated.

As a kid, he had thought the dragons were cool - their breath setting fire to fields, straw houses, and other combustibles. He had wished he could do that.

He heard Candace read countless stories to Amara about princesses, princes, dragons, chivalry, and knights. He certainly understood fantasy. When he was a boy, he fantasized all day long, back and forth, between being a war hero, a baseball star, or just a decent citizen stepping into a horrific situation fraught with peril and overcoming terrible odds to take out some despicable bad-ass. He would be showered with honors and receive glowing tributes. And maybe a girl would be impressed, too. He would welcome that result. In his own way he would be a prince, if you stretched the definition. And he would have been very happy to be a prince who faced the dragon and saved the damsel.

A girl needs to know there are good men out there, and those prince stories were the purest form of what a girl needed, what Candace desperately needed way back when but didn't get. And it left her scarred, and wanting.

One particular night, as he was arranging his clothes in the bedroom for a three-day away install trip, he overheard Candace and Amara as Candace tucked her in for the night.

"Mommy, are there any dragons anymore?"

"Not like the ones in those pictures."

"You mean there are other ones?"

"Some times. Time for sleep now."

"You're just kidding," she squirmed. "There are no dragons anymore."

"No."

"Mommy, you're like a beautiful princess."

"Thank you, dear."

"Is Daddy your prince?"

She didn't know Chester had come upstairs and was in the other room. He stopped folding a pair of pants and listened.

"A prince is tall and chivalrous and waves a mighty sword, and saves the damsel in distress," she said in a sing song way. "Saves her from the dragon."

"Daddy's tall and…"

Candace's voice took on an otherworld quality. "And then the prince takes her on his magnificent horse to his beautiful castle in a far away, romantic land…"

"Daddy drives a big truck."

"And they have magical kisses."

In her voice, Chester heard a soul that longed for magical kisses.

"And Daddy buys us things," Amara said.

"And they live happily forever."

"And Daddy buys us things," Amara said again.

"Yes."

Only quiet followed. Chester heard the squeak of the bed, Candace rising. "Good night, Amara."

Chester slowly folded a shirt and laid it in his luggage. He felt a sadness that he had felt often lately. He wanted to be to Candace what Candace was to him – everything. And he wasn't. He wasn't a prince. He wasn't even in the running.

Things would be so much easier if he were a prince and there were dragons around. Love would be simple and straight-forward, just riding around on a steed all day in a suit of armor on the lookout for any damsels who might be in a predicament of one kind or another, preferably one involving a large reptile.

But life wasn't princes and castles, and Candace under-stood that, of course, at some level, for the most part.

But still, a part of him worried that she bore a deep unspoken need for someone other than him, a prince who awaited her – chivalrous, brave, charming, and loaded. And a prince's love, unlike a regular guy's, unlike Chester's, was surpassing.

CHAPTER 9

BEFORE

Chester had worries.

One day he saw Candace with an open piece of luggage on the bed and loose clothes beside it and she was putting those clothes into the luggage.

"What are you doing?" he said.

"What's it look like?"

"Packing."

"Right."

"Are you going somewhere?"

"What's your guess?"

"I guess...likely."

"Right."

"Okay, where?"

"I don't know."

"Candace, tell me what's going on."

"I don't want to talk about it."

Later that evening she unpacked her bag, all without explanation.

He figured it was the dissociative disorder thing that had moved her to do that, detaching her from her real self to cope with some painful thing, taking her to some place that wasn't her home and her family.

But where was it? She didn't talk about it. Or maybe, when it came right down to it, she didn't even know herself.

So that was one worry.

He was also worried she was seeing someone.

Now and then at home the phone would ring and he would answer but he would hear the person on the other end hang up. Candace had no cell phone, had never wanted one. Said it interfered. 'In what?' Chester had asked. 'My inner life', she had said. 'And for that matter, my outer life. If someone has something to say to me, they have the home number.'

It had happened a few times, the person on the phone hanging up when he answered. Four times to be exact. He came to realize it always happened at times when he was not supposed to be at home but on the road but the trip was cancelled. Or when the boss changed the schedule at the last minute and a scheduled work day turned into a day off.

She would sometimes call him from somewhere, without a cell phone, when she had been out for a long unexplained time. "Would you pick Amara up? I'm running behind."

Behind what? She didn't have work that day and it didn't take six hours to get her hair done. In his mind he would see her with some hunk with curly locks. What other kind is there?

She had animal attraction for sure, some would call it magnetism. She was sometimes like a lioness. When he was anxious, which was more often lately, he would see her in his mind as on the prowl for another lion, which he was not.

He didn't want to confront her because he thought he might be just imagining things. If he accused her, she might just pack up and leave. And take Amara.

But still, he was full of anguish when she'd come home late some evenings from 'nowhere in particular.' He would find himself analyzing her hair. Was it mussed? Hard to tell because of the way she wore it - long, straight, always shiny. As an experiment, he manhandled it, mussed it up, to simulate someone else having been with her.

"What are you doing?"

"Just playing with your hair."

"What a stupid thing to do in the middle of a conversation, reaching way over like that."

"Well…it's nice to play with."

It made her huffy. "I'm not a ten-year-old girl in the schoolyard."

She grabbed her hair brush from her purse and in three quick strokes her hair was salon perfect. Her lips, eyes, face - an easy cleanup job, he knew, even if she'd just had it rough in the sack.

But what about sweating? Did she take a shower somewhere before coming home? Maybe she had applied more deodorant. Did he smell more deodorant than he should after she'd been out that long, like a just-applied smell instead of an after-walking-four-hours- in-a-mall smell? He put his nose close to her and sniffed, but that didn't produce anything that you could remotely call evidence.

Thoughts of her maybe cavorting with some other guy plagued him. One evening a sense of desperation come on, a feeling of falling apart like a cheap suit. He said to her, "How much do you love me?"

Instead of answering in a way he expected, she countered with, "How much do you love *me*?", as if she was uncertain of his love.

"No one could love you more," he said.

"But if I was someone who no one could love, then saying 'no one could love you more' could mean you just barely love me."

"A gold star for logic, Candace. But you're not right. And who says you're someone who no one could love?"

"I do, among others."

"What others?"

"Well I don't have the list handy, but it stretches back a very long way."

"To your childhood?"

"Easily."

"But come on, Candace, you know you're lovable."

"No. I've got big doubts about that."

"Candace, you know I love you."

"Some days I do, some days I don't."

"How's that?"

"Lots of days something deep inside me sinks, like the bottom's falling out. Or it's soon going to."

"Bottom falling out of what?"

"Well, stuff. Like what I'm made of, for starters. Or what I'm worth, when you get right down to it."

"Well for starters, you're everything to me. And for more starters, you're everything to Amara."

Her voice softened. "Chester, one thing I know, and have known since day one with you, is that you're a good man. And when you say you love me, I hear you. And it warms me. But sometimes something inside me sinks."

"Like what?"

"Well I already said. Something inside me. It's just a feeling."

Chester didn't want to appear not to be understanding. "Like what you're made of, or what you're worth?"

She nodded. "But you don't really understand, Chester. And you can't. And it's not your fault. You just can't ever understand. I'm sorry."

In time he came to believe her. Wrenched from her mother at a tender age, set among strangers, that's got to set a child spinning at a much deeper level than thinking, at a level that thinking can't fix. He figured that in every part of her when she was young she felt unwanted, and it twisted around in her head over time like a tight knot in your shoelace that you can't undo, a knot that shouted, 'You're not lovable, Philomena. Not ever. People just come and go in your life. So give up the hope. Too bad. So sad'.

Later that night, after she had gone to bed, Chester sat in the TV room with the TV off, wondering about her out there in the world, roaming places, maybe calling out to a prince who might care to take up a sword and slay her conviction that she was not lovable.

Later still, as the clock struck midnight, and as his mind had begun to settle and calm, he found himself wondering what the boys did to her back those days when she was 'a ten-year-old girl in the schoolyard'. He knew that she had been teased, and mercilessly. A foster kid, Philomena, a name that pinned a bull's-eye on her back. The boys would see her as easy prey. And he knew boys. They would make her cry, and then they would cheer the way boys do when gas is thrown on a fire.

He felt a pain rising in his heart and wished he could have been there to help her.

She would go home from school and she would cry in her bedroom. And she would cry herself to sleep those nights.

He ached when he thought of her pain back then, and her unending feeling of loneliness.

Back then she was scared of that other kind of aggression, too, the so-called dads, a target even in her own home, and helpless to do anything about it.

Like a rabbit.

CHAPTER 10

BEFORE

It was a Saturday night and Chester was tucking Amara in bed.

"Mommy said that a long time ago there used to be dragons," Amara said.

"Right."

"And princes could kill a dragon. But she said there aren't any dragons anymore, really."

"I guess they got killed off," Chester said.

"By the princes?"

"Some by the princes. And some by just regular guys who knew they had to do what they had to do to protect their families from getting eaten."

"Not just princes killed them?"

"No, not just princes. Regular guys, too. Like dads who loved their daughters like I love you. They had to protect their families from the dragons."

"Did they live in castles?"

"No. Small wooden huts in the forest."

"Did they have a big fast horse like a prince?"

"They had big horses because they had to be big to pull a heavy plough through a field. But they were work horses so they weren't fast when it came to running."

"So the dragons were faster and could catch them?"

"Yes. But the regular guy didn't have a choice. He had to fight the dragon even riding a slow work horse, work with what he had, do whatever he could."

"He might die, though," Amara said, now genuinely worried for the regular guy.

"He might, Amara. But he had to try."

"Did princes die?"

"Maybe once in a while."

"Okay, maybe the dad could ask a prince to kill the dragon instead of him trying."

"The problem was there were a lot more dragons than there were princes. So lots of the time the dad had to try to do it himself. He had no choice."

Amara's eyes roamed the room with a worried look. "Well, lucky there aren't any real dragons anymore."

"Ya. One less thing to worry about."

"Because mommy said there aren't princes anymore like there used to be."

It hit Chester, and he was quiet a moment. "No. I guess not."

He heard the phone ringing downstairs and heard Candace shout, "Chester, it's for you."

It was a co-worker, Clement, who told Chester he really needed Chester and Bob to come over to his house right away. There was an edge of crazy in Clement's voice, and he was crying.

When Chester drove into Clement's driveway, Bob was already there waiting in his car.

"What'd he say to you?" Chester asked as they stood together in the heavy darkness outside the front door.

"Just that he's falling apart," Bob said.

When Clement let them in, his hair was all mussed like he'd been pulling at it, and he clutched a glass of bourbon like a life-line thrown to a drowning man. It was clearly not his first drink of the evening. And he hadn't tried to clean up his face from the tears. Or maybe he had, Chester thought.

Chester and Bob followed Clement in silence to the kitchen where Clement burst out loud. "I got back home at supper...from away on the road...," his voice wavy with emotion, "out three days on an install."

He walked to the counter and picked up a small sheet of paper with handwriting on it, his hand trembling.

"Michelle left this." He choked up, swallowing audibly. "She's left me, and took the kids."

Chester and Bob were standing at the kitchen table and Clement shoved the paper at Chester. "Here, read it."

Chester held it so both he and Bob could read it together. The note read:

'I've gone, and taken the kids. I told you but you wouldn't listen. I've had enough. I'll be making arrangements. Michelle.'

Clement was lightly sobbing but trying to be quiet about it.

"I'm very sorry, Clement," Chester said. "We understand how bad this must be hurting you. Did you want to talk a bit?"

"Ya," he said and kind of collected himself.

They all took a chair at the table.

"How old are the kids?" Chester asked, sympathetic.

Clement got up and brought back a framed picture and set it on the table and turned it to face Chester and Bob. It was Michelle and two happy-faced toddlers. Clement blew his nose into a tissue. "Two and three. My little darlings. Want a drink?"

Chester gave a quick shake of his head, knowing he would not get through this if he added alcohol to what was already swimming in his head. But Bob was quickly up and poured himself one and sat back down.

"What is it that Michelle told you but you wouldn't listen?" Chester asked.

"I don't know."

Chester glanced at Bob whose eyes went to Clement's glass of bourbon and back to Chester. Chester nodded, unnoticed by Clement.

"Must have said something, Clement," Chester said.

Clement didn't look at them, just kept rubbing his hands together.

"Did you ever try some marital counseling?" Chester asked.

Clement took a drink. "Did try that. A while ago."

"What happened there?"

"Not much."

"Well, what was the topic?"

"Drinking."

"Meaning?"

"She said I drink too much."

"Well do you?"

"I don't know. Didn't think so."

"But Michelle thinks so?"

"Ya."

"I know you love Michelle."

He choked up and his eyes watered heavily. "Ya." He put his forearm on the table and hid his face in it and sobbed.

"I know it hurts, Clement. Really, I do." Chester put his hand on Clement's back and gave it a pat.

Bob threw back the rest of his drink and got up and fixed himself another. Chester glanced to Bob looking for some help but Bob's frozen expression, very like a deer's in the headlights, and not a smart one, told him he was now useless.

Chester pushed on. "So, Clement, Michelle says she's had enough."

"Ya."

"Do you believe her?"

"I don't know. I don't want to."

"I think you have to."

Clement's watery eyes wandered the room a moment.

"You have wonderful kids there, Clement."

Clement turned the picture toward himself and looked at it. He nodded and his face pained and his hands clenched.

"Is Michelle a good mother?"

"Ya, pretty good."

"You helped bring those two beautiful kids into the world. You're the most important man in their lives."

"Ya."

"They really need you, Clement."

Clement swallowed hard. Chester registered that maybe Clement thought he was a failure, like Chester sometimes thought of himself as a failure, but he didn't want Clement to think that. Chester could think to ask and say all these things and march along like this because all those thoughts were usually close to him, so close that, at times, here at this table, he felt like he was talking to himself.

"I know it's hard, really hard," Chester said. "But I also know you don't want to let them down. Those little ones. Do you?"

"No."

"You don't want to let Michelle down either."

"No."

"You can be strong for them."

"Ya."

"You'd do anything to make it right for them?"

"Ya."

"Keep that idea tight to you, Clement. Tighter than anything else."

"Okay."

*

Clement didn't show up at work on Monday and didn't call in, and wasn't answering his phone. His supervisor learned about his domestic troubles from Chester and Bob and the supervisor informed the office higher-ups. The troubles probably explained his absence and the higher-ups weren't unsympathetic.

There was still no word from Clement the next day. The manager decided to make a trip to Clement's house to give him notice that his absence, whatever the reason, could not be tolerated without some communication by him to the office.

As the manager rang the doorbell, he rehearsed a line, 'Clement, we're not unsympathetic, but you still have a job to do. Clear arrangements have to be made.' He rang the doorbell a lot of times but there was no answer.

He found Clement's front door was unlocked. He entered, calling out Clement's name. The television was on in the living room.

He found Clement in his bedroom, in bed. Clement had already made clear arrangements. He, too, had acquired a Beretta, and now his brains were on his pillow.

It beat at Chester, wondering if he and Bob could have done something else. But he knew in his heart that over the years drink had made Clement weak, too weak to stand up and fight the dragon (because, when you're older, Amara, you'll learn there are still dragons), and maybe win, and maybe save his family.

The whole episode girded Chester, made him determined never to be like Clement. He would never lie down and die. If it ever came to it, he would do anything it took to keep Candace from leaving him.

CHAPTER 11

BEFORE

Seeing what happened to Clement worried Chester. He remembered the day he had come upon the note Candace had
written when she was in tenth grade, about leaving her home
when she was sixteen 'in search of the light'. Hearing Candace
reading so many fairy tales to Amara about princes made him
think she just might do that again.

Maybe he was just being oversensitive. But maybe not.

An idea popped into his head. It occurred to him that
princes very probably knew poetry for wooing, and that
Candace would know that, too. He thought it might add to
his stature with her, open up something new in their relationship, if Chester knew some, too.

Chester knew *about* poetry. That's not to say that he actually knew any poetry, only about poetry, as in he knew it when
he saw it once a year on Valentine's Day.

He was in Carbondale, Illinois, on an install, and decided that was a good place to wade into it. Carbondale was far enough from Columbus that no one would know him there. He did the best he could to get all the lithium grease from under his fingernails before going into the local library one evening.

A woman about thirty and thin and with long black hair stood behind the counter and smiled as he approached. "May I help you?"

"I'm not familiar with your set up here," Chester said. He looked around to see if anyone was close and lowered his voice. "I'm looking for some particular poetry."

She showed new interest in him, a broad-shouldered poet, maybe worked with the land, in touch with the larger harmonies.

"A particular poetry?" she asked, an alluring quality now in her voice.

"Well, not Valentine stuff. Good stuff."

He sensed her body change, maybe stiffen, her brows furrow. "I see. Classical love poetry perhaps?"

"Sounds good."

She walked him to an area that was in a side room, far off the main room, empty of people, quiet. She scanned a shelf then reached and drew down a tome of poetry selections. It was inches thick, thicker than Chester expected, an amazing number of pages. He could never get through a hundredth of it.

"I don't have anywhere near that much time to read. Could you maybe point out a couple of poems that you wish someone had written to you?"

He didn't understand what her body language said at that moment. Maybe she was ruffled, and he sincerely wished he had said something different. "I'm sorry..."

"That would be very personal, wouldn't it?" She was looking at him, but he saw she didn't say it like she was ruffled at all, just...curious.

"I'm sorry, didn't mean anything by that, really. I guess I just mean maybe you could show me love poems that are top-rated in the industry kind of thing."

She considered him a few moments, more curious, then opened to the table of contents and her eyes ran down the list of poems. She looked up at him and he saw she was hesitating, calculating, like maybe she wasn't sure, was it a 5/8th or a 9/16th she needed?

She looked back to the list like she now knew for sure. He admired that in people, people who really knew their craft and could eyeball a calibration. She flipped to a particular page in the middle of the book.

He was surprised when she began to read aloud. She read slowly and her voice was low. And Chester soon felt her emotion.

Nothing in the world is single.
All things by a law divine
In one another's being mingle.
Why not I with thine?
See the mountains kiss high heaven,
And the waves clasp one another;
And the sunlight clasps the earth,
And the moon beams kiss the sea -
What is all this sweet work worth
If thou kiss not me?

She stopped, her eyes down a moment, then her head came up and she looked into Chester's eyes, enquiring. He now saw she was a person of some sorrow. She had been kind to him to read that, something that touched her, and he knew she had a longing.

He also knew she was a hell of a good librarian.

"In one another mingle," Chester said.

"In one another's *being* mingle," she said. "It's deeper. Embraces everything."

"Meaning like your *whole being*," he said. "In one another's *being*... mingle."

He knew what that meant. He felt it often in himself, a want, a longing for Candace that way, to mingle with her whole being. But she wouldn't mingle like that with him, he knew that for sure.

She read the last lines again. "What is all this sweet work worth, if thou kiss not me?"

"Thank you for reading. There've been times, lots more lately, when I felt what that's saying, not that I'm sure I got it all. But I remember parts, like 'sunlight clasping the earth.'"

He remembered that part because he used clasps in his work all the time, small metal mechanisms that worked with ingenious interlocking parts.

"Life's a splendid thing," he said, "sunlight clasping the earth. Everything meant to clasp something else. For example, each other. But what's it all worth if your love says they don't want you? And you're all alone."

She nodded, and the particular way she did, for a moment he thought she might have been on the wrong end of love once. He hoped the cut didn't go too deep.

"A little while ago, a fellow at work took his own life with a gun. I was with him a couple of days before that and he was in terrible shape. I tried talking to him, thought it was doing some good. But you never know what's behind tears."

She was watching him closely, her eyes sympathetic.

"His wife, she maybe had good reason to leave," Chester said, "but she didn't know what it meant to him not to have her. I guess he thought just like the poem, what's it all worth if she ... well, he made his decision. Not that it was her fault."

Her eyes were on his and she gave an almost imperceptible nod, and Chester knew she understood, maybe even more than he did.

"Maybe there's some happier stuff you can show me?"

"Most of that's in Valentine stuff. Real love poetry - that carries heartache."

She slowly flipped through some more pages, glancing to see the lines, and stopped, looking carefully at a particular page to satisfy herself. She looked at him again a moment, then back to the page.

She began to read.

Had I the heaven's embroidered cloths,
Enwrought with golden and silver light,
The blue and the dim and the dark cloths
Of night and light and the half-light;
I would spread the cloths under your feet:

She quietly closed the book and her eyes went down. But Chester knew from her look that the poem wasn't finished and she knew the rest by heart.

But I, being poor, have only my dreams;
I have spread my dreams under your feet;
Tread softly because you tread on my dreams.

Chester felt it immediately, an ache. He had wanted to tell Candace that very kind of thing but hadn't really put his finger on it. He had spread his dreams under her feet; he had done that for sure. Everything he had, everything he had ever had, everything he would ever have, all his hopes, all his dreams, yes, he would spread under her feet because he loved her without limit. He should tell her that, in that way, and she would understand him. Tread softly, Candace...

He realized the librarian was watching him. There was a knowing in her eyes and her voice was quiet. "Are we getting close?"

He nodded, and his voice was quiet, too. "Ya, pretty much bang on."

CHAPTER 12

BEFORE

Chester had been doing two things. Number one, trying to memorize the two poems, and it wasn't easy because, other than 'clasps', there wasn't anything remotely mechanical in either of them. And number two, mulling about what princes and damsels and dragons might all mean to Candace in some deep down way. There was certainly something there, and he felt a lingering threat in it.

But he also felt a little crazy to be even bringing it up, as if damsels and dragons and princes should be a topic of serious consideration between two grown adults. Still, he felt some strange vulnerability in her. Maybe he was oversensitive, but he couldn't shake the danger it presented to him.

He had mulled things to a certain conclusion and stiffened his spine and walked into the kitchen where Candace was mopping the floor.

He put it to her bluntly. "Think about it, Candace, all those stories about damsels and dragons only have a prince because the damsel's in distress and needs rescuing. She's imprisoned in a cold, dark dungeon, getting badly abused and about to be dinner for an ugly reptile. That's gotta be seriously traumatic."

She swished the mop around and around the floor. "No doubt."

"The point is, distress is the key ingredient for the whole set up. If you have a damsel just merrily doing laundry or cutting hay in a field and there's no distress, no prince comes along, because what would be the point? No distress, no prince. Can't have one without the other."

"Right."

"So, let me put it another way. If a woman's going to get a prince, she has to have traumatic distress first."

"You said that already." She bent and pushed the mop into the side compartment of the bucket and pulled the lever to rinse it.

"So, really, does a woman want to go through all that agonizing, traumatic distress just to trigger some prince to come along?"

She finished rinsing and lifted the mop out and began to swish it around the floor some more. "I'd have to think about it."

"Really? You'd have to think about it? Would you like the feeling of being tied in ropes on a hard floor with a slimy dragon slobbering hot saliva nearby as it thinks about you as dinner?"

"Of course not." Swish, swish, deep into the corner where Chester knew he sometimes dropped toast crumbs in the morning. "But like you said, twice already at least, no distress, no prince. I get it."

She rinsed the mop again but now leaned it against the stove.

Chester had expected that his clever, clear-eyed analysis would have scored total victory by this point. But she turned from the stove and looked at him for the first time in the conversation. "I don't think you understand those stories, Chester."

She went to the closet and retrieved a duster-on-a-pole. He followed her into the living room where she adjusted the slatted window blinds on the big window and began to ply the pole along each slat.

Chester said, "What's it that I don't understand?"

She didn't answer at first, but then set the pole down, and her eyes looked out the window, far away, like her eyes had looked the day he had first met her in the restaurant when she was thinking back on being taken from her mother, and on what her real name was before she changed it.

Still looking out the window, she said, with a seriousness that alarmed Chester, "A brave prince hears her cries from afar...races to where she is... sees her and is smitten...battles the mighty dragon... saves her from its clutches... slays the dragon...pledges his undying love...and they ride off to his far-away castle..."

It was the same voice he had heard in Candace the night Amara had asked that question, a kind of rapture to it, transported as if a mystical wind had swept into the room. But her rendition, delivered now in front of him, and with such feeling, kind of swept him too. But more importantly, it was as though a curtain had been drawn back on Candace and he glimpsed into a room in her soul, a room made when she was young and very alone, a room that begged to be occupied, to be warmed. To be loved.

She turned and looked back at him. "Yes".

"Yes, what?"

"Yes, a woman would go through that distress to trigger a prince."

Chester had to work to throw off the rapture and regain his feet-on-the-ground. "That degree of distress? Really? Come on. But then, you're thinking there's going to be a favorable outcome after the prince arrives. That you're not going to be chomped to bits."

"No. If I knew the outcome would be favorable, then I wouldn't have to think about it. I would endure the distress. It's only if I didn't know whether the outcome would be favorable that I'd have to think about it."

"Come on. You'd *still* have to think about it? Risk a *bad* outcome on top of the distress. Bet there aren't many of those fairy tale endings."

She moved away from him and sat down on the sofa. She seemed to be contemplating things much more deeply than he had ever anticipated she would, or that he cared to see. "Whether the prince saves her or not," she said quietly, "the prince puts his own life on the line, purely to save hers." And then she said words, a hunger, that Chester heard in his head over and over later. "Something nobody has ever done for her in her entire life."

Surprised by the general turn of the conversation, Chester sat down on the sofa, regretting he had ever brought any of it up. But, on the other hand, they were connecting, and he was understanding something, sort of, although painfully. But still...

Quiet, thinking it through for herself, she said, "The key ingredient is his love. And I have no doubt whatsoever his love is not because she has a nice shape. It's true love. And I have no doubt whatsoever... she feels that message deeply."

Chester shifted a moment, still catching up to the heavy drift of it all. He said, respectfully, "So even if the prince isn't successful, and dies trying, and she isn't rescued…and she dies…"

"She dies. But she dies knowing she was loved. Truly. The supreme happiness of life."

"Candace, I love you. Truly."

"I hear you, Chester."

She got up and began plying her duster on the slats of the other window.

Chester watched her, seeing the young girl who for so long and so deeply had longed for security, for love, but it had always been denied, and it had turned off some switch deep inside her.

"Candace, I would do anything to be a prince for you. Fight any dragon for you."

She moved her head like it was a nod of acknowledgment, or maybe it wasn't.

New words were in his head. 'I'm only a poor man, no prince. I have only my dreams. But I have laid my dreams under your feet. Tread softly…'

But he couldn't say that stuff now because, in the talk of a life and death struggle of a prince and a damsel, it seemed pretty lame when Candace needed something much, much more.

He watched her quietly plying the duster. If she ever left him… he thought a moment about poor Clement, a sobbing mess of a man. He knew he could never live without Candace. What is all this sweet work worth, if thou kiss not me.

CHAPTER 13

BEFORE

Chester had memorized the two poems, but it really depended on where he was as to whether he could say them totally right.

When he was alone in the truck cab, he could say them no problem. He would even say them out loud, with feeling, thinking about Candace, as he once did at a truck stop waiting to refuel. It wasn't until he had recited the whole thing to himself that he realized his window was down. He saw the service guy looking at him with a big smirk on his face. But the smile wiped off smartly when Chester produced the Beretta.

Chester didn't know exactly why he had memorized the poems because he had no precise action plan on how to use them. He thought something would just occur to him, but it didn't, so now what?

He was scheduled to go out the next day on a five-day install run into Canada, into Ontario to Toronto. He thought that maybe over wine at a restaurant tonight, say at the El Hombre, he would surprise Candace and recite one of the poems to her. And it wasn't even Valentines. Not that he had ever done it then either. Or ever.

"How about dinner out tonight, Candace, at the El Hombre?"

She seemed evasive, not looking at him, or like she was in some mood. "Might not be able to get the sitter that quick."

"Is something wrong?" he asked.

"No." But he felt there was a dodge in her voice.

His imagination fired up like an acetylene torch. Was she seeing someone and they had been to the El Hombre? Or were they going there when he was away? Or did he work there? Or, or, or?

"Just a little date before I go away again?" he said.

She looked at him now. "Well...let's keep it short. I'll check with the sitter. Amara has a major project to finish for school."

"She's in kindergarten! How long can it take?"

"That's not the point. It's quality."

He didn't want to argue, especially when he had no idea what she was talking about.

The El Hombre was busier than Chester hoped it would be. As they studied their menus, he kept rehearsing in his head the lines of the poem he had chosen.

Nothing in the world is single.

All things by a law divine

In one another's *being* mingle.

Why not I with thine?

He could feel his nerves coming on as he thought about actually saying it out loud. He noticed the tables were a lot closer together than he remembered. There were people all around who could listen.

He ordered wine. The waiter filled her glass first, then his. Candace's fingers wrapped around the stem and she was in the act of raising the glass to her lips when Chester said, "Stop."

She looked surprised, and annoyed. And very thirsty.

Chester leaned across the table and kept his voice as low as he could.

"Nothing in the world is single."

"What do you mean?"

"All things mingle together."

"Sure. And I'd like to mingle with this wine."

"Why not I with thine?"

"Ya, why not? You've got your own."

An older woman at the next table, bored with her husband, had noticeably craned her neck toward them. Chester knew he had already mangled the lines and knew from when he memorized it that unless he started over again from the beginning he wouldn't remember it.

But he started in anyway, out of order, his eyes mostly on the menu. "The sunlight clasps the earth."

"Where are you reading that?" She looked at the menu. "In the special?"

"What's all this sweet work worth?" he mumbled. He saw the woman had turned full in her chair toward him.

Candace looked at him. "What are you talking about?"

"Nothing," he said.

*

The next morning, May 29th, he was up and out the door at 5:30 a.m. and on the way to Toronto, Canada. Candace hadn't wakened to say good-bye, although he knew she had heard him. Well, she knew he would call her that night, so that was okay.

But before he left the house, he wrote out the whole poem on nice paper with a nice pen and left it on the counter.

That evening, after driving half the day and finishing late on a difficult first install, and getting back to the motel and showering, he quickly phoned Candace, his heart beating faster than usual, excited to know if she liked the poem.

After talking casually for a few minutes about usual stuff, him not mentioning the poem, and her not mentioning the poem, he finally said, "Did you see I left you a poem?"

"I saw that paper." Her voice seemed flat. "Did you write it?"

"I wrote it, ya. But I didn't make it up."

"You copied it from somewhere?"

"Ya."

She didn't seem moved like he hoped. He thought that maybe it was because, since reading that poem when she was in tenth grade, she'd decided she didn't like poetry. Maybe she wouldn't be impressed even if he had actually made it up.

She said abruptly, now with energy, "I'm changing Amara's dance class to a swim class."

That surprise, plus her lack of response to the poem, had Chester off balance. "Why? She loves dance."

"Yes, dance is wonderful, sure, but swimming is a life skill, a survival skill. She can't be doing both. So survival trumps."

"How'd this idea come about?"

"I heard from someone about the swimming class. I took Amara to the pool this afternoon after school."

"Ya?"

"And so we watched the class. About a dozen parents were there. I met some."

"Ya?"

"Amara was really excited. She really wants to do it."

"She doesn't mind giving up dance? Really?"

"No. Not now. Now that she made a new friend, a really nice girl her age. I talked to one of the parents afterwards over coffee to get a good feel for everything."

"What did the mom say?"

"It was a dad, actually. Not a mom."

Chester imagined that there would be ten moms there for every dad, it being right after school. "Why in particular talk to a dad, not a mom?" he said.

"Because he's a fireman. He gets a lot of time off."

Neither of those points made normal sense as a response to his question. But it made good sense when it came from Candace. Chester said, "The mom was working so fireman husband takes the daughter to swim class?"

"No. They're divorced. He has joint custody and has a lot of time off. His daughter's the same age as Amara."

Chester saw the glimmer of possibility that it was all innocent, that Amara connected with the daughter *before* Candace talked to the dad so that explained why it was him that she talked to. "So you kind of introduced yourself to the dad of the girl Amara was making friends with?"

"No. I introduced myself to him before. That's when I learned he was a fireman. Amara made friends with her after."

"There were probably ten moms to every dad there."

"Yes."

"So why be talking to him?"

"I did talk to a couple of moms first. But I talked to him because he's a professional fireman. Rescues people."

"From fires. What's that got to do with swimming lessons?"

"No, he rescues people from all sorts of things, including water - like lakes and ponds and rivers."

"But why exactly be talking to him about the class?"

"Isn't it obvious? He's a professional. He knows best how to judge the quality of the instruction. He knows safety things and so forth."

"You mean ten mothers can't see that for themselves? They just stand around the pool hoping their kids don't drown from poor instruction?"

There was edge in her voice. "He was very helpful."

Well Chester was ruffled, too. "How long did you have coffee?"

"An hour. Or so."

"It took *that* long? The fact that his daughter's in the class should already tell you everything you needed to know, like that it must be good. And he knows 'cause he's a professional."

"Ya, well I needed some more detail and reassurances."

"And what did he need?"

She paused, and to Chester it seemed she was dodging a bullet. "Nothing." Her voice was defensive and sharp.

"I see."

He heard more edge now. "His daughter's really nice," she said. "Amara starts next week."

The conversation quickly tapered to a cold and bare 'good night'.

So much for poetry, Chester thought. Scrap that overrated rigmarole.

But a professional rescuer of people in a handsome fireman suit, a modern-day prince on a steel steed, now that's something. Slays poetry any day of the week. Leaves the wordy words lying flat on the page, dead.

CHAPTER 14

BEFORE

Chester crawled into the motel bed near Toronto still ruffled from the conversation. But worry soon overtook ruffle until there was only worry - heavy, heavy worry.

After a few hours, he finally drifted off to sleep and had a dream.

He was eating a bowl of cereal at the dining room table watching Candace watching the morning news in the living room when her head suddenly swiveled towards him and she said, over the volume of the anchor-man, 'Roderick finally asked me to move in with him. He's the fireman I mentioned who specializes in rescuing people. You're nice and all, Chester. But Amara and I, we've got to be moving on. I know you love her, and she loves you. I wouldn't keep you from seeing her... now and then.' Her head turned back and she continued to watch television.

He was staring at the back of her head when he woke up, his body in sweats. He realized he was panting. It was still fully dark outside and inside, the red dot of light on the mini-fridge the only thing he could see, staring back at him like a silent warning.

He sat up and threw his sheet off and couldn't stop his arms from shaking as he stared at the red dot. He was so very grateful it was only a night nightmare and not the hellish day nightmare that it would be if she ever said those words. But still, he couldn't stop shaking. It was too real, the weight of the breakfast spoon still in his hand, her eyes looking at him as her mouth said those terrible words that hurtled at him like rocks.

If she ever uttered those words... he knew with a certainty he would never be able to put one foot in front of the other. He would be only a weeping, stumbling, mess of a man, one of the live dead.

He would do anything to prevent those words from ever being said. *Anything.*

She had given him purpose and joy in life where before he had been aimless. She was the instrument of his deepest happiness even if she couldn't love him the way he loved her, or even at all. He felt he should be grateful, not in the least resentful. Life isn't perfect, people aren't perfect, so why should marriage be any different? Marriage isn't the same thing as 'I'll put up fifty percent and you'll put up fifty percent.' Sometimes you have to put up the whole hundred percent, take the whole thing onto yourself, give thanks for the good in it and hope something comes of it, something like love.

The next evening, as soon as he finished another install, and before getting any supper, he phoned her and the phone rang and rang and rang. Finally, someone picked up. The fifteen-year-old babysitter, Sarah.

"Where is Candace?" he asked.

"She said she would be out for the evening. Back by 10:30 or so," Sarah said.

Candace hadn't said anything to him about plans for an evening out. "Did she say where she was going?"

"No."

"Like a show or something?"

"I don't know."

"Like dressed casual for a show or something?"

"No. A nice dress. Glamorous sort of."

Chester's heart sank. "Oh, okay," he said.

For hours he lay in the motel bed, desperation eating him. He finally drifted off.

He dreamed again. This time a train chugged down a long straight track toward him, and he couldn't move. At first the train moved slowly, but he soon saw it was accelerating. Still, he couldn't move. Why couldn't he move? He looked down and saw his foot was wedged between two heavy railway ties. There was nothing he could do to free it. The train was now barreling full bore and closing on him. He was going to die. He saw only one option - cut off his foot. A hacksaw was in his hand and he set its bristling blade on the skin just above his ankle and heaved.

The covers on the bed flew up as he lurched forward and grabbed for his ankle. The red dot of light on the mini-fridge was staring at him again.

It didn't take Freud to understand his dream. She was going to leave him, he was sure of it. His deepest knowing knew it. His eyes brimmed with tears. His head dropped and hung loosely and he wept loudly, a pitiable man. Candace was moving on, and getting to it quickly.

For the rest of the night and the next day his mind was filled with dread: Candace was leaving him.

He knew it wasn't just two fantastical dreams that kept him trembling. One day, one terrible day and soon, she *would* turn in a new orbit and leave him, and take Amara, move on, in search of the light.

As he drove back to the motel that evening, his mind was feverish. He would be alone, separated from the only two people in the world he loved. He would be forever in darkness. But that wasn't even the major point. She would have someone else with her. Someone who didn't understand her the way he did. Someone who didn't have a calling to care for her like he had. Some animal, selfish and cruel, who would not love her. Mate with her, yes. But not love her. He knew that with a burning.

And this animal would cast a shadow over Amara, and she would never again live in sunshine. Turmoil would stir her soul until it could never again find stillness. She would grow up to be like Candace. Without Chester there to love and nourish, there would be no other outcome. And the cycle would repeat with her own child from who knows who.

The stakes were supreme. It was a plain case of *survival*. The jungle was at hand, intent on snatching his wife and daughter and committing unspeakable horrors. He couldn't live with that looming. He would fight hammer and tong, tooth and claw, nothing held back.

But exactly how? What could he do?

As he passed through the lobby of the motel to go to his room, he paused at the newspaper stand and picked up a free copy of the Toronto Star, hoping to make an attempt, however feeble, to shake his mind from his boundless sense of desperation.

He went to his room and took a cold beer from the mini fridge and slumped in a soft chair in the corner. He flipped a few pages of the paper erratically while he took a couple of gulps. A large headline jumped at him, striking him like a slap on the head:

Silk-Tie Murders Still Unsolved

Maybe it was the terrible need to escape, but he was soon immersed, losing himself in the article.

A serial killer was operating in what they called 'Cottage Country', about two hours north of Toronto. Three murders, all women, ranging in age from twenty-five to thirty-five. The killer had struck once a year in each of the last three years. Three years, three women.

Always the murders took place by a lake, three different lakes, dozens of miles apart, but all in the same region. All in warm months, between May and September. One had been in broad daylight, the other two in the dark of evening. It was believed the women's routines had been studied.

All died by the same method, 'ligature strangulation using a garrote'. Not something thin like a shoelace, certainly not a wire, either of which would leave distinct markings at the point of pressure. If a rope were used, there would have been a distinctive burn on the skin, which there wasn't. Possibly a smooth thick cord, but not as likely. There were no microscopic fibers of any kind.

The authorities speculated that the women were strangled with something flat, probably a tie, and probably a silk-tie, hence the 'silk-tie' in the headline.

There was no clear motive, certainly not robbery, nothing was ever taken, nothing disturbed. There was no molestation of any of the women. The motive seemed simply the killing itself.

The victims were not transported, each left where they had died. The killer was skilled at leaving no evidence - no clothing fibers, no hair, no fingerprints, no footprints.

And then there were the strange facts. Not one of the women showed any sign of resistance or struggle. A meticulous medical examination revealed no external mark of injury or strike to the head or anywhere else. Blood samples showed no trace of any anesthetic chemical that might have been administered, for example by a cloth to the mouth from behind. There was nothing under the fingernails, no microscopic piece of skin or blood from scratching at an attacker's face or arm or neck or hand. No red marks on knuckles or hands that could indicate a fighting moment. No bruising on legs or feet from a kicking struggle. No markings anywhere apart from very faint bruising around the neck caused by a soft ligature applied tightly over a period of time.

So how was there no struggle? How were they each so overpowered without any sign of force? Was the killer known to each of the victims? Was there some element of trust, the victims not feeling threatened? Or was a gun held to them? But no, in any of those cases those victims, all healthy young women, would nevertheless have fought mightily once strangulation began. Some physical evidence would surely show if they had given resistance or been struck.

That all led to the belief they must have already been unconscious when strangulation began. But how?

The investigation led only to dead ends, and the police admitted they currently had no active leads.

Cottage country. Pristine lakes. Pristine woods. Primitive killings.

A very unusual idea began to float in his mind. It gripped him. He set his half-finished beer on the side table and carefully read the article a second time, slowly digesting all of the facts.

Then he sat back and for two hours contemplated its many angles, its many possibilities.

The idea seemed extreme to him, the idea of hiring a hit man. *Actually* hiring a hit man - well, you don't do a thing like that lightly because it is extreme, and very dangerous. It takes a high degree of commitment to the idea, and very careful planning, because the police tend to investigate a killing pretty darn thoroughly. And they might just think that he was behind it, that it was he who had hired the hit man, which would be correct.

Yes, the police would think that the husband was behind it because the husband is always suspect numero uno. So a husband would have to be not just desperate, but stupid.

But still the idea persisted in his mind. And he found new pieces began to fall into place unbidden, like loose pieces of a puzzle falling through the air in slow motion, piecing together just as they landed on the table surface, making a fully finished puzzle.

The idea was more inventive than anyone would attribute to him - the hit man would take on the MO of the serial killer: use a silk-tie, not molest the victim, not take anything. A hired hit man wouldn't be a hired hit man if he was the crazed serial killer instead. Yes, the police would believe that it was the serial killer striking again. An open and shut case. So nothing would come back to him.

It was a stroke of genius, and that didn't happen a lot, and he felt lifted by it.

He took a few deep breaths and considered it all again. His plan had two things going for it: the serial killer thing, and a second thing. And that second thing - well that was just so ingenious and unimaginable that the police would just never imagine the second thing.

He realized he felt calm, and he hadn't felt that way in days. He was calm now because he had a plan. And he saw that his plan was good, that he wasn't helpless, and that, no, he wasn't coming unglued.

*

He woke up the next morning and felt unusually different. Well it wasn't every night you planned that kind of thing.

But, no, it was something else. He felt charged by a sense of purpose, of mission.

He looked at his watch. It was 6:00 a.m. He could finish today's install well before noon, rent a car, and be on the road. Cottage Country was just two hours away. And he needed a cottage.

*

It was 2:00 p.m. when he parked his one-day rental car in a small town in the middle of Cottage Country. He knew that the cottage he needed would have to be one where there was privacy, no one too close by to witness anything. So the cottage would have to be privately owned, not some cottage camp place where cottages were stacked side by side like cordwood.

He knew that most private cottage owners used a rental company to rent out their properties - advertising on the net, the perfect photos, the communications with renters, the rental contracts, the money collection – the company taking maybe fifteen percent of the action.

Before leaving Toronto, he had phoned the biggest cottage rental company in cottage country, 'Cottage Country Cottage Rentals', to get their address.

He now walked into their office located on the main street of the town.

"Hi," he said. "I'm the guy from Ohio who called earlier."

"Yes," the woman said with a big smile. "I remember. We get lots of your people up our way. This area's one of the premier vacation spots for your people. And ours, too."

"How's business?"

"Always hopping around here."

Sure, thought Chester. With a crazed killer on the loose, I'll bet cottage rentals are soaring. Add a little something to your vacation experience by dodging a serial killer.

"How can I help you?" she said.

"I'd like to rent a cottage in this area for my family, three people, just my wife and I and our daughter. So we don't need anything with five bedrooms or anything."

"For when?"

"Week of July 8. I realize it's only a month away."

"No problem. We have a few left that would suit three people precisely."

'Precisely', Chester thought. Three people, not four. Such precision. In his world, precision in a machine part meant metal tolerances within 1/1000 of an inch, thinner than a thin piece of paper.

"Could give you a real deal on a nice place on Ring Lake," she said.

"Why Ring?"

"No particular reason. The owner's motivated, that's all."

Were the other owners not motivated? Like were they saying 'who the hell cares'? Doubt that. No, owner motivation would be running very high around here. Maybe they'd even throw in a fridge of beer.

He knew which three lakes the killer had killed on and Ring wasn't one of them, which was good because the killer had never hit the same lake twice. So when it did happen on Ring, the police would see that it fit the pattern - a new kill, a new lake.

"Let's see some pictures," Chester said.

He reviewed them. The cottage interiors had been shot in wide-angle to prevent you from having any possible idea of actual room sizes. There were glamorous shots of sunsets from the properties, one showing some happy-faced guy at the beach holding up a fish on the hook with the seeming message that at this cottage you won't go hungry.

He viewed pictures of three other cottages as well.

"Drive out to the cottages and do an on-site inspection of each of them," the rental woman said. "Walk the properties to see the views. But the cottages are locked up at the moment. The owners are not around, and no renters are there just yet. You're free to peek through windows."

It took him three hours to get to the lakes and carefully inspect all four cottages. As it turned out, the one on Ring Lake best filled the bill - it had the most privacy from neighbors, the best concealment, the best layout of land and roads and hiding places. Even the price worked. And it had a really nice beach for Amara.

He returned to the cottage rental company and signed up for the week of July 8.

He had enjoyed the drive, a fine bright June 1st, beautiful blue lakes, deep green forests, birds lively in the trees. In about five weeks he would be back with Candace and Amara. In the meantime he had to get Candace onside with this cottage rental idea, plus hire a hit man, plus come up with a lot of money for the hit man.

As he drove from the picturesque town nestled in idyllic cottage country, he thought about the notorious and mysterious silk-tie serial killer. Who would sneak about and kill people in an area as beautiful and wholesome as this?

CHAPTER 15

BEFORE

For five years now he had lived in what was called 'Cottage Country', a land of lakes a couple of hours north of Toronto. His place was a quaint chalet-style cottage on a tree-studded property on Fox Lake. The road followed the whole way round the lake, quiet and winding, feeding to a hundred cottages that dotted the shoreline, some of them winterized and lived in all year round, like his.

The first of his three kills, the one in July three years ago, had not been planned, and because of that he had assumed greater risk. He learned not do it that way, impulsively, ever again.

He had had thoughts of a killing for years, but had never acted on them. But that morning a special opportunity had presented itself and he found the idea overtook him, the urge irrepressible, rising from that deep dark place, and he could not push it down.

He knew Cindy's car and had seen it through the cottage window, through the trees, passing by on the road behind. He knew her kayak strapped on the roof. The day was calm and quiet, perfect for kayaking. And he knew where she was going - Craig Lake, a large lake about five miles away.

He had a good-looking face, boyish in a way, which he knew was attractive to women. It conveyed no threat, a face they could trust, which made things so much easier.

She was the only one of his kills who knew him.

"Hi there," she called out, a big smile, her voice welcoming as his canoe rounded the edge of the isolated cove on the un-cottaged island in the middle of Craig lake. He saw her wave. He knew she would be here, resting and sunning on the small sand beach.

He also knew she would be alone.

The cove was set back deep, sheltered from winds by rock heights projecting out into the water and covered with low conifers. At the rear of the beach a slope climbed quickly into a dozen acres of dense woods and bush. It was a calm beach of respite and relaxation in the middle of a long paddle.

He noted all the elements of isolation like ticking the boxes on a questionnaire: there was no one else on the island, no cottage with a sight-line to the cove, no cottage even close to shouting distance, no one on the lake itself, since it was a quiet Monday morning.

He knew she parked her car at the public boat launch at the end of the lake two miles down. He would never use that launch, of course. He knew hidden points of access.

The urge was hovering in him like a cobra fixing a rabbit in its stare. A question penetrated his mind like a flash of lightning opening a dark sky – was he the cobra? Or was he the rabbit?

He turned his canoe toward her and after a few strong strokes let it glide gently, the bow brushing into the sand at the shore and coming to a gentle stop.

"I like this spot, too," he said, still seated. "Away from things."

"Yeah, it's great." She was upbeat. Very upbeat.

He stepped out of the canoe and with a strong hand drew it a further yard up onto the sand. He would have to remember to sweep the sand later to remove the print of the bow. The same for his feet.

She was all smiles, about thirty, nice enough looking, dark brown hair in a pony-tail, her white one-piece bathing suit showing her brown tan and good figure.

Scattered pieces of gnarled bleached driftwood lay by a rock face. A circle of rocks ringed a deep hollow in the sand, a fire-pit filled with blackened charred wood bits, the remnants of a teenage party. An axe or hatchet had been employed, clean unburned wood chips scattered near the pit, the wood scavenged from the offerings of dead limbs and fallen branches in the bush behind.

"Day off?" he said.

She was a dental hygienist, one of three who worked for his dentist in town. The office was always open Mondays. She had once cleaned his teeth.

"Yeah," she said, smiling. Her own teeth were perfect pearly whites and he figured she would be under instruction to flash them often at patients to raise the whiteness bar.

She removed her sunglasses even though the sun was brilliant. Why did she do that? he wondered. He had noticed from the dental chair that her eyes were attractive.

"We get three-day weekends all summer," she said. "I get Mondays off. The other two hygienists get Fridays. We put in the extra hours on the other four days. The work days are longer, but so's the daylight."

She was separated. He knew her husband, although not well, from playing pick-up hockey with him in town. The talk in the change-room was that she was headstrong and selfish, and that explained everything, guys not looking too deeply into relationship analysis or too hard at another guy's shortcomings in the loving department.

"I need a dip," he said. "It's hot on the water even without the paddling."

"For sure. I was already in. The water's great."

He was wearing only a bathing suit, no shirt. He walked into the water a few strides then dove. He swam out, swam for minutes, mostly underwater, and mostly in circles.

*

Earlier that morning he had sat on his cottage deck alone, for he lived alone, untouched breakfast toast and coffee on the round cedar table in front of him. He could only stare at the lake, his mind dark and troubled, agitated from the nightmare that had awakened him. His mother still reached him in his dreams.

Would he ever shake her? It didn't seem so. If anything her tentacles strangled him more. Much more some days.

The memory of a day when he was eleven crawled like a pestilent rat into his mind.

School had been let out an hour early for some teacher meeting. He had told his mother about it the day before and that he would be home early.

Maybe she had forgotten. Or maybe it didn't matter.

He had come straight home. He had wondered where she was. Not in the kitchen, not in the laundry room. Not watching TV. The car was there. The door had not been locked. She should be home. But the house was quiet like she wasn't home. He looked out the window to the back yard. She wasn't in the yard.

He heard a noise upstairs. Bed springs? Then a groan. Was she sick?

He saw a bottle of rye, half empty, beside the kitchen sink. His mother didn't drink rye. She drank gin. His father didn't drink anything.

It made him nervous. He climbed the stairs quietly. He walked down the hall, stepping past a pair of big pants lying on the floor, approaching his parents' bedroom door, which was half open.

He heard his mother giggling. He didn't look in.

He took a step back in the hall and it made a squeak.

A man's head suddenly appeared at the bedroom doorway.

They looked at each other, eye to eye, for a long moment. The man had an air of authority, a no-nonsense kind of look, not angry, not even surprised, just a no-nonsense look. Not the least put out. No shame. No unease. No words.

The head withdrew back into the bedroom and he heard him say, offhand, 'Tomorrow?'

He went downstairs into the kitchen because he couldn't think of what to do. Nerves. Fear. Like an automaton he did what he always did when he came home - he took a cookie out of the tin in the corner of the counter. The man came down the stairs into the kitchen. He looked now like he wanted to have conversation.

'Hand in the cookie jar, uh? Me, too,' he said in a heavy eastern European accent. He gave off a chill like an open freezer.

'School cut short?' the man pushed. 'Hope that's it and that you weren't skipping.'

He didn't answer, just looked along the floor. If I was skipping school I wouldn't have come home early and been so obvious, stupid. And how the fuck is that any of your fucking business anyway? You're not my father. What the fuck are you doing here?

The man turned without further word and walked on out of the house like he had finished a service call.

His mother came down stairs into the kitchen wrapping a satin housecoat over a black baby-doll silk negligee. 'Don't tell your dad. I will. I've been seeing him for a while. His name's Nick. He loves me.'

So what? Dad loves you! I know that for sure. And doesn't that carry a little more weight? Like...wake up!

But he didn't say a word because he felt his insides dissolving into a liquid slush and he had no bearings.

Where was his life now? Where did he fit into this? And what about Dad? Where did he fit in?

Dad, of course, didn't fit in. When he came home and found out, he was gone the next day. The house was an inheritance his Mom had got, so it was hers, so she could stay put, so his dad was out, and Nick was in, officially a step-father, who liked alcoholic drinks more than any human company.

His dad paying support for his mother meant he couldn't afford anything but a rooming-house room, and that was no place to raise a kid the judge said. So his Mom got custody.

His Mom also told the Judge that a filthy rooming-house room with nut bars down the hall hollering at one another about who bought the beer anyway, banging walls with things that were most certainly lethal weapons, and TVs too loud at all hours of the night, and trash all around the front door and hallways, was no place for a father to have access visits to his son. Which was probably true.

So he saw his dad on Saturdays at the shopping mall in the food court. Fries and a coke.

But the visits became harder and harder, his dad so angry with his mom, always asking him questions about Nick, the lover boy Serb. He would try to get his Dad to talk about something else, like going fishing together, but his dad said it wasn't in the cards. Or maybe they could try camping together like they always talked about. But that wasn't in the cards either. And one way or another, it always came back to upsetting talk about his mother and lover boy.

The visits became fewer, the visits became shorter, because they were just two people sitting across a table from each other, quiet and hurting.

Two months later his dad left for out west. For better work, he said. Can I go with you, Dad? No. He was too bitter to give a real thought to taking him along. He didn't even say if he would ever be back.

He clung desperately to the hope that his father would return.

But he never did. Sometime later, maybe a year, he was killed in a car accident speeding headlong off a country road into a tree because, for the first time in his life, he took up drinking, and he knew he couldn't handle it a bit.

His father was dead. Gone forever.

But it was no accident.

His mother had killed him.

And over time that had coiled in his mind like a deadly snake.

*

When he came out of the water, dripping, he grabbed a towel from the canoe. He dried off a bit, noticing Cindy didn't hide her eyes admiring his strong body.

"I'm glad you came in here," she said. "I know you know Neil from hockey. I know that can be embarrassing in its own way. I don't want you to feel embarrassed or anything, being here with me."

He nodded as he toweled his arms.

"We've both decided to move on," she said.

He nodded again, observing in more detail what was around the cove, and out toward the lake, like maybe he was embarrassed and someone might see him with her. She seemed not the least bit concerned that he knew Neil and that there could be awkwardness. Her flirt dial was cranked high.

Well no loving's coming from me, baby doll. On the contrary, your train's about to pull into the station.

He tossed the towel into the canoe. He came close to where she sat in the sand and looked down at her. "Mind if I sit down?"

"Not at all." She seemed both relieved and cheered that he was being sociable. She smiled and patted her hand on the sand beside her to show him where to sit. Controlling, he thought.

He sat just beyond the spot. "We've been this close once before," he said. "In your professional capacity."

She laughed. "Yes, I know." She said it like, 'it's not like I'd forget you'.

He looked out far across the lake, still quiet, still empty.

Not a soul stirring.

There was now a pounding inside him. A growing and surreal feeling of detachment from himself, a sense of being irretrievably possessed. The cobra rising.

He scanned the lake once more. No one in sight.

A large bird was flying high, far out. "Do you see that?" he said.

She put on her sunglasses and peered into the distance and picked it up. "Yes."

She was four feet to his right. She had to turn her gaze to her right, away from him, lifting her head slightly to follow the bird's flight. Her neck was perfectly exposed.

"A blue heron?" he asked, shifting slightly toward her. "Long neck?"

He needed no weapon. He formed his right hand. Open, flat, firm, the fingers tight together.

She squinted, concentrating on the bird. "Yes, I think so."

Lightning quick, the knife-hand strike, leading with the hard knuckle at the base of his little finger into the soft white flesh of her delicate neck. The brachial stun - shocking the carotid artery, the jugular vein, the vagus nerve. He knew she would either drop unconscious or suffer an involuntary muscle spasm or paralysis. Either way Cindy would drop, and she wouldn't be able to stop the next blow.

She fell straight back and her head thumped the sand. She was out cold and would be for twenty to forty seconds.

He looked out and around. Still nobody anywhere.

He got in front of her and tucked his left hand behind her upper back and raised it a foot, her head lolling backward. He firmed the fingers of his right hand again, raised it, and struck hard at the side of her soft neck. She wouldn't be conscious for at least a minute now, and would be woozy even then. He let her head fall back down onto the sand.

He walked to her kayak and carried it across the ten yards of sand and up the slope into the thick bush just enough that it couldn't be seen from the water. Then he went to his canoe and grabbed up a quart-sized white plastic water-proof container and unscrewed the lid. He took out a bunched dark-brown silk-tie, let it drop its length, and wrapped it once around his neck like a scarf as he walked back to her.

Her white one-piece bathing suit reflected the brilliance of the sun. For a moment he admired her brown, well-turned legs.

He lifted her still-limp body and carried her up into the bush only a few yards until he was sure he could not be seen from any-where. He had to work quickly now because she would come to very soon, and he was no torturer. He didn't want her to know her end.

He laid her down flat on dry, pine-needled earth. He lifted her head and neck and laid the brown silk-tie crossways under her neck then turned her over so he was not looking at her face but the back of her head and neck. He wrapped an end of the tie in each of his hands and wound it tightly around her neck once and began to pull. He was strong, the tie squeezing into the soft white flesh, but not so much as to leave much mark observable later.

After a full minute he released the strangling grip. He waited a few moments to let his hands and arms settle and relax. Then he drew the tie tight again and pulled another full minute.

He repeated the sequence once more.

Three minutes - a very long time.

He unwound the ends of the tie from each hand and wrapped the tie once around his own neck as before and carried her farther into the woods. About fifty yards on he found what he needed, a shallow depression in the ground behind a wide clump of low cedars. He would find a similar place for the kayak.

He laid her down. She wouldn't be visible to anyone standing on the cove's beach or even venturing into the bush for firewood unless they were almost on top of her. He decided not to cover her with bows of spruce or pine. He wanted her discovered, just not today.

He bent and held her hand and gently pressed a finger on her wrist for twenty seconds to check for a pulse. Negative.

He took a pen light from his pocket to check her pupils' response to light, lifting the lid of first one eye, then the other. Negative.

He stood back and looked at her for several moments. This was a woman who was not coming back to life.

He wondered how it would appear in the papers. Cindy? Or Cyndy? Or Cynthia?

CHAPTER 16

BEFORE

Getting Candace to agree to go to the rental cottage for a week's vacation was, of course, indispensable to Chester's plan.

But when he talked to her, she seemed to be in an edgy mood. He feared that she really just didn't want to be cooped up at a cottage with him for a week, even though it would be with Amara, too. He feared also that she might have better offers elsewhere.

"Why did you rent it without talking to me?" she said.

"I wanted to surprise you. And you'll love it. It's amazing up there in cottage country."

"Cottages have mice and I grew up in places with mice and never again. They're just little rats. I'm not exposing Amara in her tender years to rats marauding in her bedroom. She'll have nightmares supreme like I did."

"There aren't any mice at this cottage. Not a one. I got assurances."

"Oh, sure. What do you think they're going to say? I suppose they also told you the mosquitoes there are real friendly and don't feed on people, just stay to themselves in the bushes."

"Candace, it'll be fabulous."

"I would like to have choices. Maybe we can cancel and reconsider this."

"I can't. We're outside the window for cancelling."

"No refund?"

"No. Because the demand is so high."

"If demand is so high they can rent to someone else."

"No, what they do is they get our money, which they've already got, and if we cancel, they keep our money, and also get someone else's money. Two weeks rent for one week. Sharp operators up there."

"So you've already paid it?"

"Yes."

"That's stupid not to have asked me."

"But that's what a surprise is."

"There's good surprises and there's bad surprises."

Ya, Chester thought, more than you know.

"You still haven't got your bonus check," she said.

Truth was he did get his bonus check, just two days before, but didn't want to tell her because he needed that $6,000, and a lot more, for the hit man he was sourcing out.

"A cottage costs money that we don't have," she said.

"But not as much as you think. You pay rent of $1,100, all in. But then there's savings."

"What are you talking about?"

"Well, because you're not at your own house that week, you're not racking up electricity costs for everything, like expensive A/C. And not using water either. Or gas for the water heater and stove."

"Big deal."

"Yeah, but I haven't told you the real savings yet."

"Okay, what?"

"The rent. $1,100. That's Canadian money. In our money, it's like half that! You could go shopping there."

Candace had never been to Canada, and Chester thought it would sound attractive to her as a country with prices, after currency conversion, equal to permanent going-out-of-business sales.

But she didn't soften. "You've still got all the extra costs of gas for the car, plus wear and tear, just to get there."

"But it's somewhere different, a faraway cottage place. New experiences. It would thrill Amara, playing in the sand and in the clean water at a clean lake, plus camp fires."

"And fighting off little rats."

The next day he felt Candace's mood had lifted somewhat. He took Amara for a walk to visit a certain friend down the street. When they came back, Amara asked Candace if they could go to a cottage, like her friend, Rebecca, down the street, and swim at their own beach and have a wiener roast and boat rides and look at the stars at night, like Rebecca, down the street.

Candace looked at Chester. "Recruiting a five-year-old neighbor as an accomplice is not beneath you?"

"I guess not."

CHAPTER 17

NOW

In Detroit, Chester hung up from his phone call with Roly. They had now had two conversations, and today he would deliver the further $8,000 to Chantelle at the laundry to bring Roly up to the ten grand up front deposit he wanted. The arrangements for the payment of the final $40,000 had just been settled - the first $20,000 in a shoe box under the bed in the cottage just before doing the hit; the last $20,000 three days after the hit, delivered to Chantelle as per usual.

But who really had the serious kind of coin lying around that Roly was demanding? Not Chester. And it wasn't going to fall from the sky anytime soon.

When he first struck his plan, he knew a hit man was going to cost serious money, and he wasn't far off in his guesstimate. He had a good credit rating and knew he could get a bank loan. But he also knew he would have to answer a lot of questions at the bank, one being 'what do you want the loan for?'

His mind had wrestled with the bank loan question one day and that night he had a dream. He was seated in a small office in the bank with the bank woman and had told her that he needed to borrow $30,000 to $40,000. Her extremely long polished manicured fingernails tapped rapidly for over a full minute without her saying a word to him. She looked more like she was finishing an important e-mail to her boyfriend about what they should do tonight, or maybe entertaining him about the goof she had in her office right now, all the while showing businesslike concentration like she was going through eight security walls to get to his measly file particulars.

Then she poised her long fingernails above the keyboard and said, 'would this be for a particular purchase like a car, a boat? Or is it for an investment?'

'An investment'.

Her fingernails pounced on the keyboard with amazing accuracy even though it was like typing with a set of knives, clickety-clackety, the nails scurrying all over the keys and hitting far more of them than are required to spell 'investment'. Then she looked at him. 'The thing is with investments, even what you think are sound investments, you always have to ask yourself if you can handle risk. There's always risk. So can you afford to lose it?' She leaned forward to him the way bank people do so they can look right into your financial soul. 'Lose even all of it?'

'I already know I'm going to lose all of it'.

'You do? All of it? What kind of investment is that?'

'I'm hiring a hit man to take somebody out'.

'Oh'

'So I'm going to lose it. All of it'.

'Yes, I would think that's the way it works. I see you have a good equity position and a great credit score, so I don't see any problem.'

When he woke, though, he realized it wasn't going to be that easy. If the police ever did conclude it was a hit man and not the serial killer at their rental cottage, they would look directly at him, and that, *coinciding with him recently borrowing a large sum of money,* could lead to a lot of suspicion, especially because the money wouldn't have been used for the thing he said to the bank that he was going to use it for, whatever that was. Yet the money would be clean gone, and he couldn't say where it went. Well yes, he could say where it went, as in make up where it went, but he would need proof, which he wouldn't have. So how would he answer all those awkward questions put to him by clever police investigators?

He had concluded that there was no answer to the amazing coincidence of him borrowing an unexplained large sum of money just before a hit man appeared out of nowhere without a very big finger being pointed at him.

It was then that an ingenious idea hit him like a bolt of lightning. He didn't need a *large* sum of money. Why didn't he think of that earlier? He needed a *small* sum of money, so much smaller that he could get by without a bank loan.

The $2,000 cash he had paid to Clyne came from money he had secretly been hiding in a coffee can in his basement workshop and which formerly had contained bolts. He had been saving for a surprise trip to Hawaii in the hopes of improving his relationship with Candace. He had been hiving off amounts from his paychecks for two years and had accumulated $3,500. But Hawaii was now, pretty clearly, off.

After paying Clyne, that had left him $1,500. He had received his annual bonus check of $6,000 several days ago, but hadn't told Candace, naturally. He had not deposited it, instead just cashed it, so it wouldn't show on their joint account, the only account they had.

That brought him to $7,500. $2,000 of that had gone to Roly a few days ago, leaving Chester with $5,500. So he had needed another $2,500 for today to get to $8,000 for the rest of the deposit for Roly to keep the wheels turning.

So where to get the $2,500? Chester's mom had loved Westerns, like he had told Candace way back, and over time his mom had accumulated a collection of rare Western Whiskey bottles, fourteen to be exact, empty of course, in pristine condition and in different shapes and colors of glass. Chester had been seventeen when he inherited the collection from his mother's estate, which had consisted solely of the said rare Western Whiskey bottles. Chester hated to do it, but a week ago he sold them to a Detroit antique dealer for $1,600. That had left him short only $900 for the $8,000 he needed for Roly. He produced that $900 via a cash advance on his American Express.

That left him with no cash, which was a very long way from the balance owing to Roly of $40,000.

From the time Chester was ten to the time he was thirteen, he had had a paper route. Sixty papers, sixty houses, six nights a week – rain or blizzards notwithstanding. Most of the paper route money he collected Friday nights was in coins and he wanted to build a proper rare-coin collection. The brown leather pouch bulged by the time he got home and he would dump it out onto the kitchen table and spread the coins for inspection. He never found much.

The thing was, his father had had a paper route when *he* was a kid and valuable coins back then were much more common and he had amassed a respectable rare-coin collection and it was passed on to Chester when his father died when Chester was eight.

Chester had always assumed that he would have it until he was ninety years old when it would be worth an unimaginable fortune, and he would show his kids, grandkids, and great grandkids what he had been able to achieve by just carefully checking each coin on collection nights, giving credit, of course, if asked, to the coins he inherited from his father.

When Chester had delivered the papers all those nights, well over 1000 nights, although he had dreamed about what the fruits of his labor, and his father's labor, might buy, and although he had a lively imagination in that regard, he never imagined it would be to buy a hit man. An action figure hit man maybe, but not a real one, like Roly, who would coldly strangle a person to death for cash payment. Mercifully, that had been left out of the range of his imagination at eleven.

But it had now come to that, the sale of his beloved coin collection to buy a hit man.

The same day he sold his mother's Western Whiskey bottle collection, he had wrangled for an hour with a rare-coin dealer in Detroit, selling the coin collection for cash of $1,320.

That still put him nowhere close to the $40,000 he needed for Roly. But that's where the ingeniousness of his revised plan came in. The plan neatly whittled that $40,000 down to a measly $2,520. With the $1,320 he had from the sale of the coin collection, he was short only $1,200 to get to the $2,520. A couple of American Express cash advances of $600 each would produce that. And if anyone was asking, well, it was for the cottage holiday in Canada, just walking around money.

No big deal.

CHAPTER 18

BEFORE

His second kill, two years ago, had been different from the first in one significant respect - he had planned it with prudence.

With Cindy - the kill at the cove - he hadn't planned it at all. He had been impulsive, and that had attracted unforgivable risk. A kill in broad daylight, an unprotected view from the lake, a canoe jaunt across open water to get there, another to leave, all fully exposed. Never again.

He would never again surrender prudence to that vaulting urge.

There had been self-lashing, yes, but not self-loathing. That required the presence of another concept, a recognition of immutable good to stand as a measure of what he did, something his mother had destroyed in him long ago.

His luck had held. No one in the whole year after had come knocking at his door to ask him about Cindy and his whereabouts on that given day.

After Cindy, he had believed he would not kill again. She had sufficed, the urge satisfied and shoved back into the jar, the lid turned.

Or so he thought. As time passed he found he was drawn back ever more powerfully to the memory of that day at the cove, the feelings it produced - the thrill, and the soothing - like no other.

Within a year after Cindy, the unrelenting impulses fed him again, his mind restless. He knew he couldn't outrun them.

And he knew there was only one cure.

He noticed certain women all the time, but for months now he had sifted which ones actually fit his needs, secretly learning more about them, creating a ready pool from which he would one day have to select and draw.

But which one? And when? He hadn't settled either question until one day, by pure happenstance, the triggering event occurred.

She was someone he had noticed many times around town and had taken that special interest in her. On that one particular day he overheard her in the grocery store in conversation with a woman who seemed a colleague. They were at the deli-counter, glancing into the glass case at the special meats and cheeses as they talked, their backs to him.

"I heard about the drama yesterday in geriatric," she said.

"A regular boxing match," the colleague said. "One was having a psychotic episode and the other one stepped right into it swinging."

"An even match?"

"Pretty much. Bruises to both. Took two orderlies to pry them apart."

He knew she was a nurse and worked at the hospital. He knew her name was Diana because he had made a point of finding that out. He knew where she lived - on a lane on a lake with no street lights - and that her boyfriend was a Ron and that she had no children.

When he circled back in the grocery aisle and stood feigning indecision in front of twelve kinds of dish soap, his back to theirs, fifteen feet away, Diana was saying, "No, Ron's away then."

"Oh?"

"Ya, has to go to Montréal for five days. They're training him on a new process. Back late on the 14th, the Saturday."

"Then why don't you and I do something the Friday night? We're both on days."

"Don't think it'll work. I'm creating a little surprise for him. I'm going to paint the living room and dining room while he's away. So I'll be up to my elbows those nights."

"Okay, then how about we do a couple's thing at our place after he's back? Like dinner. Then dessert in the hot tub."

"Great. Let's do it."

Later, when he checked his calendar, he saw that the 14th being a Saturday corresponded to May. It was now the last week of April. With grim satisfaction he noted that the Friday was, of course, the 13th. He would target that night. It would excite the superstitious. But it would more importantly allow him a few nights to case the place when Ron was away and she was alone.

*

He lifted the canoe off his shoulders and slipped it into the water almost without a sound. He swatted at another black-fly, blindly because it was dark. It was May, and in cottage country that meant black-flies. Especially in the woods. No point complaining, or even being annoyed. Things are what they are.

He had switched off his cell phone two hours before when he was still at home. Not only did he not want to be disturbed, he didn't want his location anytime in the hours that followed to be known, a digital fingerprint archived at the telecommunication company. He wanted to be able to say he was fishing and so naturally didn't want to be disturbed. So he left his phone at home.

Twenty minutes earlier he had parked his truck three hundred yards away in a small grassy stretch off the quiet bush-side road, his truck not visible from the road unless you were both walking and observant. But no one ever walked there. And it was dark. And there were no cottages on this part of this side of the lake. And he had seen no vehicle on the road on any of the four separate nights when he drove the road and parked in the past two weeks.

After parking tonight, he had strapped on the backpack, shouldered the canoe on its yoke, hooked an empty fish bucket to one of the canoe's cross-members, and grabbed up his fishing pole. He walked two hundred yards along the dark road, lit only by moonlight, then turned off onto an indistinct path that in a hundred yards gave access to a tiny, eight-foot wide, shallow pebble beach.

He had canoed dozens of the lakes in this particular region of cottage country in the past years and knew all of the official, public access points. But more importantly, he knew the obscure, known-only-to-locals ones, hidden from casual observation from road or water.

He had been here to fish last night as well, to provide a cover if needed tonight. The season had just opened and he had caught two trout not far from shore. He had quickly put them into the cooler full of ice in the truck, then into the freezer at home, then back out into ice in the cooler in the truck today.

An hour before parking earlier this evening he had taken them out, wrapped them in plastic, and put them in the backpack. They were pristine, and thawing.

He filled the fish bucket with water, set it in the canoe and slipped the trout from their plastic sheaths into the bucket water. Out of ice for an hour and a half now, they gave every appearance of newly caught and clubbed. He unstrapped the backpack and set it in the canoe.

He looked out across English Lake, dark but for moonlight tracing a wide and shimmering silver path on the water, only a small breeze stirring. Diana's cottage home was on the opposite shore, a mile away, a twenty-minute paddle. He shoved off.

Unbidden, the words of a long forgotten school poem rose to his mind. 'The moon was a ghostly galleon tossed upon cloudy seas. The road was a ribbon of moonlight over the purple moor. And the highwayman came riding, riding, riding.'

*

Her home was a one-storey cottage with cream-colored aluminum siding, a cedar-shake roof, three-bedrooms, and a big deck facing English Lake.

He had determined on an earlier night she had no dog.

The neighbors on both sides were absent, the homes dark, just as they had been dark the three previous times he had been here in the past two weeks. Those neighbors probably lived in Toronto so blew in for the May 24 long weekend and for weekends and holidays thereafter. So for now, May 13, they were not around.

In three earlier reconnoiters he had cased her property as well as the adjacent properties and the wider neighborhood. He had watched Diana's and Ron's windows late at night to establish the interior configuration of the house and determine any habits he could.

Two nights ago, he had observed only Diana. Ron was already away in Montreal. From different vantage points in the dark yard he had watched her painting. Painting demands bright lights and open windows, blinds open, fresh air circulating.

He had heard the music - rhythm and blues - drifting out from her open windows and had seen the music propelling her paint roller up and down, up and down. He found she kept her front and back doors locked even before bed-time. He was no lock-picker, so that was out. Tempting though it was that last night, he wasn't going to do a smash-his-way-in home invasion while she painted. That wasn't planning. That wasn't prudent. That was messy and stupid.

Tonight, there was no music. He had seen the lights go dim in the living room and the dining room. No more painting. The window blinds were also closed everywhere, including the bedrooms. Everything seemed more buttoned up, as if she were getting ready for bed.

But still, in the interests of not being overcome with fumes, she had left windows open a few inches at the bottom. When he got close enough, he also heard a fan going.

Now he saw the bathroom light come on. He knew which room that was, of course - the only frosted window. It was open two inches at the bottom. He brought himself close and listened, his ear only inches away. He dared not try to see in; he wasn't a voyeur, and he had no practical need to see her.

At first he heard only quiet sounds - a little water running, a tapping on ceramic - maybe Diana at the sink. Then, after moments of complete quiet, a loud bursting of water spray on tile. The shower.

*Thank you, Diana. That was going to save a lot of trouble.
He had planned that his entry would be through a window, but
hadn't decided which window. Now he knew.*

*He slipped on thin gloves. On the last visit he had scouted a
fat stump from the neighbor's woodpile. He retrieved it now and
carried it across the rough lawn. A narrow flower garden with
fresh earth ran tight against the side of the house directly below
the master bedroom window. Careful not to leave footprints, he
placed the stump into the soft earth to give him the two feet he
needed to climb up and work the window.*

*Even though the blinds were closed he could see at their edg-
es that the light was on inside the bedroom. He could also see
the window was open two inches at the bottom. He unstrapped
his backpack and set it in the grass. He took off his shoes, light
boat shoes with flat soles, no signature treads, and put them in
the grass.*

*He stood on the stump and with a short knife punctured
a corner at the top of the bug screening just enough to receive
the wire mesh cutters. With those he snipped along the top of
the screening, then down both sides, then along the bottom. He
threw the square of freed screening onto the grass.*

*He placed his fingers under the window frame and lifted
carefully. It slid easily, quietly, and held in place when it was all
the way up. He raised himself and climbed in, lifting the plastic
blinds out of his way as he did.*

The house smelled strongly of fresh paint.

*All was quiet. He made sure to reset the blinds as they were
before. He shut the bedroom overhead light off. No other light
was on in the room and it was dark but for weak ambient light
from further down the hall.*

*He stepped from the bedroom and looked down the hall to
locate the bathroom door. The noise of shower spray was clear and*

loud, not muffled as it would be behind a closed bathroom door. The noise was coming from the left, twenty feet down, the bathroom door a third the way open. The hall floor was hardwood, not carpet. Her steps would give more sound.

He went back into the bedroom. She would soon come along the hall, perhaps in a robe or housecoat, and maybe stop and wonder why she had shut the bedroom light off. He didn't think it would cause panic and turn her away from the room. Who can be sure if they left a light off or on in a room?

He considered how she would enter and flick the switch with her right hand on the right-hand wall. He wanted her attention pulled to the right, away from where he would be on the left, pressed behind the bedroom door.

He saw her discarded clothes on the bed and had an idea. He laid them on the floor in a row leading off to the right. When she entered the room and flicked the switch, the clothes would jump at her in the sudden light. She would be momentarily distracted from anything on her left.

He took the gloves off and put them in his pockets and waited.

He soon heard an abrupt shudder in the water pipes, the shower being turned off.

A full minute later he heard an elongated squeak, the bathroom door opening wide. Then very slow padding of bare feet on hardwood coming down the hall. Why so slow?

It was twenty feet from the bathroom to the bedroom. The padding approached, slowed near the door, and stopped.

Had she noticed something? What was she doing?

He pressed his body against the wall in the narrow space behind the door in the dark room.

Her loud voice broke the silence as sharp as an ax cuts wood. "Hey, I was in the shower. Just saw your text. How's Montréal on a Friday night?"

She was still in the hall, right at the bedroom entrance. Only an inch of hollow door separated her from him.

"Not too much fun, I hope," she laughed. After a few moments, "Ya, right. Sure."

Her voice so close was like a hand slapping him in the face.

The bedroom light flicked on washing the room in brilliance.

"What the...?", her voice rose in sharp surprise. Her head appeared in his view, wrapped in a white towel, looking down at the floor. She stared, trying to process why her clothes were strewn on the floor.

Her voice was quiet when she said, "Just a sec..."

She took a small step forward, her head now lifting toward the window straight ahead at the far end of the room, the phone still at her left ear, the towel pushed slightly up on her ear to hear. Her left arm in that position would happen to block a neck strike.

Her head begin to turn left, toward his position. When only her left eye was visible to him, opening wider, his firm right hand flew, a lightning strike hard into her nose, his second choice. Her head snapped back.

The cell phone dropped from her hand and she buckled to her knees, her brain stunned, her eyes watering, open but staring without seeing.

He could hear a tiny yelling voice on the floor. He bent and yanked the towel off her head. He positioned a finger in the towel to prevent a finger print then tapped the 'end call' on the screen.

She was slumped on her knees. He stood in front of her and grabbed her hair with his left hand, pulling her head backwards. Even in her stunned state her eyes were open. She gave an 'ahhh' exactly as you would expect if someone's hair was being pulled. The front of her soft neck now fully exposed, the thick, hardened edge of his right delivered a brute force chop. Her eyelids dropped shut. They would stay shut long enough. He lowered her head to the floor.

She was wearing a light-blue cotton wrap that came down to mid-thigh, loosely tied.

He heard a tiny ringing from the phone. He let it ring. Ron would try calling a couple of times before calling 911. But he was in Montreal. It would take some time, perhaps two minutes, before details were taken and recorded in Montreal, then relayed to the Ontario police, and then on to the local detachment. Then a police car would be dispatched. Out here in the boonies, the response time of the nearest car would be at least five minutes. So that gave him at least seven minutes.

He pulled the dark-brown silk-tie from his jeans' pocket, and with one hand lifted her head and laid the tie crossways under her neck. He rolled her over so he wasn't looking at her face.

He wrapped an end of the tie around each of his hands and drew the tie tight to her neck and pulled, his knee resting on her back as he did. His forearm muscles bunched under the steady effort he applied for two and a half unbroken minutes.

He checked her pulse. Negative. Then her pupils. Dead.

From the time the cell phone had hit the floor, three minutes had elapsed.

He climbed out the bedroom window and eased himself down onto the stump as lightly as a ballet dancer, although he was 160 pounds. He stepped lightly off the stump out onto the grass, avoiding making a print into the soft garden earth anywhere.

He rolled the stump away. From his backpack he lifted out a single rubber boot. Days earlier he had poured concrete slurry into the boot which was now hardened, the boot very heavy, and two sizes too small for him. He rammed it down onto the garden *earth once with all his strength, then whacked it once more on the grass before throwing it back into the pack. Forensics would measure the size of that footprint, a footprint heavier in the heel, evidently made when the killer dropped from the window.*

He was fifty yards offshore in the canoe before he heard the wail of a siren. By the time he saw the blue light flashing at Diana's, he was three hundred yards out, silent and unseen, even in the moonlight, for he was skirting the path of its silver illumination.

He stopped paddling a moment and slid the cement-filled boot into the water and let it sink. With the bail bucket, he silently scooped once for new cold water for the fish bucket, the two trout fully thawed.

He resumed a steady paddling. In fifteen minutes he would arrive at the opposite shore with his fresh night-catch, if anybody was asking.

CHAPTER 19

NOW

Darkness had just settled and the headlights on their green Jeep Cherokee washed the narrow gravel cottage road and swept along the thick pine tree stands that hugged on both sides. They were close to the rental cottage on Ring Lake in Ontario cottage country.

The gravel road rose and fell like a shallow roller-coaster which made Amara threaten to be sick. "I can't hold it forever."

"If you're going to throw up at least put your head out the window," Candace said.

From Columbus, they had driven all afternoon and all evening, the equivalent of days for a child of five.

It was Saturday, July 7, and although their rental didn't officially start until the next day, they got permission to check themselves in early.

"Just another couple of minutes," Chester said.

Amara groaned. "But how do you know?"

"I was here once before. It's just up here."

Soon Chester announced their arrival and turned the car off the road and onto two dirt tire tracks with tall grass growing between them swishing under the car as it passed over. Pine trees were everywhere. And pine cones too, and granite slabs of rock jutting from the earth everywhere, primitive-like.

The car bumped to a stop twenty feet from the cottage and three car doors flew open. At last.

"I need mosquito stuff," Amara squealed, slapping at her arm.

"Well it's packed," Candace said. "Tough it out for one whole minute and carry your bag into the cottage. They attack more if you complain."

As they unloaded and humped the luggage and groceries in, Chester's mind was more on the bundles of cash and the three burner phones that were going to stay in the car, hidden.

*

At eight o'clock the next morning, everyone refreshed, Chester fried bacon while Amara and Candace explored the property and shore.

The cottage was brown siding with pleasant yellow trim, a sizeable living room, two good bedrooms, a well provided kitchen, and nice wood floors. Candace said it was 'clean and quaint' and she liked the view of the lake, an expansive mass of clear blue water. She said not a word about little rats.

There was a wide sliding glass door that opened from the living room onto a large cedar deck that ran across the front of the cottage. The deck was about ten feet off the ground. Cedar steps led from the deck to the ground which was open and grassy and sloped quite steeply down to the water. A long series of stone steps took you up or down.

A twenty-foot dock jutted out from the shore, a paddleboat and small aluminum fishing boat tied there. To one side of the dock was a good stretch of fine sandy beach, just for them, just as Chester had promised.

There was a large deep back yard of grass and smooth granite slabs. Stands of thick bushes and mature trees clumped at the very back of the property. The two dirt tire tracks of the lane traveled through the grass a hundred and fifty feet from the cottage out to the road.

"Isn't it so quiet and peaceful around here?" Chester called from the deck, waving them up from the shore for breakfast. He served bacon sandwiches at the picnic table on the deck. There didn't appear to be any life at the cottages on either side, which weren't that close anyway, maybe a hundred and twenty feet away, with lots of shrubs and trees as property boundary markers. Good privacy.

The distant shorelines showed stretches of pristine pine forest and jutting outcroppings of rock. Where cottages had been built, they had maintained good setbacks from the shore and so retained the lake's natural treed beauty. Chester saw a fisherman in a small boat midway in the lake, the sun flashing like silver on his line when he cast it into the pure quiet.

"This is God's country," Chester said, taking a bite of bacon sandwich while he contemplated the serenity of the wide calm lake, the pure blue sky stretched to the horizon, the warm morning sun so brilliant. Yes, he thought, remembering, 'the sunlight clasps the earth'.

"Ring Lake connects with Round Lake way over that direction," Chester pointed. "From the map, it's about half as big as Ring."

While Candace and Amara chatted about playing at the beach and making sand castles, Chester's mind turned to the other thing. As he had discussed with Roly, the big day would be Wednesday at the earliest because they had to be here at least a few days to make it appear like Roly had been scouting for a random victim and had seen her. Otherwise, it would appear more like a prearranged hit.

But they couldn't just prearrange Wednesday without knowing the weather first, because if it was raining, that would mean, as he had told Roly, he and 'the husband' couldn't go golfing. Of course, there was no husband but Chester, and there wasn't going to be any golfing either. Rather, Chester was going to be out for a walk as part of his alibi, and he wouldn't be walking if the weather was inclement.

But his walk had to be a well-established daily routine as part of his cover. Otherwise, the police might find it suspicious that he just happened to be out just when the bad things happened. Back in Columbus, to build the walking alibi, he took up walking after coming home from work, telling Candace his back was acting up a lot lately, twinges and the like. He did a little reading on lower back issues and explained that driving long hours in the truck was pinching the jelly out of his discs, like squeezing a raspberry-filled donut. He needed to walk, every day, to put his vertebrae back in a straight line and keep the raspberry filling in place. At different times, in front of her, he would suddenly grab his lower back like he had just been shot, then do a series of stretches to cement the notion in her mind that his back was in a precarious condition and needed daily walks.

After their breakfast on the deck, Chester turned on the television in the cottage to check the weather because there was no Wifi there, and no cell phone service either. He worried about how to contact Roly with a burner phone. He remembered there was a golf course about two miles away, and maybe somewhere near the club house they would have cell service.

"What are you doing?" Candace asked.

"Checking the weather for the next few days. But they don't seem to have it anywhere on these channels. Maybe only certain times of day."

After twenty minutes of flipping channels and getting nothing, Candace called to him from outside. "Forget that, will you? It's beautiful weather right now and Amara wants a boat ride."

Apart from the weather and the cell phone service issue was the squeaking hinges of the door into the cottage. That had to be fixed or the big day could go sideways.

"What are you doing swinging the door open and shut like that?" Candace said.

"That squeak bothers me."

"Come on, Chester, lighten up. You're on holiday. And it's not your cottage."

"It bothers me *because* I'm on holiday. I don't want to hear that squeak all through my holiday."

"Boy, you really need a holiday."

He heard Amara calling from outside, antsy for a boat ride.

The three of them putt-putted along the shore in the little aluminum fishing boat. Chester kept a sharp lookout to memorize the distinctive features of cottages and landscape that he could use to tell Roly exactly where their cottage was if Roly decided to come by boat, not by road, on the big day.

"Can you tow me in an inner tube, like Rebecca's dad does?" Amara asked.

"This boat's motor isn't powerful enough," Chester said. "And besides, we don't have an inner tube. But I can take you fishing. Would you like that?"

"I would rather have an inner tube ride."

"Not going to happen. But if we catch fish, we can have a fish fry tonight."

"Is that fun?"

"It can be," Chester said. "But more important, it's eating."

*

Chester and Amara were in the fishing boat fishing a hundred yards off shore in a small bay. Candace, sunbathing on the dock, waved to Amara, who waved back.

"I guess Mom doesn't like fishing," she said to Chester.

"Or she just likes sunbathing more."

There was a tug on Chester's line. "Amara, feel this! A fish is on the hook."

Chester loosened his grip on the rod just enough to let Amara feel the pulling. "See the tip bending way down. Grab the net."

It was a three-pound walleye, or what he heard the Canadians called a pickerel, flopping madly in the bottom of the boat. Amara was laughing at what she thought were the fish's antics.

"He's jumping funny. Oh no! He's going to touch me," she wailed and slid away three feet along the seat.

Chester said, "The fish is going to suffocate because he can't breathe out of the water."

"Then let's put him back in."

"But you said you wanted a fish fry."

"Ya, but not him."

"Another fish is the same as this fish. The one's in the store are the same."

"Ya, but not him. He can't breathe"

"I don't want him to suffer. Do you?"

"No."

"But we want to eat fish for dinner."

"Ya." She was watching the walleye intensely.

"See, he can't get his breath. I don't want him to suffer," Chester said.

"Me either."

"So what a fisherman does is hit him over the head with this little club when he's not looking, and they never know what hit them and they're dead. Okay?"

"I don't know."

"You point at something over there, and when he looks, I'll hit him over the head."

She kept looking at the fish.

"He's going to suffer if we don't do it now," Chester said.

She raised her hand and pointed her finger into the distance, but her eyes stayed on the fish.

"You have to look that way, too, Amara, to fool him."

Her eyes went in the direction of her finger, flashed back to the fish, then to her finger, then...

Chester whacked. It startled Amara.

"See, Amara, the fish isn't suffering now."

"Is it dead?" Her face showed dread.

"Yes, but that's okay. That's what life is. Some things have to die so other things can live."

A small tear formed in her eye. "He wasn't looking at my finger. He wasn't fooled."

"Well, with a fish... it's sometimes hard to tell."

He knew she was still feeling a little dread. He said, "Amara, now you know that whenever you eat something, it's a good thing to remember to say 'thank you.'"

"But he's dead."

"Well, somewhere he can hear you."

When they got back, Amara played at the beach with Candace. Chester took the opportunity to fillet the walleye alone out back on a rock, blood and guts strewn aplenty. He figured one nature lesson was enough for today.

In the kitchen he egged and floured the two large fillets for lunch. He fried them in butter, along with some potatoes and chopped onion.

"We have to say thank you to the fish," Amara said to Candace at the table at lunch.

Candace looked at Chester. Chester looked at the fish and said, with a degree of solemnity, "Some things have to die so other things can live. Thank you, fish."

*

Candace decided that, given the early mornings and all the fresh air and exercise, Amara should have a nap every day at 1:00 right after lunch. Chester said that would be the ideal time for him to take his hour long walk every day for his back. Like a steady routine.

So at 1:00, after slipping into the car to grab one of the burner phones, he walked north along the cottage road toward the golf course. His real purpose was to check where he could get cell phone service.

About half a mile along, a path left the road through the woods and he figured that was a shortcut to the course. Following the path a half mile, he crossed a narrow creaky wooden bridge that spanned a wide creek. Not long after that, he climbed a fence, and, still within the shelter of woods, came into view of the clubhouse about a hundred yards away.

He tried his phone. He had service. And he had privacy to talk. But he wouldn't call Roly yet. Not until he had more to say.

When he got back as far as the bridge, he took the phone's battery out and threw the battery into the creek. Even a burner phone's location can be traced. Better to err on the side of caution at every stage.

When he got back to the cottage, Amara was just waking up. Chester said, "Let's try the paddleboat out, Amara."

Two hundred yards offshore, making sure Amara's attention was elsewhere, he slipped the burner phone from his pocket. It was wrapped in a tissue that he had earlier used to wipe his prints off. He slipped his hand under the water on the side of the boat away from shore and let the phone sink. He drew his hand from the water and wiped his head with it as if cooling his head had been his purpose.

Suddenly something occurred to him, and it was like someone gave him a zap from a stun gun, his nerves humming like steel threads filled with electricity. How the hell was he going to deal with Amara being in the very next bedroom when all that terrible shit was going down? Why didn't he think of that before? Yes, she would be asleep, but, come on! And what else didn't he think of?

An idea occurred to him. What was that stuff Candace always bought for Amara for colds and cough that knocked her the hell out? Bill something? Ben something? He had to get some, and some WD 40 for the squeaky door. But not at the general store. People would talk to you there and remember you, especially if his face became known in the news. The police might ask questions there about odd purchases he made. He would have to come up with some excuse to go into town to an anonymous place where the cashiers don't have time to look at you because they're too busy just shoving product by the scanner as fast as their little hands can move.

At the cottage, he kept checking the television again for the weather because the weather would structure the game plan.

"Looking for the weather on television every half hour isn't going to change anything," Candace said.

"Ya, but it's our holiday. I want good weather. I like to know whether to feel good or bad."

"If you're going to feel bad, I don't want to hear about it. Gee, you almost seem jumpy."

"Well out here it's like we're living in the woods. Got to know the weather. And for boating and stuff."

"It's not like we're going to venture off for a four-hour adventure in our dinghy. It's not complicated. If it's good weather, we do stuff outside, nearby. If it's bad weather, we're inside."

He finally caught the weather on the channel. Monday was perfect, but too early. Tuesday was rain. Wednesday was iffy. Thursday was guaranteed sun all day.

Thursday looked like the day.

CHAPTER 20

That evening, Sunday, Chester made a campfire and they waited for the fire to reduce to red hot coals so they could roast
the wieners over them on skewers. Each had their own skewer.
Chester was armed with three for himself. But he needed a
beer while he waited so headed for the cottage.

Amara was sitting on a block of rock that served as a chair
near the campfire, bouncing her empty skewer on her knee.
"When will it be ready to roast them?" she said, her eyes staring eagerly into the dying flames.

"Soon," Candace said quietly, sitting on a similar rock, her
eyes also absorbed in the flames, meditative, not turning to Amara
to answer, more like her mind was reflecting on something.

"Mom, did you ever have a wiener roast at a cottage with
your mom and dad?"

Chester heard the question as he came down the last of
the stone stairs. He walked over to his block of rock and sat
with his beer.

"I never had a dad," Candace said quietly, still staring into the fire.

Amara's mouth dropped open. "You didn't? Where was he?"

"I don't know."

Chester noticed Candace's skewer now gently rocked up and down in her hand, and he knew it was a rush of old feeling, a sadness.

Candace continued. "He left our house, left my mom, before I ever knew him."

"You never saw him?" Amara said.

"Maybe when I was one or two." Candace's voice was quieter, and her eyes were still, like there was no fire burning right there. "But I don't remember anything."

Amara looked at her skewer, now without enthusiasm. "You didn't see him after that?"

"No. He never came back. Ever."

"Why did he go?"

"I don't know."

"Was he mad at someone?"

"I don't know."

Chester figured another mother would handle this whole thing a little softer with her young child. But he knew that Candace, when she was remembering things, sometimes lost a sense of what others might be feeling, consumed by her own feelings.

Amara looked at Candace who was still looking at the fire. Amara's eyes wandered the landscape in answer of her question, but saw no answer.

After a few moments, Candace said, "Then, when I was five, they took me from my mom. I had to live in another house."

"Why?"

"They said my mom couldn't look after me. She had some sickness in her head."

There was sudden concern in Amara's voice. "Do you have that sickness?"

"Not that I know of. But who knows?"

Chester knew Amara was processing the 'but who knows'. For that matter, Chester was, too. He had never thought about it before.

But Amara moved on. "Did you see your mom after you had to live in another house?"

Chester saw Candace's skewer rise an inch and fall, rise an inch and fall, in a rhythm. "Only once, a while later. She was crying and holding her arms out for me and calling, 'Philomena, Philomena, please hold me'. Then a man took her away."

"Where did he take her?"

"To a hospital."

"Why was she saying that name?"

"That was my name then, 'Philomena', before I changed it."

"You can change your name?"

"When you're eighteen, an adult, if you really don't like it."

"Oh." Amara's face told Chester she was assessing her own name as she stared at the fire. "I don't want to change mine."

"That's good," Candace said.

"Who lived in the other house you had to live in?"

"Strangers."

"Were they nice?"

Candace's eyes wavered a bit. "I don't remember much at that first house, even though I was there for a year."

"A whole year with strangers?"

"That was just the beginning."

"Did you miss your mom?"

"Every minute of every day. That's what I do remember."

"Then where did you go?"

"Another house. More strangers. Then another house. And then another house. And then another house. And more strangers, and more and more strangers."

The last flames had ceased and Chester got up and spread the glowing red embers around to increase the surface area for roasting. He sat back down but didn't make a move to skewer the wieners, knowing their conversation wasn't finished.

Amara was looking at the red coals. "How come you had to change to another house and another house?"

Candace looked away from the fire pit, her eyes drifting to the side where low conifers stretched their branches out like arms. "Sometimes I asked to change. Sometimes they asked."

"Why?"

"A bad match."

"What's that?"

Candace ran a hand absently along her leg. She hadn't made eye contact with Amara the whole conversation, her eyes now shifting back to the red coals. "You know how you like Rebecca?"

"Yeah."

"That's a good match. And you know how you don't like Philippa?"

"Yeah."

"That's a bad match."

"You had to live with someone like Philippa?"

"Sometimes."

"I wouldn't want that."

"And other times the mom thought I was like Philippa. So they wanted a change, for someone more like Rebecca."

"But you're not like Philippa, though."

"Well, Amara, maybe sometimes I was like Philippa."

"No. Philippa's crazy a lot."

"Ya, well..."

Chester didn't look up from the fire but knew Amara was checking Candace's face to be sure there wasn't some Philippa thing hiding anywhere there. Chester had wondered the same himself on occasion.

But Amara changed direction. "Did your mom die?"

There was full quiet, Candace remembering. "One day a man came to the house. He spoke to the woman who was my foster mother at the time."

"What's a foster mother?"

"A woman who takes over as your mother. Then the man left the house. I was in the living room watching television. My foster mother came to the living room and stood in the doorway scrubbing a pot. 'Philomena,' she said to me, 'you're a big girl now that you're seven, aren't you?' I said 'yes'. She said, 'So... your mother died yesterday at the hospital.'"

It hit Chester. He had never heard that before. He found himself seeing the expression on the face of little Philomena, only two years older than Amara was now, being told her mother was gone forever, her only relation, her only connection to real love.

Amara's voice was very quiet, her face full of concern. "Then what did your foster mother do?" There was hope in her voice, just as there was hope in Chester's heart.

"Nothing. Stood there."

"What did you do?"

It took long moments for Candace to answer, a memory, a hurt, stretching back over twenty years. "I asked permission to go to my room."

There was silence among them, Chester so still he could feel his beating heart. Amara slid off her rock and walked to

Candace and held her arm. Candace put her hand on Amara's hand, both gazing into the coals.

There was emotion in Amara's voice. "I always want you to be my mom. No one else."

"You'll always have me, Amara. No one else."

"But what if you died? Like your mom did?"

"I'm not going to die, Amara. I promise."

CHAPTER 21

BEFORE

His third kill had been last September.

He had unscrewed the bulb in her front porch light a half hour before she got home.

She was a massage therapist. He had never met her, or any other massage therapist for that matter. But he had heard of her.

There were houses on both sides of her street, all set deep back. But the houses on her side backed onto Big Crane Lake, their back yards sloping down to it and set with fine rock landscaping, and, in her case, a swimming pool.

Her yard was fenced solid on both sides running all the way down to the water so neighbors had no opportunity to observe the goings on in her back yard, summer parties that invited skinny dipping that neighbor children should not have to witness.

It was now too cold for swimming, being late September. And it was dark by 7:30.

He had touched her shore with his canoe at 7:45 p.m. Full dark.

From a telephone enquiry he had made from a payphone that morning, he knew her clinic hours finished at 8:00 p.m. and that her last appointment today was 7:15. He knew that because he was told: 'Sorry, last appointment is 7:15. Can't squeeze you in today.'

He knew she would be home no earlier than 8:10, maybe as late as 8:30 if the appointment ran long.

The street lights were widely spaced, the nearest light three houses down. He had needed nothing more than a chair to stand on the porch to open the light fixture and unscrew the bulb. Several chairs had been available in her backyard. It took him two minutes.

As he did it, two cars had driven by, but all they would notice in the darkness, if anything, was a guy with long black hair wearing a low cap and loose sweatshirt changing the porch light bulb in plain view, no doubt one of her new 'friends', if they knew anything about her at all. Nothing to cause suspicion, or even memory. Across the street, an old fellow who did a slow walk down his long driveway to the curb to collect his garbage can didn't even notice him.

Now he was waiting in the back yard in the dark, sitting in a lounge chair. He soon heard her car pull into the driveway. He heard the car door open, then shut. He heard the side door of the house open, then close. He watched the lights come on in the house, one at a time.

Time for a change. He pulled the low cap off, then the black wig, then the loose sweatshirt. He threw them all into a bag in the canoe he had beached in the grass at the low end of her yard. He combed his hair neatly, then walked to the front door and knocked.

She answered the door with a look of impatience, tired, just getting home from a long day. The light was poor because it came only dimly from the hall. But when she observed his face, a handsome man, clean cut, wearing a fetching wool sweater, she softened very considerably.

"Yes?" she asked, now pleasant, smiling, not the least impatient. And not the least afraid. She snapped the porch light switch up and down twice trying to make it come on. "Sorry, damn light seems burnt out," she muttered.

He stood well back on the large porch to act even less a threat, perhaps even timid. "Good evening. Thank you for answering the door. I'm canvassing for Jim Franks, the local Liberal candidate. Maybe you know him?"

She liked the sound of his voice. "Heard of him, ya. I tend to be more NDP. But I've gone Liberal before," she said, suggesting promise.

"Well," and he held up a sheet of paper, the top half showing the smiling mug of Mr. Franks, the lower half full of tiny bolded print. He held a small bundle of these sheets in his other hand, as if a copy was to be left with each household.

"What we hope is that you'll let me read to you just three quick highlights from his platform to inform you of his top three priorities."

"Okay."

He looked down at the tiny print, unreadable in the shadows, his brow furrowed, then, apologizing, "I know I should know it by heart, but...not enough light."

"Yes, yes. Why don't you come in?"

"That's kind of you."

He made sure the door came almost fully closed behind him as he stood in the front hall. "I'm supposed to show you the sheet as I read it. Like reading it together."

"Sure. I don't have my glasses, but let's do it."

He set the bundle of sheets down on the floor, holding just the one sheet. "I'll hold it out a little further then."

"Okay."

She stood on his right. He held it with his left, well out in front of them so they could both see the wording.

She thought he held it a little higher than he needed to, above her eye line. But he was taller. And maybe it was for better light. Her head tilted slightly up.

"Priority one," he said. "Tax the hell out of the top one percent."

She laughed.

"I'm paraphrasing," he said.

She laughed again.

At his side, his right hand opened flat and firm, the fingers tight together. He saw her concentrating, her eyes trying to discern the print.

"Priority two..." He raised the sheet another inch and her head followed.

His right hand flew into her soft neck, the knife-hand strike. She fell to the floor, a sprawl, and lay there. No movement in any limb, eyes woozy, unfocussed.

He pushed the front door closed all the way. He bent over her, his left hand in a tuft of her hair, lifting her head and neck slightly, his right hand, like a blur, making another hard strike to the neck.

He hauled her into the bedroom and took the dark-brown silk-tie from his pocket.

CHAPTER 22

It was Monday and Chester was on his 1:00 p.m. walk. He was hidden in the woods a hundred yards from the golf course clubhouse when he called Roly on another of his burner phones.

"Thursday's the day," Chester said. "Weather looks good. But I'll still call Wednesday at this time to be sure."

"I've been thinking more about it," Roly said.

"Like pulling out?"

"No, relax. First a small thing. Are the door hinges quiet?"

Roly was sure thinking ahead. "There's only one door. It's quiet as a mouse. I WD40'd it." He hadn't, but he was soon getting to it.

"Really? Must be visiting pretty regular."

Roly was quick, and probing. Chester said, "I dropped in to see the husband yesterday."

"With a can of WD40?"

"No. I told him about the door being so squeaky. Like a problem."

"And he had a can of WD 40?"

"Found one on a tool shelf in a closet in the cottage. And one more thing. There's a big sliding glass door out onto a deck at the front. Don't use that to get in. It's often locked and anyway it makes a heavy rolling noise when you open it. So use the door."

The long pause here said Roly was trying to connect some dots, and to Chester, the pause was endless feeling.

Finally, Roly said, "I've also been thinking about something else."

"What something else?"

"I'm worried it's going to look too clean."

"What do you mean?"

"If it's too clean, if the cops don't see some other motive for the killer being there except to kill her, it might look a whole lot too much like a hired kill. So they look around for who wanted her killed. The husband's always suspect numero uno. That line of thinking has a much bigger chance of coming back on you."

"Very true," Chester said. But he was thinking fast. Roly wasn't aware of the silk-tie serial killer working in the area, of course, and Chester was counting on the police believing Roly to be that killer, that belief overshadowing anything else the police might speculate. But the reports of the serial killer had made no mention of any other motives at play other than an outright deranged desire to kill. Chester said, "So…what do you suggest?"

"How about killed in the course of a break and enter? Didn't know anyone was there. She saw me. Things got out of hand. I had to do it. I'd have to turn the place upside down on my way out. And hit her around a bit to look like we had an encounter."

"Roly, I really appreciate this."

But there was nothing in any of what Chester read in that newspaper article that talked about the killer being interrupted while doing a supposed break and enter. In fact, the article said that robbery appeared never to be the motive.

"But I don't *know*, Roly. I'm not too sure about that."

"Or a rape thing," Roly said like he already had considered a better alternative. "The police thinking I maybe saw her sunbathing and watched the property."

"Rape thing? What would that involve?"

"Well hold on. I'm not actually going to do it, okay? It's not in the price."

"I know, Roly. Don't want you to go above and beyond."

Chester could tell Roly was thinking, drawing on a cigarette, the long pause, the exhalation.

"But, you know what? A B&E in the middle of the day probably wouldn't fly," Roly said.

"Why not?"

"What would I be doing carrying around a silk-tie with me if that's what I was up to? Are they going to think I was wearing a suit? The middle of the fucking day."

"Not likely."

"Listen, Ken, how about I don't use a silk-tie but just shoot her. So much easier."

"SHIT NO, Roly. That's NOT the deal. Silk-tie or nothing. You won't be getting another cent from me if you shoot her. You could hunt me to the ends of the earth and I wouldn't care."

"Real fixated on the tie thing."

"TOTALLY. Non-negotiable."

"But you get my point. Why would I have a tie with me unless I knew I was there to kill her? Hey, unless, maybe, there was a silk-tie already hanging on a hook there, real handy, and it can be traced to the husband."

"No. I don't like it," Chester said. "Cottage renters aren't going to bring silk-ties with them in the heat of summer. My friend hasn't, I'm certain. And I really don't want to have to run out and supply the murder weapon."

More inhalation, then the sound of a cloudy exhalation. "Okay, so back to why I have a tie with me. Maybe make it appear like I wanted to rape her, then kill her, so had a tie along, but must have been interrupted so couldn't manage the rape part."

"Interrupted by what?"

"Nothing they can pin, just speculate, a sudden noise nearby on the lake. Or maybe she was a real fighter."

"That's good because she will be."

"I could rip her clothes off after I strangle her, pose her in some way, like I was going to do something really sick but then had to skedaddle like I heard something."

"You don't have to do all that for me."

"Well it isn't all for you. Believe it or not, I'm looking out for myself, too. See, looking at it from my point of view, the less suspicion that falls on the husband or you, the less chance that it's ever going to get back to me."

"How do you mean?"

"Well if you're ever nailed, don't you think it might cross your mind to try to get a little leniency from the law and tell everything you know about me? Not that it's much, but it could be inconvenient. And for Clyne, too."

"I would never do that."

Roly laughed. "No, you would never do that. Of course not. Not after all the free advice I'm giving. And after we've become such pals."

Chester knew Roly was blowing out another cloud of smoke. Roly's voice now became hard, unlike Chester had heard before. "If they ever pin you, Ken, and you talk, or the husband talks, I just want to tell you, between Clyne and me, you won't see the light of the next day. We've both been around a good while because we know how to look after numero uno. Am I clear?"

"Clear, Roly. Ya. Clear."

*

Chester got back to the cottage and found Amara in the water and Candace reading a magazine and sunbathing on the dock. The sun was hot. He changed into his bathing suit and joined Amara a few minutes in the water, then said, "How about another paddleboat ride?"

"Sure!"

Off they went and Chester donated a second burner phone to the bottom of Ring Lake.

As they paddle-boated their way toward shore - slosh, slosh, slosh - he saw Candace stand up on the dock to stretch and apply some more lotion. She was a siren. The particular luminescent pink of her bikini sent a radiant beam across the lake, the visual equivalent of a foghorn, unmissable by even distant craft.

He wondered if Roly had already seen her, not that he would know it's her. It was a big lake, hundreds of cottages, but her signal was pretty strong. Roly knew the cottage was on Ring Lake, but that was all. But if he had seen her, he wouldn't forget anytime soon.

When he and Amara got back, he said to Candace, "It's going to rain tomorrow. Soak up the rays while you can."

"Working on it," she said lazily, and rolled a perfect 90 degrees.

*

Chester saw him first, a guy late thirties, handsome, tall, tanned, muscled, without a shirt, canoeing about seventy yards out from their dock, looking their way, intently, and why ever would he be doing that when Candace was only doing an exercise routine in a luminescent pink bikini on the dock.

Maybe it wasn't Chester who had noticed him first.

The guy carried on down the lake, southward, then cut in toward shore and disappeared from their sight.

But shortly, it was him again. Chester began to think of him as Mr. Bronze World. This time, he was wind-surfing, a bright blue sail, the wind whipping him back up the lake toward them, the board slapping fast through the choppy water.

He passed by them a hundred yards out. Then, just a bit north of them, spun the board around and turned back their way, south, to pass again, performing a couple of little jumps as he did. He slipped right on by and again cut into shore south of them and disappeared.

It certainly wasn't Roly, Chester thought. Roly would never be that stupidly obvious. Moreover, as Roly had once said, he was from Detroit, not Minnesota. He would hardly be zipping around so expertly on a windsurfer if he was uncomfortable just handling a canoe.

Soon Chester heard what sounded like a plane engine revving up a few cottages away to the south, unseen, though, because of the contour of the shore. It was him again, this time in a powerful looking bow-rider. It surged across the water, deep-throated, gurgling, really impatient, wanting to bellow and roar and slice a deep line across the lake like a butcher's knife cleaving through a side of beef.

Then the boat turned sharply and came roaring toward them, so fast and so straight and getting so close that Candace jumped off the dock. The engine cut and the boat plowed water, slowing, begrudging, impatient, like it would much rather have sliced the dock in half.

"Hey," Mr. Bronze World shouted. "Didn't mean to startle you. Just thought I would say 'hi' to a neighbor. And a fellow Ohioan." Chester thought it odd the guy didn't seem to smile.

"How'd you know that?" Candace said, a big smile, now not put out by the muscle antics.

"Saw your car plates."

"Oh."

"Saw you guys out in the fishing boat the other day and thought maybe the little girl would like an inner tube ride. I know your little boat there couldn't pull a bicycle tire. I could show her how it's done."

"That would be nice," Chester said. "I know she'd like that."

Although it was Chester who spoke, Mr. Bronze World hadn't taken his eyes off Candace.

After introducing himself as Dennis, they all piled into his boat and roared around the lake a few times so fast they couldn't have conversation. Then he rigged up the inner tube for Amara.

"Let's keep it under fifty," Chester said. "She's only five."

"That would be too fast for a little girl," Dennis said seriously, not realizing that Chester was making a joke.

Chester climbed into the inner tube with Amara for a few rides to let her get the feel of it. Then Dennis did endless sweeping circles with Amara in it alone, Amara beside herself with joy.

"I do enjoy thrilling a girl," Dennis said to Candace, his words and look not lost on her, or on Chester. Chester began to think of him now more as Dennis the Menace.

What was astounding was the fact that he was a dentist. His practice was in Toledo. Dennis the Menace the dentist. Chester wondered how he got those big hairy hands into any patient's mouth. And a dentist who didn't himself smile didn't say a lot for dentistry.

After the boating, Dennis invited them over to his cottage - a jaw-dropping edifice four cottages down - 2,800 square feet of squared cedar timbers, two storey's tall, cathedral ceiling with rising glass and stained-glass windows, not unlike a real cathedral, a sprawling deck more like a grand balcony offering wide panoramas of the lake. Out from the deck and thirty feet below it was smoothed rock shore and white sand beach running three hundred feet across in front, ending at his enormous dock where there was a kayak, a canoe, a 20' sailboat, a windsurfer and the bow-rider.

Inside, the whole place was bright and airy and leather and rattan, granite fireplace and counters, a decorator's expensive hand evident everywhere, and everything matching. The main floor bathroom was so full of marble and shine that Chester knew he would feel terrible if he ever had to actually use it. The whole place looked like something out of a glossy cottage magazine.

In the middle of the living room, Dennis, with his muscular suntanned arms folded, watched Candace and said, offhand, "People want to photograph this place for a glossy cottage magazine, but I'm not interested."

"Do you cottage here alone?" Candace asked, jumping past all small talk.

"Yes."

"Just you and the servants?" Chester joked.

"I have no servants," Dennis replied seriously, as if Chester was being serious. "But a woman cleans once a week, brings premade meals and other necessaries. A landscape company handles everything outside."

"You live alone in Ohio, too?" Candace plied, ditching small talk and redirecting it to big talk at high speed.

"Yes. No one in my life now," he said, cutting to the chase. He looked at her like he was looking at something of interest in a high-end catalogue. "No one at all. Divorced. No children. All alone."

"Oh," she said, and Chester thought there was sparkle in her eyes.

"I got this cottage, the house in Toledo, and my dental practice. She got the plane."

"The plane?" Candace gasped.

"Lear jet. She travels a lot."

"Well, well. My, my," Candace said. "We're certainly neighbors, only four cottages away from ours. How convenient for everyone."

Not quite everyone, Chester thought.

Dennis almost licked his lips. He walked to the fridge/freezer, pulled out an ice-cream bar, took off its wrapper, and handed it to Amara whose eyes lit up in surprise as her hand reached and took it.

Dennis said to Candace, "Hope that's ok?" his voice full of false concern. Not kid-smart, Chester thought, sticking ice-cream in a kid's hand and *then* asking the parent if it's ok. What a dork. Probably pulled out patients' teeth without asking, then said, 'Hope that's ok?'

Dennis said to Candace, "Would you like an ice-cream bar?" He stepped a little closer to her like they were alone in the cottage, like Chester was nowhere to be seen.

"No, thank you."

To Chester, her smile was so broad, her eyes so bright, so

out of proportion to what was asked, he wondered whether she even knew what he asked.

Dennis turned to Chester. "How about you...Charles?"

"It's Chester."

"Oh, didn't hear you right before. I haven't heard that one since I watched *Gunsmoke* on re-runs. It's a western."

"Ya, I know. No thanks to the ice-cream, though, Dennis. Amara, you say thank you to Dennis for the ice-cream."

"Thank you."

Dennis bent down to her. "You're welcome, Amara-little-darling-so-very-pretty-like-your-mother."

A certified class-A jerk but loaded to the hilt. Could give a woman anything she wants back at his castle.

"We'd better be going," Chester said, taking Amara's hand.

Chester saw Dennis's eyes trace up, down, and around, Candace's body. She caught his eye and smiled. He was unabashed. For the first time he gave a smile - a big, hungry, shark smile, his teeth whiter and more perfect than Chiclets.

"Tomorrow's going to rain and I have to do some business in Toronto anyway," Dennis said. "But maybe Wednesday we could do something ...neighborly."

Candace said, "How about we return your generosity in giving us the boat ride and have you over at dusk for a marsh-mallow-roast and a drink on the beach?"

Dennis nodded as his eyes toured Candace again. "I'll be there."

Chester saw the teeth flash again.

CHAPTER 23

The weatherman was right. Rain fell all Tuesday morning, dripping endlessly from the pine trees, the sky grey and gloomy and no end of it in sight.

Chester desperately had to get to town for the WD 40 and child's cough syrup.

"Since it's so rainy, how about I mosey into the town and get us some ice cream?" he said.

Candace was reading a magazine on the couch. "Why not just go to the general store and not all that way into town for just that?"

"I was thinking we might need pork chops, too, for a barbecue. I forgot to bring some. General store won't have good ones."

"You've never barbecued pork chops in your life. And we've got lots of meat here."

"Well something different. Pork chop memories, made here."

"Well do whatever. It sounds like you just want to take a drive."

"Ya. That, too. Cabin fever."

"I want to go, too," Amara said. "It's getting boring with the rain."

Candace said, "Ya, take Amara. Make it an outing. I'm happy to just relax here."

He would need a pharmacy, a hardware store, and a grocery store. And Amara had to be kept in the dark about the purchase in the pharmacy and the hardware store. Two out of three.

"Amara," Chester said, "wouldn't you rather just relax here with mom?"

"No."

The drive into town took about twenty minutes. Chester kept his eyes peeled for places. He kept wondering how to pull one over on Amara. He circled through the town twice.

"Why are we driving around and around? There's stores," Amara said.

"I'm looking for the best one."

He saw a sign, 'Jacob's Hardware, Pharmacy, and Grocery.' Three out of three. You had to hand it to little towns.

The ice cream and pork chops were easy to find, but the other stuff was impossible. The thing was, he didn't want to have to ask out loud for WD 40 or Cough syrup. Amara was a sharp cookie and would blab to Candace and Candace would ask him about it and he would be hard pressed for answers and would blow his cover.

He took out a pen and wrote on a piece of paper, 'child's cough syrup? WD 40?" He handed it to a clerk and put his finger to his lips. The clerk read it, looked at Chester, then looked at Amara, then nodded conspiratorially to Chester, although Chester figured the guy would wonder why the secrecy about the WD 40. Maybe thought good for an ear ache.

"How about we get a bit of candy, Amara?"

"Okay."

At the checkout, Chester put the ice cream and pork chops and candy on the counter and the clerk slipped the WD 40 and Cough syrup on ahead of it.

To keep Amara occupied for the transaction, Chester showed her some of the Canadian bills. "Look at the funny Canadian money, darling. All kinds of different colors. Like Monopoly. Maybe that's where they got the idea."

*

It rained the rest of Tuesday and on into Wednesday morning, but cleared nicely by noon.

After putting Amara down for her nap at 1:00, Chester left for his daily walk, but not before grabbing the last burner phone from the car.

Hidden in the woods a hundred yards from the golf club-house, he called Roly. "So it's on for tomorrow. Weather looks perfect."

"Good. It's getting boring around here. So where's the cottage?"

"Do you know that big marina, Shelby's?"

"Ya."

"The cottage is on the other side of the lake from that, but quite a ways more south. The address is 2210 Ring Lake Road. Not all the cottages have numbers posted at the roadside, but this one does. But it's hard to see. I had a time finding it the first time. If you come by boat, it's a brown cottage with bright yellow trim and has a long deck across the front."

"That's really great, Ken. Like only ninety percent of the other cottages on the lake. I could end up doing the wrong woman.

Maybe I should ask, 'Mam, before I strangle you to death, I need to know if your love's on the rocks and you're the wife of a friend of Ken.' That should clear up any confusion."

"There won't be any mistakes. Taking the road, it's the twenty-fourth cottage going south from the general store. And there'll be the husband's green Jeep Cherokee parked in the driveway, Ohio plates. When we golf, we take my car."

"Okay."

"Now, if you're coming by boat, it's about a half mile south of the marina, but on the other side of the lake, like I said."

"Okay."

"First, you're going to see a dark-brown cottage perched really high up from the water, can't miss it. And it has two flags on a really tall green flag pole down by the dock: An American flag on top and a Canadian flag underneath that."

"Is that one of those red and white flags I'm seeing everywhere with a big tree leaf in the middle?"

"Yes. So you go about five cottages down and you'll see a big clump of tall birch trees standing all on their own. Know what birch trees look like?"

"Ya, Ken, I do. White bark. Indians supposedly made canoes out of it. Good luck with that."

"Okay, so it's the fourth cottage down from the birch trees. Brown with yellow trim. Big deck across the front."

"What time?"

"1:15. The husband and I will leave for golfing at 1:00. That's exactly always when the little daughter goes down for her nap so the wife will be alone."

"Daughter? What daughter?"

"She'll be asleep…"

"What daughter? Some little kid tugging at my leg screaming blue murder?"

"Nothing to worry about. I'm going to fix it. Really. She'll be sleeping like a baby."

"You didn't say anything about a kid. You said they just got married. This pisses me off, Ken. Fuck."

"The kid's from a previous thing. She'll be in her own bedroom asleep with the door closed. She'll be out for the count. I guarantee it."

"How?"

"A sleep drug for kids. Knock her out like Muhammad Ali."

"Fuck." But Roly's tone suggested he was accepting the added wrinkle. "You're some talented guy, sneaking in money under the bed, oiling squeaky doors, putting the kid out for the count. Makes my part a cakewalk."

"Still gotta do the walk. With the tie."

"Ya, the damn tie. You doing everything, what's the husband doing in all this?"

"Staying in the clear."

"You must be a real pal. Look, what if the wife isn't there, or is out for a walk or something?"

"That's the great thing about the daughter. Keeps the mother there where you need her to be. I guess you're not a father, Roly."

"You're right."

"When the daughter's napping, the wife doesn't traipse off walking anywhere. Mothers don't do that when their baby's napping. She won't be leaving the cottage. She'll either be reading on the couch, or watching TV, or napping in her bedroom herself. She might go so far as to sit outside on the deck. But I know you can handle an extra wrinkle like that."

"There's always wrinkles."

"That's why the big bucks."

"Yeah. And what about those big bucks?"

"I'll be putting the money in the main bedroom at lunchtime tomorrow. Under the bed."

"Which side?"

"Closest to the window."

"You really know this place. All planned out."

"Ya. A thousand $20 bills. In the shoe box. Ten bundles with a hundred 20s in each."

"American money?"

"Of course."

"It better be American money. That kids' play money the Canadians use isn't worth shit. Looks like Mexican money."

Chester heard what sounded like Roly cracking his knuckles. Then Roly said, "The doors will be unlocked, right?"

"Right. But there's only one door."

"How will I know for sure this thing's still on?"

"I'll hang a blue-and-white striped beach towel over an aluminum lawn chair down near the water's edge by 11:00 a.m. tomorrow. Can't miss it. I assume you have binoculars."

"Maybe the wind will blow it off."

"Give me some credit. I'm using a clothespin."

"Credit? I give you credit and up pops a kid. And now a lawn chair. I'm not giving you any credit. A fucking clothespin? This whole thing feels like it's held together with a clothespin."

"Screw it all if you want. Tell me now. But I'll want my money back, or I'm taking it out on Clyne."

"Relax," Roly said. Another pause, then, "You said you'd tell me about the neighbors."

"No one has been at the three cottages on either side of this one all week. You won't be seen if you come ashore at the cottage next door. Or you could drive in and park in the grass two cottages down."

"I'll figure that out for myself, Ken." A long pause, then his voice was edged, and very serious. "The hairs on my back are tingling. Means I'm smelling something or my curiosity's running. Let me just say this, Ken, if this doesn't go as you say it's going to go, if you screw anything up on your end, or if there's something you're not telling me, I give you my word, someone else is going to get themselves killed."

Now Roly's voice was shrill. "Understand?"

"I understand," Chester said.

CHAPTER 24

It was Wednesday and almost dusk. Dennis the menace would soon arrive for a marshmallow roast and a drink.

Chester noticed that Candace had taken extra time in the bathroom getting ready. When she came out, she looked stunning - hair perfect, eyes and make up like she was ready to go to a fancy ball. Except it was only a simple campfire. So she didn't wear an evening gown, just a purple top that clung to every curvaceous part as hard as a drowning swimmer, and white slacks that gripped her legs like paint to a wall. Everything in every department turned to best advantage.

Chester got the fire going down at the beach, the orange flames more brilliant as dusk came on.

Chester saw Dennis sauntering through the nearest neighbor's yard. Candace stood from her chair to shake hands. "Welcome."

"Brought the stuff for Smors," Dennis said, holding out a bag of marshmallows and some chocolate and honey wafers.

"Wouldn't expect a dentist to encourage that kind of thing," Chester said, joking.

"The better to rot your teeth with," Dennis said, not to Chester but to Amara, and said it like the big bad wolf.

Amara laughed.

And a big bad wolf he is, Chester thought.

He turned to Chester. "Hey, it's not like we all don't do things we shouldn't. Even dentists."

"Ya, ain't that the truth."

They sampled Canadian rye whiskies and ate Smors while Dennis impressed Candace talking about his luxury property in Florida.

"Do you go often?" Candace asked.

"Regularly in winter. It's just by a long white sand beach. Great for long walks on an evening like this."

Chester's mind wandered as he tended the fire, moving the embers around. Things felt different now that Roly knew which cottage was theirs. Chester felt more tension, a hired killer knowing where you are and coming the next day. He might even be watching the campfire tonight with binoculars. He would see two men and a woman and little girl and he'd think - Ken, the husband, the wife, the little girl - the cast assembled, the target locked.

"That's how Cinderella got her name," he heard Amara saying to Dennis.

"Who's that?" Dennis asked.

"Cinderella, the princess. She was the one who always had to clean up all those dirty black chunks," she pointed to the fire. "They're called 'cinders'. And her step sisters made fun of her. They called her 'CINDER-ella.'"

"Why would a princess have to do that clean-up?" Dennis said surprised. He turned to Candace. "No princess I've ever known does anything like that."

Chester thought it odd that an educated dentist wouldn't know who Cinderella was.

"She had to do that *before* she was a princess," Amara instructed.

"Oh, I get it. Started at the bottom," Dennis said. "Worked her way up."

Amara struggled to educate Dennis on the main points, although Dennis was more intent on Candace, feigning occasional interest in poor Cinderella's story, flashing his perfect teeth now and then at Candace like he was really listening to cute little Amara.

The job of explaining it to Dennis wore Amara out and she began to yawn a lot.

"Time for bed, Amara," Candace said. "Say thank you to Dennis for the Smors."

"Thank you. Did you like the story?"

"Ya. Except for the glass slippers. How dumb. They'd shatter right off."

Amara looked perplexed. "That isn't the point."

"Okay. Maybe I missed something," he said and flashed a goofy look at Candace.

Candace said to Chester, "Would you mind putting her to bed? This rye whiskey is making me a little…and those steep steps up."

Chester glanced at Dennis who looked like a kid who had been handed the key to a candy store but was trying very hard to look nonchalant about it.

Chester carried Amara to the cottage and while she brushed her teeth in the washroom, he glanced down to the beach from the bedroom window. Dennis was talking, but Chester couldn't make out what he was saying. Dennis was putting his head close to hers and Candace wasn't pulling away.

Maybe innocent. Maybe not.

Had he made a grand mistake? Should he just call the whole thing off, not leave the blue and white towel on the line, call Roly on that last burner phone that he hadn't yet sent to the bottom of Ring Lake and just tell him to go home?

Amara came into the room.

"Time to tuck me in, Daddy."

Chester did, slowly.

"Daddy, my feet are getting cold."

"Cold feet?" Chester said. He knew the feeling well.

She pointed to her bare feet. "You moved the blanket off them."

"No, I think the blanket wiggled away by itself."

"Daddyyyyy...blankets can't do that!"

"Why not? Blankets can surprise you."

"That was just my toes wiggling. Seeeee."

"Have you ever seen blankets on the clothes line?"

"Yes."

"Haven't you seen them moving? With nobody around?"

"Daddyyyy...that's just the wind."

"But you can't see wind. You see the blankets moving. That's all you see, and you just *think* it's the wind. But they're wiggling around, all by themselves, trying to get off."

A conspiratorial look slowly appeared on Amara's face and her eyes twinkled. The game was on. She forced her smile to disappear. Now her voice was an acting-serious voice. "Or maybe...the blankets were...shivering", pathos written all over her little face, "cause they were wet and cold."

"I've seen them do that. Poor, poor blankets," Chester said with sentiment. "With nothing to keep them warm. They keep children warm. And Moms and Dads warm. But they have nothing to keep *them* warm. Life...can be cruel sometimes."

Her eyes went to the blanket, a note of play sadness. "They just want to keep people warm."

Her eyes returned to Chester's.

Chester sat back slowly, looking at her, too. But now she knew the game had stopped. A real sadness was now in Chester's face and eyes. "That's all they want," he said. "Just want to be there for you. With you. Always keeping you warm."

He gave her a long hug, much longer, much tighter, than usual.

"I love you, Daddy."

"I love you, Amara."

More than you'll ever know.

A child's innocence. A child's trust. That's what counted.

And it wasn't that Candace didn't love him. It was that the love she had, the love she could give, was a good deal smaller than Chester's, but was still there. Smaller because the love she got all her life was smaller. And even at that, sporadic. She never meant to hurt him. It was just that sometimes she felt herself slipping beneath old waves.

He had come this far, spent all the money he was going to spend anyway. He couldn't let Amara go, couldn't let her innocence die. He couldn't let her live with a Dennis. He couldn't let Candace go. Not without giving his plan a good shot.

He kissed Amara's head, shut off the light, and shut the door behind him.

CHAPTER 25

The day that Chester had been planning for over a month had now come. He had to get hopping on his very secret to-do list because Roly would be here at 1:15.

But first he had to go down to the beach with Candace and Amara as was their habit after breakfast each morning. Today had to appear no different from any other day here. He couldn't risk Candace having any suspicions.

They carried the assortment of playthings and towels down the stairs and across the lawn to the beach.

It was not long before he said, "Darn, I left my sunglasses," and got up from the chair and climbed the terraced set of stairs and went into the cottage.

Roly was expecting to find ten bundles of cash in a shoe box under the bed with a hundred $20's in each bundle, $2,000 per bundle, $20,000 in total.

Chester hurried to the bedroom and opened the bottom drawer of his dresser. From under the underwear and two pairs of folded pants, he lifted out another pair of pants. He felt in the front two pockets. From each one he took out two fat wads of bills, each tied with an elastic band. Four bundles of one hundred $20's in each, $2,000 per bundle, $8,000 total. Or so it appeared.

He quietly opened the cottage door, glancing down to Amara and Candace, who were oblivious. He went to the car and opened the glove compartment. From a black, zippered pouch where he kept the car insurance and ownership papers, he withdrew another two bundles of a hundred 20's each. Another $4,000. Or so it would appear.

He was now at $12,000. Seemingly.

In the trunk he lifted the flap that covered the spare tire and drew out another four bundles, another $8,000, if someone wasn't looking too closely.

That brought the cash to a total of $20,000. At least he hoped it would appear that way to Roly.

Chester hadn't been able to actually produce that much cash without going to the bank for a loan, and he had decided against doing that for damn good reason. Instead, he had created bundles that had three 20's on the top, three 20's on the bottom, and two 20's in the middle slightly extended out from the rest. All the rest were 1's. 92 $1's. The real total per bundle was $252, not $2,000.

Ten bundles of $252 made the $2,520.

Time would be tight for Roly. Chester hoped Roly would just count that there were indeed ten bundles, probably check tops and bottoms as well, hopefully be fooled by the 20's sticking out a little from the rest in the middle. And something more - Roly would be thinking that Chester would never be so stupid as to try to cheat a hit man who was clearly going to count the money after the job anyway.

He slipped back into the cottage and went to the small utility closet where he had set the shoe box on the floor at the back, hidden from view by rain gear they had brought along and hung up on low hooks. He grabbed the shoebox.

He went to the bedroom and placed the ten money bundles into the shoebox and slid it along the floor under the bed.

He came down to the beach. Candace and Amara were making a sand castle.

"I was looking for those sunglasses everywhere," Chester said. "Finally found them in the car."

"I was wondering what took you so long. Amara says she's thirsty. Would you mind?"

"No problem."

Now he could do the gun, the Beretta M9.

He went to the cottage. The Beretta was tucked under heavy blankets on the top shelf in the front hall closet, wrapped in a black plastic bag. He had loaded it last night, but certainly wasn't going to leave it outside overnight. He reached up and grabbed it and slipped out of the cottage into the rear yard, again unobserved. He hid it under pine needles at the base of a pine tree at the far end of the laneway right near the road, a spot he would have to pass by when he took his walk at 1:00 after lunch. He had left the gun in the plastic bag because you don't want unexplained pine gum on a gun when you know you'll have to turn it over to the police for examining.

He slipped back into the cottage and got the water at the kitchen sink. He came back down to the beach.

"Here's the water, Amara," he said, handing her the pink water bottle with frolicking bunnies on it. Candace was now lying on the dock sunning.

Amara sang to herself and dug in the sand with a plastic shovel, filling a big plastic tray to which she added small scoops of lake water then stirred it around and scooped the thick slurry into a pail to make round turrets for a sand castle. "I need a square pail, too," she said.

"They don't make square pails," Candace said, turning a half rotation into the sun.

"How do you make square things then?"

"Just make round things for now." Candace was listless. "I'll find something later for you."

"They'll be too many round things."

"I'll deal with it later."

"But they'll be too many round things."

Their back and forth carried on, but Chester tuned it all out. He had to consider the thing he hadn't decided on yet. First, he had to have a reason that would satisfy the police as to why, very coincidentally, he was not at the cottage right after lunch when the terrible thing that was going to happen was happening. That part was easy - his one-hour, every-day-at-1:00 walking routine would cover that.

But *this time,* he had to have a damn good reason to turn around in his walk and come back after ten minutes. By design, he never took his wallet when he took his walk. But this time his plan was that he would need his wallet, but would forget it in his other pants' pocket, a simple mistake anyone could make when they don't normally take their wallet on their walk. It would naturally mean he had to return to the cottage unexpectedly to get it when he remembered.

So the question was *why* need the wallet *this* time? He needed it to buy something at the general store a mile down the road, but what? It had to be something that *needed* buying, otherwise it could look suspicious. It couldn't be just a candy treat for Amara because they had loaded up on those before. He had put off giving it the serious thought he should have, instead believing something believable would just pop into his head, which hadn't happened.

Everything he thought of seemed forced, stupid, suspicious. They had pop and chips already. And it couldn't be something frozen because it would melt on the walk home.

Think outside the box. His nerves had been rising all morning, and now he felt the muscles in his chest tightening and his brain seizing. He couldn't think either outside *or* inside the box.

He tried to see it from the police perspective. 'Mr. Carter, did you really need more marshmallows when I see three bags in that cupboard?'

His mind was so preoccupied with this new question that he missed hearing Candace saying something to him.

"Chester?" Her voice carried annoyance.

"What?"

"You're like in dreamland. I asked you a question. I said, are you walking today?"

He was suddenly annoyed, too. Haven't you seen it's my unchanging routine, religiously followed? Don't go forgetting that when the police ask you about it. But he said, "Yes, of course. I go every day. My routine. My back. Remember."

"If you're going in the direction of the general store, would you pick up some potato chips. I went and ate all the other ones last night. They're not much to carry."

He could have dropped to the ground and prostrated himself to her in gratitude. *She* was asking *him* to buy something before he even said anything about buying something that might sound stupid and made up. A rock solid alibi the police would never question because *she* asked *him*. Thank you, Candace!

"Well...okay," he said. "I guess I could do that."

Then he added. "My mouth's a bit dry. I'm going up to the cottage to get some gun. Gum. Can I get you anything?"

"No, thanks."

Time to do the Cough syrup milkshake. He had hidden the Cough syrup under the blanket in the high shelf where the gun was. He put a dose into the strawberry milkshake for Amara and put it in the fridge and made up one for himself, without the drug. The colder it was, the less she would taste anything other than strawberry, the Cough syrup being cherry-flavored. The day before, he had removed the label from the bottle by running it under hot water to de-glue and then burned the paper labeling. He knew police would possibly check the garbage. Now he emptied the rest of the Cough syrup into the sink in the bathroom and ran hot water for a minute. He filled the empty Cough syrup bottle with water.

Back down at the beach, he said to Amara, "I just tasted our strawberry milkshake, just a little bit. Mmmm good. I put it in the fridge to get nice and cold for lunch."

"Oh goody," Amara said.

"Time for a quick paddleboat ride?"

"Sure."

Thirty yards out, he slipped the Cough syrup bottle overboard.

Back at the beach, he went swimming so he would need to use the blue and white striped towel. He even let part fall into the water so it would need drying. He hung it over the aluminum lawn chair. There wasn't the least bit of wind stirring, but still, he clipped a clothespin over it.

It was 10:50.

Chester thought about what he was doing, and precisely what he was going to have to do very soon.

A very high high-wire act.

CHAPTER 26

They ate a lunch of scrambled eggs and toast. He thought Candace seemed more quiet than usual. On the other hand, he thought, he wasn't exactly himself, so probably wasn't much of a judge of that.

It was 12:30 and Chester wanted Amara to finish drinking all of her strawberry milkshake, and soon. "I'm halfway finished mine," he said, "and you are, too. I think it's a perfect time for a race to the finish."

Without announcing her agreement, and dispensing with the usual '1,2,3 go', Amara grabbed her glass and gulped and gulped. Chester did the same, his eyes on Amara's progress to make sure she was faster.

She drained the glass. "I won! Ahhhhhh," she said, bringing the glass down on the table with a bang and giving a victory flourish with her hand.

"You're just too fast, beating me like that," Chester said. "Did it taste good?"

"Yummy. Can we do it again tomorrow?"

"Tomorrow? Well…we'll see."

Candace and Amara chatted as Candace started the dish-es. Chester went into the living room to the sliding glass door to the deck and locked it. Like he told Roly, it made a heavy rolling noise when opened. But more to the point, it faced the water, and he didn't want Roly coming in through that door as Chester might miss seeing him.

He went into the master bedroom, over to the side of the bed that was near the window, opposite to Candace's side of the bed. He looked under the bed at the shoe box. Candace would have no reason to be over on this side, especially to look under the bed. But, to satisfy his nerves, he nudged the box further under the bed with his foot.

At 12:53 he tucked Amara into bed for her nap. Usually she wanted to talk a few minutes, but today she couldn't keep her eye-lids open and her mouth was slack. "Good night, Daddy." She didn't even catch her mistake, just rolling over away from him, the cough syrup cocktail working its magic. He kissed her forehead and closed the door behind him.

"See you later," he called to Candace, who was flipping through a magazine in the living room. It was 12:58.

"Okay," she called back.

He walked out the door and along the cottage laneway. Near the road, hidden from observation from anywhere, he grabbed up the black plastic bag with the Beretta inside from under the pine-needle pile. He took it out of the bag, stuffing the bags in his pants' pocket. He checked again that the gun was indeed loaded. He put it behind his back, tucked under his belt and under his loose golf shirt.

He started walking. Both sides of the graveled road were heavily treed - cedars, pine, and plenty of thick wild undergrowth. He couldn't see twenty yards into the woods on either side.

After walking a few minutes down the road he came to the 'S' bend. In its middle, anyone on the road couldn't see ahead or back more than thirty yards. He slipped off the road and went into the bush twenty yards.

He heard a car moving slowly along the narrow, twisty road. He caught a look, a black Honda Civic. He couldn't see the plates as it approached, but got a glimpse of the driver, a man, who looked like a businessman, proper shirt collar. Too unobservant, not wary, not looking around. Not Roly.

He looked at his watch. 1:03.

*

When Chester left the cottage, Candace had gone to the master bedroom and stood at the corner of the window, drawing the curtain slightly open with her finger, watching Chester walk out the laneway until she couldn't see him for the trees and tall bushes that thickened at the back of the property.

After a few moments, although the trees were thick, she caught a brief glimpse of his shirt color as he walked, thirty yards down the graveled road and receding, striding with purpose in the direction of the general store.

Her finger let the curtain drop and she stood thinking. She glanced at her watch. 1:00. She looked out again. No sign of Chester.

She opened Amara's door and saw and heard she was already sleeping soundly. She closed the door and stood moments more, her teeth lightly biting at her lip.

She went to the telephone in the living room. Her hand hovered over it a moment. She picked up the receiver, looked at a small piece of torn paper in her hand, and dialed the number Dennis had written on it last night.

"Hello?" Dennis answered.

"Hi, it's me, Candace. Chester just left to walk to the general store, and Amara is sleeping. I wondered if you would care to come over for a short visit?"

*

Chester took the black plastic bag that had held the gun and put a match to it and in five seconds it was a few square inches of nondescript black shrivel and he stamped it into the ground. On an earlier two walks he had reconnoitered the best way back through the woods to a point in the deep rear corner of the cottage property where he could remain hidden. He began to walk back through the bush in the direction of the cottage, staying well off the road and out of sight.

*

Candace opened the door and let Dennis in. "Welcome."

She walked to the living room and sat down on the sofa, Dennis following. He sat down beside her. Too close. He bent and kissed her cheek and his hand went to her breast.

She slapped his hand. "Hey, stop. What are you doing?"

"Just what you want me to do."

She moved herself away on the couch. "No. That's not what I want. You don't understand. I just want to talk."

*

Chester arrived back at the deep rear of the cottage property and hid. A wide clump of thick bushes obscured him from sight from the road and from the cottage and from anywhere in the rear yard of the cottage. But it afforded him a clean view and a wide field of vision. He could see the cottage door at a 90-degree angle, the whole of the rear yard and side yards, as well as the yards of the cottage on each side of their cottage.

Now he just had to wait. And try to calm his nerves.

He had been in a sweat before but now it beaded and dropped from his forehead like a leaky faucet. He had to stay unwaveringly committed, because commitment was something that could very easily slide sideways in this situation. This was very dangerous. But it was also imperative. He felt pretty confident, although not confident confident, that he was up to it. He only hoped Candace was.

He checked the gun again.

*

"Talk?" Dennis said. "About what?"

"Well, stuff. Like why you're a dentist?"

"Why?"

"Like what your childhood was like?"

'Why?"

"Like what's important to a person like you? Why you and your wife divorced? Why you live alone now? I'm interested in those things."

"Why?"

"Well you're different from most people I see, and I like to just see what's going on out there."

"Why?"

"Well sometimes people can be interesting, you know? You can learn something."

"Why?"

"Why? Why? Why? Are you stupid or something?"

"I didn't think that's why you invited me here."

"Well I'm sorry you're under a wrong impression."

*

Chester was suddenly aware of a soft 'putt-putt' sound, a small outboard motor-boat approaching from the north, like probably a small aluminum fishing boat of the kind he had been using here. It was maybe three cottages away.

He heard the motor cut out. Maybe someone was fishing in close to shore and wanted to be quiet now. He couldn't see anything that far away for the trees and the other cottages. No one was at the other cottages along that way until the weekend.

*

Dennis seemed exasperated. "You don't wear those shorts and that top because you want to just chit-chat."

She looked at her shorts - short-shorts, a lot of leg. Her top - a lot of cleavage. "Sometimes I give off the wrong signals," she said. "Old habits. I shouldn't. I'm sorry."

"And you asked me to come when Chester's not here."

"Well yes. That's because he doesn't want to hear about any of your life. He's not interested. And besides, it probably bothers him, you being around here. But I just like to talk. That's all."

"And you care if it bothers him?"

"Of course I care."

"Boy, that's some false advertising." He was still exasperated. "I came here so damn fast, I didn't even use the washroom."

She wasn't sure what to do. But her finger half lifted and pointed in the direction of the washroom.

Dennis got up looking at her, trying to figure her out, then walked to the washroom.

*

Chester saw him. It had to be him, Roly, not thirty yards away, light-footed, short but stocky, coming across the grassy back-yard of the cottage next door to the north, wary, a hard face, white summer pants, a baggy brown T-shirt. He one-handedly slipped a black balaclava over his head.

*

Candace heard the washroom door close. She sat another moment.

Dennis would probably take his time, simmer down, maybe walk out on her. Well, that would be fine. Even for the best. She got up and went down the hall, past Amara's door, and into the bedroom and pushed the door almost closed behind her. I shouldn't have invited him over, she thought. That was playing with fire. Damn, that was stupid. Wake up Candace.

She would just tell him it was better he went home. Sorry for the signals. But she wasn't going to tell him that in her short shorts and that top.

*

Chester felt a chill run up and down his body. But then he felt strangely calm, like a switch threw on inside, a sudden focus, a visceral strength, a steeling to the task, his mind cleared of everything else.

Here he was, Roly, a cold-blooded murderer, here to strangle innocent Candace to death, a gruesome death, for nothing she's ever done to deserve it, strangle an innocent person without feeling and for nothing but cold hard cash. Death and destruction, a merciless killer. I've got to believe you've done it before, you killing bastard. But you won't ever be doing it again. Live by the sword, die by the sword. Tooth and claw. Time to pay the piper.

Sweat dripped. His hand felt for the Beretta M9, a gun reputed to be 'accurate and reliable.' It better the hell be, he thought, or things were quickly going to get damn ugly around here.

He always knew as part of his plan that he had to have a clear and compelling reason to kill Roly, a reason evident to anyone, including Candace and the police. He couldn't just blast Roly away any old time. Roly had to be in very serious progress with Candace to make Candace and the police believe he was the serial killer. Chester couldn't make a saving entrance on the scene before Candace needed saving because that could look cooked. Something like a life and death struggle had to be in progress to make this work for all concerned.

He saw Roly looking all around before sneaking along to approach the cottage door, keeping his head low. Roly was listening at the door, trying to peek in once, but Chester knew the curtain on the door blocked his view. Roly lifted his hand to the handle. Chester saw the door open out on its now quiet hinges, just as Roly wanted it. And just as Chester would need it.

Roly stepped through the doorway. Chester saw the door swing gently and close silently behind him.

The dragon was now in. The damsel would soon be in distress.

CHAPTER 27

In the bedroom, Candace looked around for the shirt and the slacks she wanted, set them on the bed, and took her top and shorts off, now wearing only a bra and panties. As she reached for her slacks, she felt the bedroom door open behind her. Damn it, Dennis. She hadn't even heard the bathroom door open.

She turned and saw dark eyes in a black balaclava close to her and the back of a thick flying hand. Not Dennis. It caught her in the mouth and cheek, hard, before any sound came out. It sent her sprawling backward onto the floor by the bed, stunning her.

She lay in a semi-concussed state, trying to figure what had happened, but couldn't, her mind fuzzy.

She couldn't see him anywhere. He must be down low, she thought. Why down low?

She heard him on the other side of the bed. Why was he over *there*?

Why was he even *here*, in this cottage, at all?

She heard something, like something small scraping or sliding across the wood floor on the other side of the bed. There wasn't anything to slide over there, so what was he doing sliding something over there?

Her mind went in hazy circles.

Long seconds passed.

She tried to rise, but thought the better of it, staying prone to appear still out of it. She kept wondering, who is he, what does he want?

She heard him say "bastard," out loud. Very angry.

She heard the toilet flush. Dennis.

Balaclava man heard it, too. He came leaping across the room into her view, his balaclava still on. She kept her eyes mostly closed. But she glimpsed he now had a hand gun firmly in his hand.

He closed the door most of the way and stood behind it in the corner of the room. He glanced to her but she closed her eyes faster.

She kept them closed as she heard the bathroom door open with its squeak that hadn't bothered Chester all week. She heard Dennis walk out of the washroom, then down the hall away from the bedroom, his weight sounding on the laminate flooring. She knew he was taking a look in the living room for her.

Now she heard him walking toward her bedroom. She opened her eyes a millimeter. The balaclava man was edging back tight along the bedroom wall, still shielded from Dennis's view by the door, watching the door, the gun pointed.

The door moved open very slowly, only partway. Dennis was in the doorway, puzzled at seeing Candace on the floor wearing only a bra and panties, her eyes on him. His hand pushed the door open further and he took a step forward.

He saw the balaclava man and the gun and stopped abruptly.

"Fuck!" the balaclava man said.

"What the…" Dennis yelled, his eyes wide

"You fucking screwed with the money," the balaclava man yelled back.

Candace saw him point the gun and BANG. A red hole appeared in Dennis's chest and Dennis's eyes went wider than before.

"You think I'm fucking stupid?" the balaclava man yelled.

Another BANG and Dennis's head threw back, a black hole in his forehead. He fell back against the wall and slid all the way down, his head resting against the wall.

Candace saw Dennis's eyes were open but there was no life in them.

She was aware of loud echoing in the room.

The balaclava turned to her.

She was too slow.

He was looking at her and she at him.

She began to cry softly, her voice trembling. "What do you want?" She tried to cover herself with her arms and brought her legs up into her body.

He walked close and slapped her across the head. He glanced once around the room and looked at Dennis again. "Bastard," he said.

He looked back to her. Even with the balaclava on, she could see his eyes were cold, hardened, set. She knew he was going to kill her.

*

Hearing two gun shots, Chester was terrified, slipping into the cottage with speed, but quiet.

From down the hall, he saw Candace on the bedroom floor wearing only panties and a bra, her face in terror, her hand at her face. But she clearly hadn't been shot. Roly was standing in front of her holding a gun, his back to Chester. What the hell was Roly doing shooting a gun twice like that?

Candace's eyes now saw Chester coming silently down the hall, the Beretta aimed.

Roly saw her eyes. He swung around, his gun-hand jumping up toward Chester.

Chester unloaded two shots before Roly could fire. The cottage filled with thunderous echoes. Roly fell to a sitting position against the wall, his gun-arm limp, his eyes staring at Chester, enquiring.

Roly's gun-hand jerked up.

Chester fired again, into the chest.

Roly slumped forward, his head lowering, the balaclava almost touching the wood floor, the gun slipping from his hand. Chester walked in and kicked the gun away across the floor, not wanting to touch it.

Now, along another wall, he saw Dennis, his body sagged, his head against the wall, looking very dead.

What the fucking hell? Chester's head exploded. What the hell was *he* doing here? And in the bedroom, Candace half naked!

He glanced to her and realized she had fainted.

Chester's mind reeled. Dennis had to have come here just minutes after he left for his walk, like it was arranged. She had asked him to pick up some potato chips. Damn it, Candace.

Did she have Dennis visit yesterday, too, turning the walk routine to her own advantage?

His brain was on fire. Damn it, Candace.

He stepped to Roly. He didn't disturb the balaclava, only raised Roly's head with one hand and looked at the eyes, an empty vacant stare, looking very dead like Dennis.

Panic reared in his head. The whole idea was supposed to be just a husband and wife and daughter enjoying time at a cottage in wonderful surroundings. The police wouldn't have had any suspicions.

But now there *would be* suspicions, on Chester, Dennis being here with Candace, alone like this in the bedroom. The police would start thinking that Chester had a motive to want Candace gone. 'Rather obvious problem in the marriage, Mr. Carter. Reason to want her dead. Hire a hit man?' It would add weight against suspect numero uno.

The whole damn plan would go crashing to hell in a hand bag.

And then what? He would go straight to prison. Up here in Canada. A very long time. A total jerk.

And far, far worse - he would lose Candace and Amara. Forever and forever.

He looked around the room, his heart and head racing.

NO. NOT GOING TO HAPPEN. GET A GRIP. A DAMN FIRM GRIP.

He looked at Candace, still fainted.

It was her face, so still and serene in the middle of this bloody chaos. It drew him in and held him from the chaos, slowed the feverish whirling of his mind, steadied him, centered him again.

He got down beside her and saw a rough redness on her cheek. But he was certain she was otherwise alright. Her eye had caught his, a clear focus, the moment before he shot Roly, so he knew she hadn't been hurt.

He saw her short shorts and tank top and a shirt lying on the bed. Her slacks were on the floor.

"Candace," he said. He held her, hugged her. His voice was calm as he whispered in her ear. "Candace."

She began to stir. "Candace," he said again.

She came to, her head suddenly moving, her eyes wild and frightened, checking the room. Her eyes registered the two dead bodies.

"Candace, it's alright. You're safe now." He hugged her tighter.

She burst into sobs, clutching at him, afraid. "Chester, I don't know what happened," she blurted.

"Are you okay?"

"Yes." But her body was shaking.

"It's alright, Candace. Everything's alright."

She was squeezing him. "I don't know what happened. Is Amara alright?"

Chester had seen her door was closed. "Yes, yes."

"I don't know what happened."

"He must have sneaked in."

"How were you here?"

"I forgot my wallet. I was almost at the front door when I heard what sounded like shots. Grabbed my gun."

She gripped him. "I would have been killed. He was going to kill me, I know it."

She saw her bare legs. "Chester, I was just changing my clothes. Honest. Honest. Dennis was here just to talk. He was in the bathroom when that man came."

"I believe you."

"Chester," she broke into full sobs, gripping him tightly.

"It's all okay."

They both heard Amara whimpering.

*

Chester said, "I'm calling the police. You stay with Amara in her bedroom. Can't let her see any of this. I'll let you know when it's okay to bring her out."

Candace, still frightened, nodded. With trembling hands she reached for her slacks and shirt on the bed.

Chester went to Amara's door and opened it an inch and saw her sitting up in bed, her head weaving a bit, woozy looking. He opened the door a little more and said, "Mommy's coming and will lie down with you. You stay right there."

"I heard bangs," she said drowsily, trying to focus on Chester.

"I know. It's all okay. Mommy's coming."

Candace, buttoning her shirt with shaking fingers, her face wet with tears, slid past him into Amara's room and closed the door.

He went to the cottage phone in the living room. He dialed 911. He had checked before they left Ohio that it was the emergency number used in Canada, too.

He heard the female dispatcher's voice. "Emergency. Do you require fire, police, or ambulance?"

"Police," Chester said. "And an ambulance. 2210 Ring Lake Road." He figured an ambulance was needed to take the bodies away.

He felt his heart racing and his voice running fast. He had always known he would be making this call and had considered that he better sound frightened and upset. It was a whole lot easier than he expected.

"What is the emergency?"

"An intruder came into our rented cottage. He shot a neighbor who was visiting here. Then I shot the intruder. Both men seem dead to me. My wife is fine."

"Is anyone else injured?"

"No."

"Are you alright, Sir?"

"Yes."

"Are you calling from that address?"

"Yes."

"Please stay on the line."

She would be relaying the information to the local authorities. After a few moments she was back. "The police are on the way, Sir. It will take them fifteen minutes to get to where you are."

"Okay."

"What is your name, Sir?"

"Chester Carter."

"Mr. Carter, do not touch or disturb anything there."

"Yes, I understand."

"Do not permit anyone into the building. Tell people to keep off the property."

"Yes, I understand. There aren't any people around anyway. Just us. The cottage number isn't well marked on the road. I'll stand out on the road to flag them down. I'm wearing a blue golf shirt."

*

In the bedroom, he looked around but couldn't see a silk-tie anywhere. He bent close to Roly, avoiding the eyes in the balaclava, and lifted the baggy brown T-shirt so he could check in the white pants' pockets.

The tie was bunched in one of the front pockets. A white silk-tie, the same white as the pants. Chester used part of the T-shirt to cover his fingers as he eased one end of the tie out of the pocket until a length of about six inches was out and showing. He positioned the shirt back to leave a few inches of tie visible. He wanted the police to see it right off, suggesting Roly had been getting it out just when all the shit happened.

Candace would easily understand how she missed seeing it - the tie was white, the pants were white. And she had fainted, and when she came to, Roly was slumped forward, dead, his baggy shirt covering most of the pockets. When she was eventually told about the tie, she would realize the agonizing death she had been spared.

Chester went to the other side of the bed. The shoe box had been moved out a foot from the bed. Four of the money bundles were lying on the floor. Roly must have been counting them when he heard Dennis coming, Chester figured.

Chester grabbed them and the shoebox and went to the open hall closet where his gun had been. He set his gun back on the shelf at the top. He took the rest of the money bundles out of the shoe box, counting that there were still ten of them. He set the shoe box back where it had been all week, empty on the floor of the closet at the back behind the owners' raincoats and boots.

On the top shelf under a blanket, his hand found the thick plastic freezer bag he had deposited there when they first arrived. He took it and slipped the cash bundles into it.

With the bag tucked behind his back, he walked to Amara's bedroom door but didn't open it. "They're coming soon. I'm just going out to meet them now. Won't be long."

"Okay," Candace said weakly.

"How're you doing?"

"Okay."

He left the cottage with the freezer bag of money now hidden under his shirt and walked along the road in the opposite direction he had taken earlier. One thing was very clear. He had known all along he couldn't risk leaving the money anywhere in the cottage or in the car or on the property. The police and forensics people would be scouring the place looking everywhere for any telling thing. $2,520 in cash would be a tantalizing first clue as to what had really happened.

After walking a hundred yards or so, he stepped off the road and entered the woods, almost across the road from the back of Dennis's property. Behind a stand of cedars about thirty yards in was a natural grouping of low granite slabs which he had discovered when exploring for just such a hiding place a few days ago on a short stroll.

On that earlier day he had found a crevice, two inches high and horizontal, in one of the granite slabs. He had jabbed in a stick to see how far the crevice went in - well over two feet. Now he knelt beside it and slid the plastic bag into the crevice, using a small stick to shove it all the way in beyond anyone's view. Unless someone actually knew something was in there, it would never be discovered. And it was in a waterproof container if any rain seeped in.

He would come back and retrieve it with long-handle pliers on a night drive up from Toronto when he was doing an install sometime in the next month or two.

CHAPTER 28

The police siren was still distant as Chester hurried back along the road toward the cottage. He took deep breaths to compose himself, to relax his flaring nerves. Not that he wanted to appear calm, of course. Well that sure wasn't going to happen anyway.

Within a minute, a police car showed up, the siren still wailing and blue lights flashing. Chester stood to the side of the road in front of the cottage, waving his arm as it approached. There was one policeman in the car.

The officer killed the siren but left the lights flashing and remained in the car. Chester could see he was on the radio, but watching Chester. Ten seconds later, another police car arrived with no siren on or lights flashing and parked behind the first. Chester figured they were communicating on the way.

Both officers got out of their cars at the same time, both warily observing Chester, both with a hand on the holster of their service revolver, both remaining on the other side of their car. After all, his report did reference shootings, and that he had shot the intruder, and maybe he was a nut bar.

"Mr. Carter?", the officer from the lead car said.

"Yes, officer," Chester said. "I'm the one who called in."

They were still wary.

"Is anyone hurt?" the lead officer said.

"Well, two men are dead, I'm pretty sure. But no one else is hurt. My wife, Candace, is in the cottage with our daughter, keeping her in her bedroom so she doesn't see anything. Amara was napping when it all happened."

He knew he sounded nervous but also sane, and they could see he had no weapon. They came forward.

The lead officer said, "I'm Officer Thomas. Where are the dead men?"

"In the master bedroom."

Both officers' eyes showed momentary wonder, as in 'what were they doing in there'?

"Is that where they were shot?" Thomas asked, and Chester figured he wondered if the bodies had been moved.

"Yes. The intruder came into the bedroom where my wife was changing. Dennis, our neighbor, was visiting and was in the bathroom. When Dennis came into the bedroom, the intruder shot him."

Chester could see they now wondered why neighbor Dennis came into the bedroom when Candace was changing. "Dennis probably heard something in the bedroom so came in," Chester said. "I was just coming in the laneway here when I heard two shots. I went in, grabbed my gun, and shot the intruder who was about to kill Candace."

Chester noticed the eyes of the policemen glance to each other as if to say, 'this is uncanny'.

The other policeman, Officer Gill, went on into the cottage.

"Who is this neighbor, Dennis?" Officer Thomas said.

"His cottage is four over," Chester said, pointing. "He's a dentist, from Toledo. We just met him Monday. Don't know his last name. We're from Ohio, too. Just renting here."

"Is anyone at his cottage?"

"No. He's single. Divorced. No kids. Nobody else over there."

"Where is your gun?"

"Back on the closet shelf."

"Where is the intruder's gun?"

"In the bedroom on the floor. I didn't touch it. Just kicked it away from him."

"Show me where your gun is."

They didn't know Chester, and Chester knew they wanted zero risk of Chester shooting anybody else today. He led Officer Thomas into the cottage to the open closet near the front door and lifted the blanket on the top shelf and pointed to the Beretta. Officer Thomas picked it up by the tip of the barrel with his fingers and put it in a clear plastic bag he took from his pocket.

"Okay," Thomas said, now somewhat impatient, "you stay outside and let us take a look. We'll have more questions shortly."

*

Officer Thomas passed by the closed door of one bedroom - that would be mother and child. He went on and saw Officer Gill in the master bedroom. He glanced around the room and took a look at the two men on the floor, the one in the balaclava, the obvious intruder, looking like three shots in the chest, heavily bloodstained T-shirt. The other one, the neighbor, Dennis - plugged in the forehead and the chest. A regular gunfight at the OK Corral.

Officer Thomas looked at Officer Gill, a nod confirming that both men indeed appeared dead. But an ambulance was on the way and a paramedic would confirm.

They noted the pistol on the floor. They noted a pair of woman's short shorts and a woman's skimpy summer top lying on the bed.

Officer Gill stayed in the room while Officer Thomas tapped lightly on Amara's closed bedroom door. "Mrs. Carter?"

"Yes." He heard a voice weak and stressed.

"I am police officer Thomas. May I open the door?"

"Yes."

He saw Candace sitting on the bed, looking shaken, her face tear-stained, one of her cheeks reddened. Amara was under a blanket, apparently sleeping, just the back of her dark-haired head showing.

"Are you alright?" Thomas asked.

"Yes."

"Sure?"

"Just a bit…unsettled."

"Your cheek?"

"He hit me there."

"The intruder?"

She nodded. "But it's ok."

"There'll be traffic in here soon so you should take your daughter outside, maybe down to the dock for now. We'll have some questions."

"Okay."

"Thank you."

He shut the door and went back to the master bedroom. Officer Gill said, "Take a look at that," pointing toward Roly's pants' pocket. It had escaped initial observation.

Officer Thomas bent and took a good look without touching it, four inches of it sticking out of a front pocket. He looked up at Gill, a sudden brightening of Thomas' face. "My God, a silk-tie," Thomas said.

He looked back at the black balaclava, the silent head bowed to the floor. "I'll be damned. He's struck again."

"Question is, who is he?" Officer Gill said. "I checked. There's no wallet, no I.D., no keys, nothing."

*

Chester walked with Candace who carried Amara down the stone steps from the cottage to the chairs at the dock. Although Amara mumbled 'what's going on', she showed exceptional tiredness and couldn't focus, her eyelids hard to keep open. She tucked into Candace and wanted to sleep.

Chester knew Candace wanted to talk but couldn't because Amara was right there. Candace got up from her chair and carried Amara along their beach a few yards and set her on a cloth chaise-lounge where Amara curled up and Candace knew she would quickly doze in the warmth of the sun.

She came back and sat beside Chester. She reached and held his hand. "Chester," she said, her eyes filling with tears, "I would've been killed if you hadn't been there."

"Damn lucky I forgot my wallet. What happened?"

"Chester, I'm so sorry. I invited Dennis over just to sit and talk. Nothing more. I mean it. I know you don't like him around, so I didn't tell you I was going to do that. I wasn't even sure myself. But it was nothing more." She squeezed his hand. "He was using the bathroom. I was in the bedroom in the middle of changing into slacks and a shirt because I didn't feel decent."

Chester squeezed her hand back. "It's alright, Candace. I believe you."

"I didn't hear anything. The man came out of nowhere from behind and hit me. I know I was stunned a bit. Then Dennis came in the bedroom wondering where I was and the man shot him. And he was about to kill me, I could feel it..."

Chester put his arm around her and hugged her close. "All that matters is that we're safe now."

"But I remember the man said something to Dennis first, something about 'screwing with the money' or something."

Chester felt sudden alarm and released his hug, but forced himself to ask gently. "What do you mean 'said something'? Said what?"

"I've got to try to remember. I think he was on the other side of the bed first, I don't know why. But he swore at Dennis, 'fuck, you screwed with the money,' or something like that."

Chester could feel his heart racing. The damn modified little money bundles didn't cut it. "Did he say anything else? Anything?"

"I don't know. But...did he know Dennis? It's like he did. It's so strange."

Chester felt tension squeezing his chest. He had checked that all of the money he had put in the shoe box was still there when he went back in. But had Roly lifted or moved the shoe box into Candace's view at any time?

"You mean you didn't see him doing anything on the other side of the bed?"

"No. I couldn't see. I was on the floor."

Chester realized that the bedspread draping to the floor on her side would have blocked her view of the floor on the other side.

He had an inspiration. "Maybe he was hiding on the other side of the bed because he heard Dennis in the washroom."

"That may be it," she said.

"Yes, that's probably it." He tried not to sound insistent.

He increasingly worried how the 'screwing with the money' thing was going to play. And besides that, with Dennis at the cottage, and in the bedroom, and Candace half-dressed in the bedroom, it would raise awkward and suspicious questions that threatened the whole plan, all a serious departure from the random, silk-tie serial murderer scenario that he had so painstakingly planned. His whole tidy arrangement could derail like a freight train at high speed.

He heard more vehicles arriving. He looked up toward the cottage. An ambulance pulled into the driveway. Two uniformed paramedics, a man and a woman, got out.

He saw another police car drive past the driveway and stop, two uniformed police getting out, a man and a woman.

Then an unmarked police car turned into the driveway. A man stepped out, much older, straightening his suit and tie, an air of relaxed authority. A detective, Chester figured.

Chester watched as Officer Thomas met the police and the detective and paramedics outside the cottage. He saw Thomas speak a bit and point, and the paramedics went on into the cottage. Thomas then spoke to the police and detective for a full minute further in words Chester couldn't hear, although he strained.

Officer Thomas pointed down to the beach to Chester and Candace. The police and detective looked, then talked more, and Chester saw excitement rising. Officer Thomas was surely telling them about the silk-tie. Thomas then escorted them all into the cottage.

Chester looked at Candace who was looking at nothing, her head down, her face badly troubled.

Chester worried they'd wonder why Roly would have a silk-tie if he was there to kill Dennis. And they'd wonder why Roly would be in *their* cottage if he was on a mission to kill Dennis instead of at Dennis's cottage? And why would anyone believe a rich dentist screwed with anyone's money anyway?

The issues were getting confusing. It might just make the police look a whole lot deeper into the case, Chester worried, and getting to the very bottom of it. And finding Chester there.

CHAPTER 29

In the master bedroom the female paramedic finished her check of vital signs of Dennis and Roly as Detective Constable Grant came in, taking it all in.

Grant was fifty-seven, a girth that was beginning to show, thinning blond hair, sparkling blue eyes, and a genial look about him.

His eyes caught the female paramedic's and she read the question. "Both deceased," she said, still kneeling on the floor.

"How long?"

"Within the last thirty minutes, I'd say."

Grant nodded. That fit with what Officer Thomas said Chester said had happened. When there's an incident with questionable gunplay, a person involved doesn't always phone 911 immediately, sometimes taking time to work out a story. Chester must have called immediately, so he seemed to be on the level.

The female paramedic said, "Appears to be a silk-tie there."

"Appears to be," Grant said, having already been informed of it by Thomas, along with everything else Thomas knew to this point from talking to Chester and Candace.

She glanced knowingly at the male paramedic whose expression told Grant that they had already spoken of the tie. Word about the tie would get out quickly, of course. It would be big news, exciting news, carrying the real prospect, finally, of the end of a very puzzling mystery, the death of the serial killer, the end of three years of terrorizing fear in the area. But as tempting as it was to believe that this was the silk-tie murderer, as tempting as it was to think of Grant himself delivering such news to the public, a full investigation still needed to be conducted with an open mind and sound evidence gathered.

The paramedics left the room. The bodies would remain as they were to await photography and forensics.

Grant naturally wanted to know who exactly this killer was but had been told there was no ID present on the body. An unknown, unclaimed parked car or boat nearby would go a long way to answering that question.

He also wanted to interview Chester and Candace immediately.

He walked outside the cottage and saw a policewoman on the road instructing inquisitive cottagers to stay well back from the cottage property. They had heard the siren. She would also be checking the road nearby for an unknown car.

A rookie policeman was down at the dock commanding several boats to keep away. The boats were turning in slow circles just beyond the dock, the boaters trying to discern what they could from the significant police presence.

Grant knew Officer Gill was checking the cottages and shoreline immediately to the north for a possible boat used by the killer. The rookie cop was now leaving the dock to make his way south to check the shoreline for the same purpose.

Officer Thomas had gone to Dennis's cottage to find anything - a cell phone, a wallet - that would provide the name of a contact person in Toledo or wherever. Thomas said Chester didn't even know Dennis's last name.

Grant saw that Chester and Candace and Amara were now huddled in chairs on the front deck of the cottage, avoiding the gawking boaters down at the shore.

Grant walked over. "I'm Detective Constable Grant," he said.

He shook hands with Chester, Candace keeping herself withdrawn. "I've been briefed on what happened. I know how very, very distressing this is. I appreciate your cooperation. I would like to ask you a few questions for now, separately, of course, so one of you can stay with your daughter."

*

Alone in the living room with Chester, Detective Constable Grant first pointed out the mini microphone on his jacket with a thin wire running from it. "A recorder. Everything we say will be recorded. My memory isn't what it used to be. Is that ok?"

"Certainly," Chester said.

Chester informed Grant that they were renters on a one week rental, Sunday to Sunday, that they had arrived late Saturday, though, and that it was their first time renting here or anywhere in Canada.

"I was told you and your wife just met Dennis on Monday. Don't know Dennis very well," Grant said.

"That's right. Don't even know his last name."

"I understand Dennis was visiting when the intruder came in."

"Yes."

"Where were you exactly?"

"I had gone to buy potato chips. But I forgot my wallet and was coming back from the road, just walking up the laneway when I heard two gun shots."

"How long had you been away from the cottage?"

"Maybe ten minutes."

"What extreme good fortune that you came back just then."

"Yes, it is. Someone up there's watching over me."

Chester saw Grant's eyes twinkle. "Yes, miraculous. So, you heard the shots from the driveway. And what exactly did you do?"

"I came in and grabbed my gun from under the blanket on the top shelf and ran along the hall."

"I presume you came in the cottage door running?"

"Fast enough."

"The intruder…didn't hear you come in the door?"

"The door's very quiet. I was also wary. But fast. He heard me only when I was almost at the bedroom door. He was going to kill Candace. She saw me, and he turned toward me with his gun raising. I shot him, twice. I had no choice. He tried to shoot me right after that, so I had to shoot him again."

Grant let it all sink in. From his observations of the intruder, it did appear that he had been shot in the front, not the back, so that supported Chester's version of what happened. Chester hadn't come in just blasting him from behind. But still, there were troubling elements here.

Grant changed direction. "You said you were walking in the laneway. You didn't take the car to get the chips?"

"No. Walking."

"Where were you going to buy the chips?"

"At the general store."

"More than a mile away, isn't it?"

"Yes. I walk distance every day to help my back. I walk when Amara naps."

"Even though Dennis was visiting?"

Chester hesitated. "I didn't know he was visiting. He came here after I left."

Grant looked at Chester several long moments and Chester knew he wondered whether Dennis had just dropped over, uninvited, or had been invited by Candace after Chester left. But Grant moved on, and Chester knew that would be a question for Candace.

"You said you were gone only maybe ten minutes."

"Yes, about that."

"And in that short time, two different men showed up. Dennis, then the intruder."

"Yes."

Grant nodded to himself, his eyes on Chester. After a moment he motioned he wanted Chester to go with him into the master bedroom. Chester followed.

"I know this may be difficult, but I have to know if you have ever seen the intruder before. The man you shot."

Grant knelt and carefully raised the balaclava enough to allow Chester a good look, including the hair. Roly's eyes were still open. Chester winced slightly at the sight. He shook his head. "Never saw him before."

"Do you have any idea who he is?"

"No."

"Or why he would be here?"

"No."

Grant replaced the balaclava as before. Photography wanted it that way.

"You told Officer Thomas that your wife was changing her clothes in here."

"Yes."

"The killer came in here when she was changing?"

"Yes, that's what she told me."

"When you came down the hall and saw her, where was she?"

"On the floor there."

"And in what state of dress or undress?"

"She was wearing only a bra and panties."

Grant paused and his eyes roamed the room a moment, scanning the short shorts and the small summer top, and moved on to the two dead men. His eyes came back to Chester, prodding. "Odd to change with a neighbor visiting."

"She told me she was just changing. Nothing more to it. I believe her."

Grant's eyes stayed fixed on Chester and his mouth made a small gesture that seemed to say to Chester, 'believe it if you want, but I'm not buying it yet.'

Grant took a breath and said, "I want to ask you about your gun. Why did you have a gun, a very lethal gun, here at the cottage?"

"I take it on the road when I'm doing installs for my company. We're tools and machine specialists. Valuable equipment on board. It's habit. I just brought it."

"Was it already loaded?"

"Yes."

Grant paused a long moment. "I suppose that was lucky. Did you declare it at the border coming into Canada?"

"No."

"Do you have a license to bring that gun across international borders?"

"No."

"That's a serious offence…"

Chester had been ready for this one for over a month. "Look, Sir, it just saved my wife's life. My life. Arrest me for entering the country without declaring the thing if you want. A small price to pay."

"We'll leave that matter for now. But we have to confiscate it, do a ballistics test, verify what gun killed whom, standard procedure to verify your story. But it is here illegally, so you won't be getting it back."

Chester nodded. "I understand." He had fully expected that. Small price to pay.

Grant said, "Your walks, let's go back to that. Were they habitual, like every day?"

Chester nodded. "Every day. When Amara napped."

"Same time?"

"Same time. My unchanging routine."

He hoped Grant would latch firmly onto the idea that the killer had observed the routine and timed his home invasion accordingly. "I stiffen if I don't walk regularly," Chester said. "Comes from being behind the wheel long hours. When Amara goes down for a nap at one o'clock, I go for an hour, about three miles. I either go south, down the road to the waterfalls, rest a few minutes, then come back. Or I'll go north, then take that trail that cuts through the woods and comes out at that golf course."

Grant nodded, maybe latching, Chester thought.

"When I walk, I never bother to take a wallet. But Candace had asked me this morning if I could make my walk to the General Store and pick up some potato chips."

In Grant's look, Chester saw the thought register that said, 'getting Chester out of the way so Dennis could come over'. But Chester pushed on. "I was about five minutes down the road before I realized I had forgotten my wallet. Thank God it slipped my mind in the first place and that I then remembered. I could have been down the road a mile and then..."

Chester felt Grant observing him more keenly than ever before. "The timing was remarkable, Mr. Carter. Really...very remarkable."

CHAPTER 30

Candace was seated in the living room, her eyes lowered, her hands lightly rubbing together, her nerves evident. Detective Constable Grant and Candace were alone, Chester out on the deck cradling the still-sleepy Amara.

Grant said, "Do you have any recollection of seeing anyone who might have been watching you? From the lake? From the road? Perhaps from somewhere at night? Anything like that?"

She thought for moments. "No, I wasn't aware of anything like that. Nobody unusual the whole time we've been here."

"I need you to come with me into the bedroom."

"I don't want to go in there. They're still there."

"I have to insist, Mrs. Carter. It's important."

He walked ahead of her into the bedroom. She was slow to follow.

She avoided looking at Dennis.

Grant bent and carefully lifted the killer's head and raised the balaclava. The eyes were still open.

She recoiled and looked away, fighting new tears, her hand at her mouth.

"I'm sorry to have to do this, Mrs. Carter, but I need to know. Please look again, carefully."

She turned her head slowly, and looked, her face tormented.

"Have you ever seen this man before?"

She looked away and shook her head. "No."

"Do you have any idea who he is?"

She was still looking away. "No."

Grant had decided to do this part before really questioning her to shake her, to put her off balance, because he had some difficult questions and wanted her vulnerable.

He replaced the balaclava and got up from the floor. "Were you in this room when the killer came in?"

"Yes."

"Your husband was not here."

"No."

"You had a guest here? Dennis?"

"Yes. But he was in the bathroom."

"Your husband said he wasn't aware that Dennis was going to visit."

"That's right."

"Your husband said you were wearing only a bra and panties when he came in here."

She looked at him. Her face grew suddenly angry. "Yes. I was changing my clothes when the killer came in. That's all. Does it really matter what I was wearing? It has nothing to do with what happened here. That man came in here, hit me and it knocked me out. When I came to he was over there, on the other side of the bed, and I heard Dennis coming out of the washroom and so did he. He kind of leaped across the room and pulled a gun and hid behind the door and when Dennis came in, he shot him. He was going to kill me, I know it. Then I saw Chester in the hall and Chester shot him. What else matters?" By the end of the monologue, her voice was a lot louder than she realized.

She looked down and began to sob and held her hand over her face. She walked from the room, out into the living room. She sat on the couch and took a tissue.

Grant took a seat across from her. "I know this is difficult, Mrs. Carter. I do. Take your time."

She wiped her eyes and blew her nose twice.

Grant said gently, "Two men died here today, Mrs. Carter. We really need your help to know what happened. Why it happened."

She felt her exhaustion now. "We just want to pack up and go home."

"I know," he nodded, sympathetic. "You have a very lovely daughter."

"Thank you."

"She reminds me of my granddaughter."

She wiped at her nose and nodded.

"An apparently innocent man has died. Dennis. We need to really know what happened."

"I just told you." She wasn't confrontational, just saying it.

"Your husband admits he shot and killed a man. He says he had no choice."

"I say he had no choice, too. The guy just shot Dennis and was going to kill me. He would have shot Chester, too. Chester's not lying. It's just so simple."

"I'm not saying anyone's lying. We would like to know who the man is. It will help tell us what happened."

"Well how does that matter to us? What do you think happened here?"

"It may be just as you say, but we don't know for sure. We want to know why the intruder was here in the first place. You must understand that we need to do more investigation, ask all reasonable questions, and get all necessary answers that we are satisfied with. The answers may not always come from you or your husband, but many will. It will take us some time."

"How much time?"

"We don't know. We'll know better in a day or two I expect."

"You mean we might have to stay a day or two?" Her voice elevated again, upset. "This is not our problem."

Grant now felt his own blood rising. "Mrs. Carter, we need your cooperation. You can't just bolt out of here and leave the country. Two men were killed in your bedroom today, neither of whom was your husband. Your husband killed one of them. We have questions."

Candace looked at him a few moments, his words in her head, 'two men in your bedroom, neither of whom was your husband', then lowered her eyes, a look of sudden resignation.

"Dennis was visiting," Grant asked.

She breathed deeply. "Yes."

"Chester said he didn't know that Dennis was going to visit when he went for his walk just minutes before."

"That's right."

"Why was Chester out for a walk?"

"He took a walk every day, when Amara's napping. For his back."

"I see. Like a routine."

She nodded. "I asked him to make his walk today go by the general store to pick up some potato chips. But he forgot his wallet and came back. That's how he was here when…" her voice suspended.

He waited a moment. "Did you invite Dennis over, or did he drop by?"

"I invited him."

"When?"

"A couple of minutes after Chester left."

"So Chester wouldn't be here."

"Yes. And I understand that doesn't look good. But it was all innocent. Chester doesn't...didn't...really like him. I just like to talk to interesting people. That was all. Dennis is...was a dentist. And as far as changing my clothes, I was putting on more decent clothes for the visit. Dennis got here faster than I thought and he was using the washroom while I changed. The killer must have thought I was here alone or he wouldn't have come in. Surely."

She looked at Grant. "Don't you see I feel guilty? Dennis is dead. Don't you see? He wouldn't be if I hadn't invited him here."

Then it struck her, and she remembered again. Maybe it wasn't her fault. In all the distress and the feelings of accusation, she had simply forgotten it. But it seemed so impossible to her that Dennis could know the killer. "I forgot something before," she said.

"What did you forget?"

"After the killer hit me and I was out of it, when I came to, he was on the other side of the bed, and he said 'bastard', to himself like. Then when he heard Dennis coming, he leaped around the bed and jumped behind the door and when Dennis came in..."

"Yes, you told me..."

"No, I forgot that he *spoke* to Dennis, said something like, 'fuck, you screwed with the money', and then he shot him."

Grant was taken aback, silent for several moments. "Are you quite sure?"

"Yes."

"Anything else? Any other words at all?"

"It was all so shocking. I don't think so."

Grant mulled a moment. "You said a minute ago that the killer obviously thought you were alone. I would have thought that, too. But perhaps that's not so. Perhaps the killer came here *because* Dennis was in here."

"Why would he do that? Dennis was a dentist. Who would want to kill a dentist?"

Grant sat back and his hand ran over his mouth several times. Even with the oddities - the remarkable timing of Chester's return (but he had seen unbelievable coincidences before) and the possible tryst thing between Dennis and Candace that could supply motive - he had been thinking that this would still all resolve as an open and shut case, most particularly given the presence of the silk-tie. The silk-tie serial killer solved. Finally.

But now, with the killer accusing Dennis of screwing with the money, well, how did that fit in with the silk-tie being in the intruder's pocket? Was he working with Dennis all this time? But doing what? None of the three women that had been killed had been robbed or extorted. Money was not a factor in any of those deaths. And none of the women was connected with Dennis the dentist in any way as far as the police knew.

A yawning gap in things now. Grant saw the lid of an open and shut case fly wide open again.

*

When Grant stepped out of the cottage, Officer Thomas was just returning from Dennis's cottage.

"Dennis's back door was open," Thomas said to Grant, excited. "And wait 'til you hear this. He's some dentist. His closet's a small armory: a Sig Sauer assault rifle, two fully clipped handguns, hundreds of rounds. There's about $50,000 in American $50 bills in drawers in a desk. And there's a big vault in the basement. A vault…at a cottage!"

Grant looked perplexed. "Candace just told me that the killer, just before he shot Dennis, said to Dennis something about 'screwing with the money.'"

Officer Gill walked up to them, coming from his search for a possible suspicious boat at the shoreline to the north. He had heard the comments from Grant and Thomas, and like them, registered the new complexion of the case.

Thomas held up a wallet. "His name's Dennis Kreig."

Grant said, "We'll print him and run our CPIC checks, but I'm guessing now it's the FBI who'll have something on him."

Officer Gill was anxious to speak. "I think I found what we're looking for. An aluminum fishing boat tied loosely to a tree two cottages over, looking all a bit temporary. No one was at the cottage. I found binoculars in a case on the seat of the boat, and under the seat a set of keys. But they're not for the boat; it's a simple outboard. They're for a rental car."

He held the keys up, dangling from a leather I.D. rental tag. The large print read 'SUPERIOR AUTO RENTALS'. Gill said, "The car's license number's right there. And the fine print says the rental agency's in, get this…Detroit!"

Grant's face showed surprise. It had always been believed that the serial killer was local to the area because it seemed he had an intimate knowledge of the lakes and would have needed to be here over time to have opportunity to scout suitable victims and observe their routines.

"The killer...from Detroit? Or somewhere in the States?" Grant considered aloud, more puzzled. "Chester, Candace, Dennis. Everybody here's from the States. What the hell gives?"

Officer Gill said, "The serial killer, if that's the dead guy in there, could reasonably be from the States. Working far from home's a lot safer. Nobody knows you."

Officer Thomas nodded at that possibility.

Grant only said, "Maybe," before pausing for a long moment. "Like with Dennis's prints, the killer's prints aren't likely to do us much good on CPIC. We'll run them anyway, but send them to the FBI too. Those car keys being in the boat suggests the killer wasn't staying somewhere on this lake, or Round Lake. He trailered here, put the boat in at a public launch and parked the vehicle and trailer."

The officers nodded. "An easy find," Gill said. "No more than four or five public parking and launch points on these two lakes. The vehicle plates would be Michigan."

"The boat and trailer have to be a rental, too. That'll tell us where he got it," Grant said. "Let's hope there's a wallet with ID in the vehicle. In any case, the rental company will have a record of who rented it. I'm very curious about this guy, whoever he is."

Although Grant said nothing more about it, he conjectured the killer was not their serial killer. It didn't sit right that their killer would be from the States. And there were the words the killer, also apparently an American, said to Dennis indicating some other connection. And there was another thing in his mind - the killer had hit Candace with his hand full in the face causing severe redness, like a clumsy strike, leaving a rough redness on her cheek. None of the three women victims of the serial killer had suffered any discernible strike. The serial killer was a consummate pro. This killer was not.

But the silk-tie? That was definitely puzzling.

So if it wasn't a random killing by the serial killer, what the hell was it?

And something else pressed his thoughts - the return of Chester to the cottage at just the precise right moment. And Candace's peculiar behavior with Dennis.

Were Chester and Candace actually the innocents they presented?

*

The place was quickly shaping into a full crime scene, yellow tape being stretched in every part of the property, a news' truck at the road, a camera man shooting footage, a reporter talking into a mike.

Nothing on the property was permitted to be moved, including Chester and Candace. So they and Amara were back in a huddle in chairs on the deck, Amara still blurry, Candace in quiet despair, and Chester more than a little worried.

When he had conceived his master plan, he had envisioned great hoopla would be happening by this point, the presence of the silk-tie creating waves of exuberance in the police at the solving of the serial silk-tie killer. There would be hand-pumping congratulations to Chester, a regular aw-shucks guy from Ohio who was just vacationing in beautiful Ontario cottage country with his little family when they were attacked, Chester coming to the rescue, taking out the brutal, notorious serial killer in amazing heroic fashion.

But there was no hoopla. The police showed nothing approaching even gladness. Nada. Nobody congratulated him for anything, not taking out a killer, not saving his wife. And nobody was mentioning the silk-tie.

He understood that Roly saying words to Dennis threw a spinning wrench into the tidy master plan. But it might also carry some deflecting suspicion away from him. On the other hand, Dennis was in the cottage with Candace, which looked like a tryst, supported by a scantily clad Candace. This sure raised eyebrows and questions and supplied a motive for Chester maybe wanting her gone, that is, if the police began to suspect Chester.

If only Dennis hadn't been there throwing things out of orbit. It was like playing a card game with regular guys and a surprise fancy pants cardsharp suddenly joins the game.

The best laid plans…so much for those.

*

Detective Grant came over to Chester and Candace on the deck. "A lot of elements to investigate."

"What elements?" Chester said, not really wanting to be that enlightened.

"Can't say yet. We're making enquiries. Need to learn more about the killer and Dennis. And because Dennis is from the States, things may move a little slower."

"But Detective," Chester said, showing exasperation, "we've told you what happened. An intruder stalked in…"

"Mr. Carter, I know that. But until we have answers, I have to insist that you both be available for more questioning."

"But we just want to go home," Candace said.

"Isn't it an open and shut case here?" Chester said.

"We hope it is, but we don't know yet. We know it's difficult for you to have to stay. But we know you also appreciate that this was a major event here. We need you to help us know what happened. But you can't stay here, of course. This place will be swarming with forensics soon."

Chester looked around. "Well where do we go?"

"I'm making arrangements to book you into a local motel for tonight, at our expense, of course."

It seemed very much like a done deal, and Chester knew things would look a lot better if he showed cooperation. He looked at Candace. "They need our help. It's the right thing to do. And we do the right thing."

Candace looked drained, bewildered, and lacked the energy to respond.

*

The police woman at the cottage informed Chester and Candace that they could remove only what they needed for one night and the next day. "Everything else," she said, "must stay here undisturbed as part of our investigation."

They were not even allowed into their bedroom but could only instruct the police woman on the essential clothing items. Then she followed them around the cottage as close as a shadow as they selected a few more things and quickly packed.

Candace just wanted to get the hell away from the place.

CHAPTER 31

Officer Gill turned his police cruiser into the gravel parking area. This was the third public boat- launch on Ring Lake that he had now visited, checking for the killer's rented car or truck. It would have a trailer attached, although most vehicles at the launches had trailers.

He drove slowly along the row of parked vehicles. He hit the brakes when he saw the Michigan plates.

He got out and tested the key that he had found in the boat. The car door opened. He looked for a moment inside, then got in and carefully opened the glove compartment. There was a wallet. In the wallet was a Michigan driver's license in the name of Ben Davey. And there was a passport. Ben Davey.

On the boat trailer was a marina sticker with an address in Oak River, more than a hundred miles away, and the phone number.

Gill radioed all of the information to the station. An officer would soon attend the marina to determine when the killer rented the boat and trailer, and for how long.

With the wallet and passport in plastic bags, Gill drove back to the crime scene where he found Detective Grant with the forensics' man, Officer Spence, who was completing photography and fingerprints on both the killer and Dennis. They would be run through Canadian CPIC but also submitted to the FBI with a request for ID assistance.

Gill showed Grant the plastic bags. "I found the car at Gordon's Point launch. American passport. Michigan driver's license."

"Good show. We'll get it to the FBI. I'll have the station put in a request to Canadian Border Security at both Windsor and Sarnia. It's likely he crossed over at one of those two. I'd like to know how long he's been in Canada."

*

It took only ninety minutes after Chester's and Candace's check-in to the motel for the news' trucks and journalists from Toronto and area to arrive in the motel's parking lot like locusts sweeping into a lush green field. Shoulder cameras and microphones popped up and clustered thick. Coiffed hair was two rows deep.

Chester ventured out of the motel to go to the car to get a cuddly thing for Amara.

The locusts surged toward Chester. "Mr. Carter, Mr. Carter, Mr. Carter."

Chester felt like the President of the United States on the front lawn of the White House. But he retrieved the cuddly thing from the car and held it in his arms before sheepishly facing the press scrum.

"Mr. Carter, Mr. Carter," one tough woman journalist plunged to the front, jabbing a mike toward him, "we have information that you killed the serial killer today."

"Nobody mentioned anything to me about a serial killer," Chester said, playing surprise well.

"But you did kill someone?" She shoved the mike closer.

"I suppose I must be careful about what I say about that."

"No, it's okay. We already know that you did. Just tell us how it happened. How you rescued your family."

Now this is more like it, Chester thought. "Well I was just walking back to the cottage. I was in the laneway when I heard two gun shots come from inside the cottage. I ran in, grabbed my gun from the shelf, saw a man in a balaclava standing over my wife. He turned to me with a gun. I shot him twice. Had to. No choice. Then he still tried to shoot me, and I had to shoot him again." Gee, Chester thought, I guess I just did tell her I killed someone.

"Yes, yes," the woman journalist exclaimed. "Now…did you see he had a silk-tie?"

"A silk-tie? No. Why would he have a silk-tie? He wasn't dressed that well."

Laughter swept through the body of reporters and technical people, microphones and cameras bobbing. This was sure going to go viral – shy, innocent family man from Ohio, the hero of Ontario cottage country.

"It's because he's the silk-tie killer!" the woman said. "He's been terrorizing cottage country for three years."

"Silk-tie killer? Terrorizing?" Chester half turned in big surprise like he couldn't comprehend such overwhelming information. His eye caught Candace who was now standing outside the motel's front door, listening.

"Mr. Carter, didn't the police tell you? About the silk-tie killer?"

"No."

"Killed three women. One every year in the last three years."

"Well…"

"You're a hero, Mr. Carter. You not only saved your family, but ridded the entire community of a brutal killer."

"It was just a reaction, really. What anyone would do. I was just damn lucky to be there at the right time. And I'm truly grateful."

"We understand there was another man, a neighbor, in the cottage at the time, and that he was killed by the killer."

Chester noticed Candace turn and walk back through the motel door. He looked at the journalist woman crowding him and he began to back away. "Thank you," he said, "but I've got to get back to my family." He moved toward the motel door. "We would just really appreciate some quiet time now, if we could."

In the motel room Candace was silently crying, a tissue at her face. Amara was watching a cartoon on television. Chester sat beside Candace, taking her hand.

"He killed three women already, Chester. He was going to strangle me, with a tie."

"It's all okay now." He hugged her.

"If you hadn't saved me…"

"It's all okay, Candace."

But now she looked pensive, not looking at Chester, just at the wall. "But he didn't pull out any tie. If that's why he was there, you'd think…I mean …that's not what he seemed to be up to. He knocked me out kind of. Why not strangle me then? Instead, he's off doing something on the other side of the bed… before he even heard Dennis…"

"Who knows the mind of a crazed killer, Candace?" Chester tried.

It was like she didn't even hear him, still thinking it through. "And then he said that stuff to Dennis. What's that got to do with strangling me?"

"Maybe in that moment you didn't hear that stuff right, Candace. That would be understandable. Anyone in that kind of moment could make a mistake hearing exact words...in that kind of moment."

"No, I heard it right. I can still hear him."

*

That evening, information from U.S. authorities on Chester and Candace came in by fax to Detective Grant's office. Chester's record was squeaky clean. Candace's was, too, except for one juvenile offence - a shoplifting as a teenager, a summer dress she tried to hide in a plastic grocery bag. Just as I suspected, thought Grant, not exactly Bonnie and Clyde.

During the night the fax machine hummed much more, carrying from the FBI a volume of information about the balaclava killer and Dennis.

At 8:00 the next morning, Grant walked into the police conference room carrying copious sheets of fax print-out. His smile said he knew something. Officer Thomas, Officer Gill, the forensics man, Officer Spence, and a young rookie, known as 'cheerful Sid', had just arrived, seating themselves.

Everyone's eyes were now on Grant. "Our balaclava killer's not our silk-tie killer," he said. "Not one and the same. Definitively."

There was silence, glances exchanged all around. "And his driver's license and passport – both false. He's not a Ben Davey."

Grant appeared to enjoy his role, playing it out slowly, everybody watching him, hanging on his every word. "And more," he said, "Dennis isn't Dennis. And he isn't even a dentist."

Much more surprise. This one was definitely one for the books.

"Okay, let's start with our balaclava killer," he said. "The prints belong to a George Long. Age 52, living in Detroit. The photo we sent matches with Long, too. He has a serious sheet. A rape/murder when he was twenty. Did fourteen years. He was out three years when he was then convicted of a restricted weapon's offence, three sexual assaults, and an aggravated assault on one of the women. Did another eleven years. Got out on parole four years ago when he was forty-eight. He got a part-time warehouse job. There were no parole reporting problems, all seemed good, so his reporting was reduced to twice a month a year ago. He just booked off work for two week's holidays starting last week. Told his parole officer he wanted to go camping, get into nature, become 'eco aware.'"

"So what says he's not our serial killer?" Officer Thomas asked.

"Because on July 14, three years ago, George Long was sitting in his parole officer's office in Detroit at noon. He was reporting twice a week at that time, and one of those days was July 14."

They looked at Grant, trying to piece it. Moments passed.

"Now I remember," Officer Thomas said. "That's the day the first silk-tie killing occurred, Cynthia Hammond, at that little cove over on Craig Lake. The autopsy report that evening stated she was killed that morning."

"Right," Grant replied, "and we can safely assume Long didn't have a jet. The FBI checked with the car rental agency in Detroit who says that the car Long was using was rented last Friday, July 5th, by a James Marlin who turns out to be a small time fence in

Detroit. FBI questioned him last night. He said he rented it for a guy he only knew as Ben Davey, who said he needed a car for a week for a holiday and it had to have a hitch for a light tow."

"Anything back from Border Security, Sir?" Officer Gill asked.

"Yes. George Long, as Ben Davey, crossed at Windsor last Friday, July 5. Don't know where he spent Friday night, but on Saturday he booked into a motel in Oak River. At a marina there on Sunday, he took a seven day rental on the boat and trailer."

"Seems odd," Thomas said, "that a hit man, if it was a pre-arranged hit, would rent a boat for seven days. Yesterday, the day of the attack, was the fifth day."

"I agree. And during those days he booked into three different cheap motels ranging from 40 miles away to 110 miles away, the last two nights being 40 miles away. Odd if a prearranged hit."

"More like cruising the area for random possibilities," Gill said. "More like a serial killer kind of behavior. It's just possible that he had heard of the silk-tie killings and was playing copycat, scouting lakes far from home, another country even. Do a rape, then kill her with a silk-tie to deflect suspicion. Scouting for some victim. Checking women out with those binoculars I found."

"Yes," said the forensics man, Officer Spence. "Candace on the dock. She looks pretty nice. He watches the place. Was watching when he saw Chester leave. I mean, the last two days beforehand, this killer stayed at accommodation nearby…"

"But still," said Grant, "all the way to Canada, and need a boat…."

"But if not that, then why was he here?" said Thomas. "Somebody paying him to do something? Or was he getting even for something, given his words to Dennis before he shot him. But then his sheet doesn't add up like a sheet for a hit man. More like a rapist. On the other hand, maybe he just hadn't been caught before as a killer, and maybe needed the work and put out the word..."

It was all very puzzling.

"And the guy we thought was Dennis the dentist," Officer Spence said. "So...he wasn't one?"

Grant's eyes lighted. "That one's really exciting. The FBI sends us a very big 'thank you.'"

*

Grant was on the phone with Toronto, HQ.

The man he was talking to was Detective Zinski, known by everyone as 'the Nutcracker'.

"I've got something strange brewing here," Grant said. "Something much more than I first thought, but I don't know what it is. Let's just say it's a very hard nut."

Grant listened for a moment to Zinski, then said, "Yes, I know you like those. So anyway, a guy from Detroit wearing a balaclava and carrying a silk-tie in his pocket sneaks into a cottage being rented by a young American couple. The husband's out for a walk at the time. Detroit hits the wife, kind of knocking her out, then shoots and kills a neighbor guy, also American, who was visiting the wife although they hardly knew each other. The husband, who's now near the cottage by amazing coincidence.....Pardon? Yeah, I know you don't like amazing coincidences. Anyway, the husband hears the gunshots, grabs a loaded handgun that he happened to have along on his holiday, and plugs Detroit dead. So at first, with the silk-tie and a young woman and a cottage, all the hallmarks, you know, I thought it was a slam dunk – our silk-tie killer. But there were some real oddities, inconsistencies, things that didn't add up. And now this morning I've learned our bala-clava killer is *definitively* not our silk-tie killer.....Pardon? Yes, intriguing, your thing exactly. And more, the neighbor who was killed wasn't at all what he appeared. A big story there, but more than I can explain on the phone. This thing is fast rising above my pay grade. So we need you here. Something isn't sit-ting right about this young American couple. I've been mostly Mr. Sympathetic with them to this point. But what's needed now is someone to really put the old boots to them.....Pardon? That's right, steel-toed and sharp."

CHAPTER 32

At 1 p.m. sharp, Detective Zinski arrived from HQ in Toronto to meet with Detective Constable Grant at the police station and take over the investigation.

"How was your drive to cottage country?" Grant said smiling and offering his hand.

"Almost agreeable," Zinski said, unsmiling. Grant didn't know whether he was being funny or not, but he figured he wasn't. Grant had never met him, had only spoken to him by phone on another file.

Grant and Zinski could hardly be more opposite. Grant was genial, like there was good in the world, with gentle blue eyes and working his way to portly. Zinski was surly, like there was no good in the world, with glaring black eyes, his body spare, and a well-known reputation as a man arrogant and haughty.

Grant took him first to the morgue to see the dead bala-clava killer, George Long, and the dead 'Dennis', Grant still calling him that just to keep things clear. Then they went to the yellow-taped cottage crime scene and walked through it all, Grant twice playing back his audio recording of the interviews with Chester and Candace for Zinski as they did. "I'll want a copy of that today," Zinski said.

Zinski then walked the whole of the cottage lot, stopping every so often to make careful inspection, his eyes flashing around like black lasers.

He made a show of going back into the master bedroom, so Grant followed him. "I am vigorously of the view that the killer didn't come to this cottage to kill Dennis," Zinski said. "It doesn't fit."

He scrutinized the room and the hall. "If he were here for that purpose, then he entered *this* cottage only because he knew Dennis was already here. And yet all his actions run contrary to that. This killer was unaware that Dennis was in the cottage, didn't even know who Dennis was, I suspect, and accordingly was here for some other purpose."

There was a triumphant flourish in the way he said 'for some other purpose'.

"But," Grant said, "what about the words Candace says she heard the killer say to Dennis, about 'screwing with the money'?"

"I'm developing a theory. But first I need a few things. I want to speak to your forensics' man and get prints of the shoes Chester wore that day. I want the property and Chester's car thoroughly searched for possible cash. I want to access and review Chester's home and cell phone calls for the last three months. I also want his bank records - proof of loans or mortgages or big credit card cash advances, any unusual activity, in the past year."

"It will take time to get the required authorizations through the FBI and U.S. agencies to produce those," Grant said.

"Not if Chester cooperates. If he doesn't, I'll squeeze him like a peach in a vice. He'll know we're onto him, and then I'll slowly rip out his entrails."

"I understand."

"We need to keep him and Candace around for several more days. We can't charge either of them yet, not until I grind them down, break them, maybe get a confession. Can't let them leave the country. We don't want to have to go through extradition nonsense to get them back here. But I certainly don't want them to clam up. Get them another place to stay around here, something comfortable, another cottage, say. Make it easy for them. But I need to keep them here until I nail this."

"Chester's something of a hero with the media at the moment."

"Good. Maybe you can feed his ego to get cooperation. But we don't tell him or the press that the guy he killed was *not* the silk-tie killer. I want to keep Chester and Candace in the dark. Until I tell them."

Zinski looked at Grant. "And just so there is no ambiguity between us, I assume you know as well as I do that the best conclusion to be drawn is that Chester set up the hit on his wife. But things went sideways and he panicked."

*

Amara was present in the motel room watching television, so Candace watched her language. "What do you friggin' mean we have to stay for several more days?" Candace said to Grant, upset, and clearly un-slept. "We want to go home! We can't stay in this box. And we're getting hounded, the media swarming us all the time."

"Everyone wants a piece of me," Chester said, huffy. "I'm told I killed some silk-tie serial killer, which I'm happy for, sure. But we just want to go home now."

Grant and Zinski had agreed that Grant should be the one delivering the news because he was genial. Zinski would stay entirely out of the picture until Chester and Candace had been suitably relocated and were made happier.

"This is crazy, asking us to stay any longer," Candace said. "What for? It's like we did something wrong."

"Well no, Candace, nobody is saying that," Grant said, projecting calm, adding warmth in his smile. "But we're waiting on forensics and other information. We just need to get to the bottom of things and we know we will have more questions for both of you."

"But we already told you what happened," Candace said. "And you recorded it all, so it's not like you forgot."

"We appreciate how difficult this is, but we need your help. I don't want to play tough here," Grant said, "but you don't live in this country and there is a complexion to this case..."

"What kind of complexion?" Candace interrupted.

"A troubling kind. Things aren't that clean."

"Like what?" Candace said.

"Well, a lot happened. Two men were killed in your bedroom, neither of whom was your husband."

"Do you have to keep saying that?"

"It does raise questions. I don't want to suggest that either of you could or would be charged..."

"For what?" Chester blurted.

"Well, Mr. Carter, you did admit shooting a man three times. And he's dead. And you used a gun illegally brought into Canada."

"Well, come on..."

"In Canada we have tighter rules on that sort of thing. We don't want to have to formally hold you. We really just want your cooperation, both of you, in answering more questions as more evidence surfaces over the next days. We just need time to tie up loose ends."

It kept pressing on Chester's mind that cooperation was the best way to avoid suspicion, given that for the police the complexion of the case was 'troubling'. What did they know but weren't saying? What did they suspect but weren't saying? It was a troubling complexion for Chester that not once, even now, had Grant acknowledged the damn silk-tie. If they were sniffing things the wrong way, or, really, the right way, he could get fried in the end. They would just come for him in Ohio and drag him back here anyway. So better to stay here and throw them off the scent, look innocent, nip things in the bud.

He looked at Candace and shrugged. "Look, they need our help. It's the right thing to do. And we do the right thing."

"You said that yesterday, too," Candace said. "What's with you two repeating yourselves? You sound like parrots."

*

They were provided a beautiful cottage, free of charge, on Great Driftwood Lake, away from neighbors, and away from the press who didn't know to where they had been spirited. 'They need privacy,' the police informed the media.

Before they made the relocate, Chester suggested to Candace that with all that was going on, it would be better if Amara stayed with the Findlays, their friends in Columbus whose daughter was a friend of Amara. Candace at first objected, but then reconsidered her own distress. Candace was not sleeping and had little hope of things improving around here. She and Chester were going to be at the police's beck and call. It was hardly a time and a place for their little girl to be here, exposed to all this.

"You'll be able to pet their furry golden retriever as much as you want," Chester told Amara, which went down well. And Amara admitted that, anyway, she was also bored of just watching television now, adding that her mom and dad weren't being that much fun anymore.

The Findlays didn't hesitate to come, whisking Amara to a happier place.

And Detective Grant, with a big smile, told Chester and Candace to really enjoy the new cottage.

As if.

CHAPTER 33

The next morning, Officer Gill, Officer Thomas, and forensics' man, Officer Spence, arrived at the new cottage. It had no laneway and no actual car access to the road. Instead, the road ran high and well behind the cottages through heavily treed and granite landscape. About every ten or fifteen cottages along the road, there was a small gravel parking lot. The cottagers parked their cars there and walked, some for two minutes, some for five or ten minutes, along the road and down over flat rock and pathways to their respective cottages. The officers had parked their two cruisers at the nearest lot, a six minute walk away.

When the three officers knocked at the cottage door, Chester answered.

"Beautiful morning," Officer Thomas said.

"Yes," Chester said, less enthusiastic about the weather than Thomas.

"So," Thomas said, "I'm here to take Mrs. Carter over for some follow-up questioning."

"Over where?" Chester asked.

"To the other cottage."

"There?" That was going to be an all-over-again big stress for her. "Well, how about at least I take her?"

"We need you here for awhile. And the Detective wants to see Mrs. Carter alone."

Chester naturally assumed it was Detective Grant he was talking about.

With some reluctance, Candace was soon ready to go with Thomas.

"Beautiful morning," Thomas said to her.

"More to some than others," Candace said, not looking at him as she walked out the cottage door. "Lead the way."

Officer Thomas and she left the cottage, Chester watching them through the window a few moments, concerned for how Candace was feeling.

Forensics' Officer Spence said to Chester, "Now what we need from you, Sir, is to take shoeprints of your shoes so we can distinguish your prints from the shoeprints of the other two guys – the killer and Dennis. It's standard procedure, Mr. Carter."

"Okay, no problem. But why?" Chester showed no upset, just asking. "You know their shoe prints, if you kept their shoes. So, you eliminate them and you know mine."

"Yes, but maybe there's prints of other people on the property, or in the area. Need to keep them all straight."

"Oh, okay, I see. Sure."

As Chester took off the thick-soled running shoes, Spence looked at Officer Gill who nodded. That was the sign of confirmation that the shoes looked to be the same as those Chester had been wearing on the big day. A good officer notes that kind of thing. Unless, of course, Chester had changed them before Gill and Thomas had arrived on that day.

"How many pairs of shoes did you bring on your vacation?" Spence asked.

"Just these and some rubber boots. I used the boots just when I was playing in the water with Amara to get things from the muck."

Gill nodded to Spence. Chester was cooperating, things under control. "I'll let you two get to know each other better," Gill said. "I'll wait down at the dock."

Spence took one of Chester's shoes, the left shoe. "Okay, I'll show you how we take a print with my handy dandy mobile kit."

Spence was a friendly sort and Chester found himself warming to him.

From a small bag, Spence took several items, showing and naming each item like a magician as he did. "Two sheets of black carbon paper. One container of fingerprint powder. One stiff cleaning brush. One soft fingerprint brush."

"I like learning this kind of thing," Chester said. "Technical know-how." He watched Spence with honest anticipation.

Spence looked around the large, pine-walled living room, then toward the kitchen. "Come with me," he said and took his kit into the kitchen.

Spence opened two of the kitchen drawers, one below the other. "I stabilize the shoe, tread side up, by putting it in there." He placed the shoe upside-down and backwards part way in the bottom drawer, then drew the upper drawer over it until it grabbed tight onto the shoe. "The drawers act like a vice to hold the shoe in place."

Chester showed delight. Spence ran a stiff bristle over the tread, back and forth, even whistling a moment as he did. When it was clean, he applied the light-colored fingerprint powder, saying "carefully" twice as he did.

"Now I place the sheet of carbon paper over the tread and rub the back of the paper using bare hands. It's like giving my wife a nice back massage, using bare hands to feel the tread beneath, somewhat more knobby than my wife's back."

"Except along her vertebrae maybe," Chester said.

"Ah, you give the wife massages, too," Spence said with a laugh. He continued to rub with smooth precision. "Not as easy as it looks, actually. You still have to know what to look for, and have the right 'touch', which my wife says I have."

"She just wants more massages," Chester chuckled.

Spence laughed. "Ya, I know."

After a full minute, he lifted the carbon sheet off, holding it up for Chester to see. "Voila! A perfect impression of the treads. Even picks up that distinct wear pattern there, and, of course, the entire width and length."

Spence had lifted a set of shoe prints from a very particular piece of ground the night before, as directed by Detective Zinski. Spence's eye was good, as was his memory. He now knew from the distinctive pattern on Chester's left shoe that the left shoe prints from the ground were Chester's. No need to look at those rubber boots.

Smiling cheerfully, Chester said, "I like the simplicity of it, and that kitchen drawer technique."

"Thank you, Mr. Carter. Now let's do that other shoe."

*

There was yellow tape stretched everywhere, but the crime scene cottage was quiet, no police car parked, no activity, not a soul in sight when Officer Thomas dropped Candace off without ceremony, without word. When she got out of the car, expecting him to get out, too, he just drove off, abandoning her.

She stood in the lane, the forbidding strangeness of the place descending on her now in the eerie quiet.

Then she saw a tall lean man with a hard face and black eyes that stared, watching her from the front deck. He made no move, no attempt at civil acknowledgment. He looked like she imagined Jack-the-Ripper probably looked, but at least this guy wasn't wearing a cape.

"Where is Detective Grant?" she called.

He waited several moments, his eyes watching her. Then he came forward and she saw his lips were very thin, and that his eyes didn't blink.

"Detective Grant asked me to take over this investigation, Mrs. Carter. I'm Detective Zinski, from Toronto HQ."

He attempted a smile as he continued to observe her. "Let's go inside and have a seat," he said.

They took seats opposite each other in the living room.

"I do understand you've been through a very traumatic experience," he said, his eyes without warmth.

For somebody who wanted to express sympathy, Candace thought, he had a cold way of showing it. She nodded. "Yes," she said quietly.

His black eyes concentrated on her. "Tell me, did your husband at any time leave the cottage during the days you were here, other than on his walks?"

She saw he wasn't into any getting-to-know-you-warm-up chat. "No, I…oh, yes, once he went into town to grab some things – groceries we were short on."

"When was that?"

"That would have been…Tuesday."

"Was Tuesday the day Dennis was away in Toronto, or at least said he would be?"

She couldn't think straight for a moment, Zinski's eyes like two chisels chipping at her concentration. The question threw her, too. What possible connection was he trying to make? Or maybe he was just trying to throw her off, mix her up, put her off balance. "Yes, it was."

"Do you and Chester have many assets, savings, investments?"

"A house with a mortgage, two cars, no savings to speak of. No investments."

"Do you both deal with just one bank?"

"Yes, always. Chase Bank."

"Did you know your husband had brought his gun on this holiday vacation?"

"No."

"Is that strange to you?"

"I don't know. I know he always has it traveling with work."

"This isn't work."

"I know."

"So isn't that strange?"

"Like I said, I don't know."

"Does he keep it loaded at home?"

"I don't know. I don't particularly like guns."

"And I surmise you like them even less now."

"A good surmise."

He nodded, almost a smile. "Have you and Chester ever rented a cottage before?"

"No. First time."

"When did you first meet Dennis?"

"On Monday."

"Had you ever seen him before?"

"No."

"Had you ever spoken to him before?"

"No."

"Did you know of him from something, anything, before?"

"No. Nothing."

Incredibly he wasn't blinking at all, his eyes always on her.

"You rented a cottage only four cottages from his."

It sounded like an accusation. "It's not like that was planned. And anyway, I'm not the one who rented the cottage. Chester did. So I don't know what you're getting at."

"You don't have to know what I'm getting at. Just answer the question."

"You didn't ask me a question. You just made an insinuation."

"Okay. So, you didn't know he had rented a cottage?"

"I didn't know he had rented a cottage."

"You didn't know where it was?"

"I didn't know where it was."

His way of becoming informed was just too damn slow, so she said, "I've never been to Canada before. He just surprised me."

She saw his eyes become keen. "When you say he *surprised* you, you do mean he had already rented the cottage, not merely surprised you with the idea of renting a cottage?"

"Right. Surprised as in done deal, cottage rented, money paid."

"Why do you think he did it that way, instead of discussing it with you first?"

Candace had wondered that, too. But she said, "He's done that before, once. Surprised me with a trip to St. Lucia."

His look registered momentary disappointment with her answer. She only wondered what any of it really had to do with what actually happened here.

"Did you tell anyone you were coming to Canada, to this particular location?"

"Just a couple of close friends, and the Findlays. Their daughter's a friend of our daughter, Amara."

"What about Chester?"

"He would have told people at work. They talk about vacations."

"Can you think of anyone back in Ohio, or anywhere, who would want you dead?"

She laughed. "No. I may not always be polite, but I don't upset people that much."

He seemed satisfied. Then he leaned forward. "I understand Dennis was from Ohio."

"Yes, that's partly why we became acquaintances."

"Partly."

"People coming from the same place kind of thing."

"I get that. It's the *other* part I want to know about."

She felt his bite. "Well, the other part is he's the only neighbor we've met here. There doesn't seem to be anyone else around here during the week. He was nice enough to take us out in his boat. Towed Amara behind his boat in an inner tube. Our little boat doesn't do that."

"And that's the other part?"

"That's the other part."

"And that's why you invited Dennis over here when Chester was going to be away, without Chester knowing Dennis was here, so you could negotiate another inner tube ride?" The sarcasm was rich.

Candace was ticked. "Of course not."

"Well what was it? Wasn't it to be alone with him?"

"As a matter of fact it was to be alone with him, and I already explained all that to Detective Grant's little microphone which I'm sure you listened to already. Do I really have to repeat myself?"

He ignored her comment, like that was a matter for later.

"You met Dennis Monday and had your boat ride. You say he was away Tuesday. Were you with him Wednesday, when Chester went for his walk?"

"No. I...we... invited him over for a marshmallow roast for Wednesday evening at dusk down at the beach. That was all."

"So he came here Wednesday evening?"

Candace nodded.

"Did he stay late?"

"No, maybe an hour after Amara went to bed. Maybe 10:30."

She saw Zinski wondering a moment. "You put Amara to bed?"

"Chester did."

"Were you in the cottage at the time?"

"No. Down at the beach."

"I see. Was it then that you invited Dennis over for the next afternoon for 1:00?"

"No. Nothing about getting together was talked about. I just...on the spur of the moment invited him just after Chester left for his walk."

"Why invite him when Chester was gone?"

So, I do have to repeat myself, she thought. "I think it bothers Chester sometimes when other men show interest in me."

"Or you show interest in them."

"That's fair."

"Why did you invite him over?"

"Just wanted to talk."

"Just talk. Not a tryst?"

"No."

"A meeting of lovers?"

"It's the same thing and I just said 'no'. Look, this Dennis stuff is irrelevant to what happened."

"I decide what's relevant."

"Well come on, how's it relevant? Some guy with a silk-tie in a balaclava comes into the cottage and shoots Dennis and he's going to shoot me and Chester shoots him. That's what's relevant. Not whether I had some tryst thing happening with Dennis, which I definitely did not."

"So, just to talk?"

"Yes, and not bother Chester with it. I know I flirt. That's…a weakness. But I just like to talk to interesting people. I thought a dentist would be different. I'm interested in people more than Chester. What makes people tick. Chester likes more what makes machinery tick. But he's not unsocial with people or anything. People like him."

"Is he possessive of you?"

"No, that's not it. He just doesn't understand me completely, all my needs. Who really can in another person? I'm sure you don't understand all your wife's needs."

His eyes changed just enough, disciplined though they were, for Candace to know she hit one home. But then the small victory turned, an infinitesimal smile creeping on his lips. He said, "So Chester doesn't really understand your needs?"

Damn, that could open a can of worms, she thought. "I mean I like to talk to people, okay, men, because I like to know what makes them tick. That's all I mean by that. There's no tryst."

"Are there problems in the marriage?"

"I suppose some."

"I mean serious problems."

"We have our difficulties. Sometimes they feel serious."

"Serious enough to separate?"

"I don't think so."

"You don't *think* so."

"Explain all that bling on '*think*'."

"Well, you don't *know* if it's enough to separate."

"Well, when you put it *that* way, I *do know*, and then the answer is *no*, difficulties not serious enough to separate because, as you may have observed in your not-miss-a-thing observations, we haven't separated."

"You have never told him you want to leave him."

"Never."

"Never?"

"Never." But she remembered a day, and it popped out. "I once packed a bag though."

"You did? But you didn't talk about separating?"

"We didn't talk about separating. I just packed a bag. Then later the same day I unpacked it."

"Chester saw you packing?"

"Yes."

"When was that?"

"About six months ago."

"Chester didn't think you were leaving by packing a bag?"

"Well, like I said, I unpacked it later that day."

"What did you tell him?"

"I told him I was… off balance."

"How's that?"

"Not great. I think you mean 'why's that.'"

"Okay."

"It's called dissociative disorder. I have a form of it. It happens once in a while. Psychologists told me it comes from being in five foster homes from age six. My mom died. Sometimes the past grips me. Something inside me makes me lose my bearings. I want to run away from things. It's not like it's logical or anything."

Zinski had a curious look in his eyes as he watched her, not something anyone would call sympathetic understanding. It made her feel small. And a little angry.

She said, "You probably came from a good home life, Detective. Probably knew love and security always. But take those away when you're little and... you don't ever get over it. And add to that some abuse, big hands touching you where they shouldn't by men who are supposed to be your foster fathers...well, that fear, those memories, they can pull you down real fast when you're not looking. And your mind... you go to a place, like you're leaving yourself behind, that's the dissociative disorder...that's what I mean by off balance."

"So, Chester could have fears you might leave him."

She remembered the prickly telephone conversation with Chester about her meeting the fireman at the swimming pool, having a very drawn out coffee with the fireman. She knew Chester was bothered. But surely...not that much. "He could have those thoughts sometimes. Maybe."

"The day you packed and unpacked the bag, was your... turmoil that day resolved?"

"Shoved back in the jar, yes. But looking back, I'm trying to be honest here, maybe Chester wasn't sure."

"He thought you might leave?"

"I don't know. He didn't say anything. You'll have to ask him." She looked fully at Zinski. "With all the crap that swirls around in my head some days, Chester's my only rock. Him and Amara. He would do anything for me. And as I sit here, today...I know I don't thank him enough."

Zinski looked at her, harder than usual, unimpressed with the little speech. He got up. "I would like you to come with me into the bedroom."

The bedroom again. Candace took a deep breath, reluctant. But she got to her feet, and they went in.

CHAPTER 34

"Why did Dennis come into the bedroom at all?" Zinski said to Candace.

"Well, he came down the hall looking for me because I wasn't in the living room where he last saw me."

"Did he call out, 'Candace, where are you?'"

"No."

"He was just going to waltz into your bedroom?"

"I...doubt it. I had already made it clear to him that there wasn't going to be any hanky panky."

"And why did you have to make that clear to him?"

"He...showed a little aggression in the living room."

"Sexual?"

"Touched me."

"In the first minutes of his arrival?"

"Yes."

"When you invited him over, you told him Chester wouldn't be here."

"Yes."

"I guess he thought that communicated something, felt it was appropriate to be sexual with you."

"I admit, I was stupid."

"And how did Dennis receive that instruction to just talk?"

"He received it... a little frustrated."

"But moments later you're wearing only a bra and panties in the bedroom."

"I explained all that."

"I heard that you said you were changing into something decent, *after* Dennis arrived. What were you prancing around in when he did arrive?"

"Listen..."

"There was a lot of male traffic in here, Mrs. Carter, and your conduct is very much at the center of the explanation of it."

"You've got things all wrong. And the thing about Dennis, I'd never done that before."

"You mean with Dennis?"

"I mean with anybody. Any man. But sometimes, sometimes I know I seemed like I might just trip off."

"A habit of acting certain ways as regards men, and maybe you hurt Chester over time and he became desperately afraid you would leave for another man, like a Dennis, and take your daughter."

She looked at him aghast, unbelieving. "Meaning what?"

"To what lengths would he possibly go, Mrs. Carter?"

"Do you actually believe...? Look, I wasn't leaving Chester to begin with, but if you think what happened is that Chester set up a hit against me, you're out of your mind. My God, if I ever believed that too, I'd not be sticking around in a marriage with him for one second more. But you're dead wrong. Chester would never hurt me. I know it in my bones."

Got to hand it to her, Zinski thought, a good performance. She could work a jury.

So he had to work her a little harder. Drop the first bomb. "Mrs. Carter, I know you are laboring under a misunderstanding, supplied by the media, that your balaclava killer was our silk-tie serial killer. Let me share a little piece of information. We know now he absolutely was not."

"He wasn't?"

"No. Your balaclava killer was in a parole office in Detroit during the morning of the first murder here three years ago. Detroit's six hours away. And balaclava man was from Detroit, an American, like you and your husband. And your husband does some work in the Detroit area, I understand. An American from Detroit, a hit man, coming to kill an American tourist in Canada; more than coincidence, wouldn't you say?"

"But, the silk-tie..." Candace was still processing. "Maybe he was a copycat. That could be it, right?"

"But you said he seemed to know Dennis. Something about screwing with the money."

"Well yes, of course, that's it. He was here for Dennis but brings a silk-tie to throw you off."

"So what's he doing in *your* cottage, do you think?"

"That's where Dennis was."

"And why would he want to kill a dentist, do you think?"

"Well I don't know. Maybe Dennis's ex-wife was behind it?"

Zinski couldn't arrest a smile. Candace understood lovers' quarrels.

"Candace, I'm going to be perfectly candid with you. Dennis wasn't a dentist."

"Not a dentist?"

"Not a dentist. Wouldn't know an incisor if it bit him."

Candace was dumbstruck.

"We've learned that Dennis, or at least the man you knew as Dennis, because that wasn't his real name…"

"It wasn't?"

Zinski shook his head 'no', "…it was Reginald Simpson, and he was wanted by the FBI. He was living here under that assumed name and identity to avoid arrest. The FBI had no idea of his whereabouts until now."

"My Gosh," Candace said.

"He worked for some powerful and very dangerous people who control a U.S. crime syndicate. He had two roles, it appears. One was as an enforcer."

"What's that?"

"If you're not doing what the organization wants you to do, he breaks your arm, or shoots you in the kneecap. And if you're still really bad…well…he does worse."

Candace's hand went to her mouth, "My Gosh…"

"Yes, not a nice man. His other role was to launder some of their dirty money, what they call an intermediary."

Candace reflected for moments. "Well, Detective, that's it! That would explain why the killer yelled at Dennis about screwing with the money before he shot him. Dennis maybe upset those dangerous people. So doesn't that wrap things up here? The killer was here to kill Dennis, and would then have killed me too, except that Chester forgot his wallet. And that would explain the silk-tie, to throw you off who the killer was…"

Zinski said nothing, letting her revel in her theory. She appeared to relax, although it was evident she was still thinking things through. "He didn't look like a Reginald. Was he divorced?"

"No. Never married."

"Did he live in Toledo?"

"Only born in Toledo. For the last two years he rented a condo in Toronto, but mostly lived here at the cottage, all to avoid U.S. authorities. The cottage is registered to a U.S. numbered company that's owned by an offshore company."

"What's an offshore company?"

"In this case a company registered in the Turks and Caicos. Shielded in secrecy. Can't trace who the hell owns it. But it'll be dirty money."

Zinski got up and began to pace the room slowly. "Let's walk through your little theory step by step, your theory that the killer was here to kill Dennis, Reginald..."

"Let's just call him Dennis."

He nodded. "If that were so, the killer was worse than an amateur, and that crime syndicate would not send an amateur. They would send a consummate pro to do one of their own. There are things we know about the killer that say he was an amateur, and his actions confirm that. Let me ask you, if you were a killer, and were here to kill Dennis, why wouldn't you just shoot him as he's walking to your cottage, or wait until he's walking to his own cottage, so as not to involve an innocent person, i.e., you?"

That did make sense, Candace thought. Why wait until Dennis was in her cottage where Dennis might hide, and ready a weapon, or jump out a window on the other side of the cottage and get away? But... "Well maybe the killer didn't know when he would come out and couldn't wait around and didn't care about an innocent person, i.e., me."

"No, Candace. The killer had been in the area five days already and had plenty of time. Time for a much better shot at killing Dennis without even being seen. If the killer was in your cottage for the purpose of killing Dennis, then he entered your cottage only because he knew Dennis was already in here. Correct?"

Candace nodded.

"But all his actions after that run contrary, strongly indicating he *didn't* know Dennis was here. You might argue he knew Dennis was in here but didn't know where he was, didn't know he was in the washroom, or perhaps he thought Dennis might be armed, because Dennis had a small armory at his house."

"My gosh."

"Okay, but what does the killer do? He enters your bedroom, sneaking up from behind, with you changing. At that point, do you think the killer's pretty sure that neither you nor Dennis knows the killer's in the house?"

"I would think that's correct."

"Then he hits you, stunning you, but you're shortly aware he's at the other side, the far side, of the bed. You hear him say 'bastard'. That's odd, isn't it, first, because if he knows Dennis is somewhere in the cottage but doesn't know where, and Dennis may be armed, he's hardly going to start talking out loud to himself."

She thought, yes, that would be odd. She nodded.

"And second, you've got to believe he didn't say 'bastard' because he was actually expecting to find Dennis hiding behind the bed and was disappointed. If he suspected that, he would hardly have bothered to deal with you first, hitting you like he did. I mean, he would just know Dennis wasn't behind the bed because if he were, you'd be there, too, not lounging about half naked."

She didn't accept the 'lounging', but accepted the point.

"Then you said, at that moment, you heard the toilet flush, and so did the killer. So now he knows where Dennis is. And the killer knows Dennis clearly doesn't know he's even here. Now Candace, if you were a killer, and Dennis was occupied in the john, and you think that Dennis might have a gun but didn't know you were here, would you hide behind the bedroom door, as you described, with the possibility that the knocked out woman behind you might come to consciousness and scream at any moment? Giving things away? Wouldn't that be stupid?"

"Ya, when you think of it like that."

"Wouldn't it make so much more sense to position yourself for a sure shot, either by throwing the washroom door open to catch Dennis in complete surprise, or just plug the unwary Dennis the moment he exits the washroom?"

"But maybe the killer *was* just stupid. I mean, gee, Dennis was a money launderer and the killer tells him he was screwing with the money. Why would he say that unless he was here for Dennis?"

"Because he thought Dennis was Chester. It was about payment for the hit."

Candace looked shocked. She was still for several moments, thinking.

"Tell me, when the killer spoke to Dennis about screwing with the money, did Dennis say anything back?"

She was still thinking. "No. I don't think so. Looked dumbfounded, shocked, like me."

"As I suspected. Had no idea what the killer was talking about."

It went through her mind that if Dennis was screwing with the money, which would explain why the killer was there, why wouldn't Dennis have shown more awareness, maybe tried to explain something about the money. But he truly looked like he didn't know what the killer was talking about. That's if she could read his reaction accurately in that moment in those circumstances. That was a very big if.

She was still pondering. "I can only say 'maybe' to that point."

Time for the second bomb. "On all the walks Chester took, did he ever come back earlier than expected?"

"No."

"Wouldn't you say that the timing of Chester's return that day was...miraculous?"

"It sure was for me. But there's a simple explanation. I asked him to buy some chips when he took the walk. But he forgot his wallet."

"Wasn't that convenient." It wasn't a question. It was a heavily sarcastic statement, full of suspicion.

"It sure was for me."

Zinski gave a very knowing look which Candace didn't like one bit because it made her feel like a child who doesn't know something that everybody else does. She wanted to kill his superior look dead on the spot. "Look, Detective, forgetting is something Chester can do. And regularly does. That wasn't miraculous. That was forgetfulness. Have you ever had to go back home after a few minutes because you forgot something, maybe that you didn't normally need? Was your return at that very moment miraculous?"

He had to hand it to her. He could well hear that question being put to a witness or jury by a clever defense lawyer, and that would produce big smiles all around. Who hasn't done that before? An everyday occurrence. Not a miracle. Not even a coincidence.

But, nevertheless, he could expunge that defense with a single stroke, take it off the table, even turn the table, because he had an ace.

He drew himself up and stood before her, more imposing. "What if I were to tell you that it wasn't that Chester remembered his wallet and just so happened to return at the very moment he did, but instead had been hiding in the bushes at the back of the property, waiting for the killer to arrive? With his gun loaded and very handy."

"But I saw him go down the road when he left the cottage. I looked out the window when he was leaving the property. He went down the road." But her nerves were firing and her face showed worry. She had wondered about that life-saving timing, but had buried that wonder under just plain gratefulness.

Zinski smiled, and his black eyes lit up like a match. "Yes, Candace. He went down the road, like anyone would do who wants to appear to be going somewhere else. But I have evidence he came back. And waited."

CHAPTER 35

Riding in the back seat of the police cruiser driven by Officer Thomas on the way back to the other cottage, Candace saw a police cruiser coming the other way. The two cruisers passed and she saw Chester was in the back seat.

"That's Chester! What's happening?" Her head whipped around to look out the rear window.

Thomas said, "Yes, Mrs. Carter. Now that your interview is completed, he's on his way for his."

"Well, nice to be kept informed!" She didn't say it politely.

*

"We know with certainty the killer here was not the silk-tie serial killer," Zinski said.

The statement floored Chester. "You do?" he said, trying to mask the sudden and terrible surprise. Roly as serial killer was the centerpiece of his plan, and it was a bit quick for that piece to vanish. He felt his nerves ramping up, and nerves and clear thinking don't mix.

"We do," Zinski said. "What do you think of that?"

"Well… good to know."

"Yes…*very* good. You show surprise."

"Well," he opened his hands and shrugged like it wasn't that big a surprise, "the television people said it was the serial killer, so…that's why."

They were seated in the living room of the cottage, yellow crime-scene tape across the sliding glass door to the deck. Chester looked out, trying to appear relaxed, as if this was just a casual visit and he was also enjoying the scenery. He saw two curious boats circling nearby on the lake.

"Mr. Carter, you kept a fully loaded handgun in the linen shelf?"

Switches direction fast, wants to throw me, Chester thought. "Yes."

"Not exactly a cap gun but a lethal Beretta. With your daughter in the cottage."

"Yes. But it was hidden. And high up."

"Your wife said she didn't know you had it along."

"Right. It was on the shelf because I didn't want to leave it in the car. Had to leave it in the cottage somewhere." Chester's voice was tighter than he hoped it would be.

"And not tell your wife?"

"She doesn't like guns."

"And loaded. Why loaded?"

Chester was again struck by how the police in Canada were so very sticky when it came to a loaded 9 mm handgun being around. He hadn't anticipated this attitude, thinking that was a minor matter in the scheme of things and to be quickly overlooked given the favorable outcome the gun had produced. But it set him on the defensive. "Habit," he said. "Keeping it loaded is kind of the point. But it has a safety."

"When you were packing for the trip here, why bring a loaded handgun?"

Now Chester thought it was sounding stupid to bring a loaded handgun so he would have to...distort the truth. "I didn't say I brought a loaded handgun. I brought an unloaded handgun. Loaded it here."

"Well you said it's 'habit, loaded is kind of the point'. I thought you meant the gun's always loaded."

"Thought wrong." Chester knew immediately he shouldn't have said it that way. Damn nerves. He saw Zinski's eyes now become like two jack hammers ready to break cement.

"When you drive your truck for work, is the gun loaded?"

"Yes. That's when I could get held up."

"So, when you're on the road in your truck, and you stay away overnight, do you unload it when you go into the motel?"

"No. You could get some crazy come after you even there, too."

"So, when you're working, it's always loaded?"

"Yes."

"But coming here, on a vacation, you weren't really concerned about getting held up, just driving your car across Ontario?"

"No. Just in the States." Chester knew a split second after he said it that he shouldn't have said that either. So here we go again.

"Did you take the I-75?"

"Yes."

"You loaded your Beretta to drive the I-75?"

He knew he had to say yes because where else would he be driving there with it loaded?

"Yes. It passes near Detroit."

"You felt a safety issue existed there?"

"Yes."

"So was it loaded when you crossed the border into Canada?"

"No. I had unloaded it by then."

"Then you reloaded when you got to the cottage?"

"Yes. Well, no actually. I loaded it a couple of hours south of here, near Toronto, because it was going to be already dark when we arrived here."

"All this loading and unloading, and your wife didn't even know you had brought it?"

"Right."

"Well where did you load it and unload it twice on your way coming here?"

"McDonald's. Two different ones."

"You were in two different McDonald's loading and unloading your Beretta?"

"No. Stayed in the parking lot. Candace got me big Macs. She didn't know I was loading or unloading. She doesn't really like guns, like I said."

"So you didn't tell her you had it along?"

"No."

"Maybe that's why she didn't know."

"Maybe."

"Why did you feel you needed a loaded Beretta when you arrived here?"

"Like I said, it was night time. Dark."

"So?"

"I don't know the area. I had to be sure it was safe. You know, wife and young daughter."

"Make sure the cottage was safe?"

"Sure."

"Would you have loaded it if you arrived in daylight?"

"Probably."

"Well what were you expecting here that made you load your Beretta before getting here and going into the cottage?"

"I don't know what's here. That's the point."

"Oh come on. This isn't the Wild West."

"Sure felt like it two days ago."

After a reflective pause, Zinski said, "When I asked you why it was loaded, on your shelf, you said 'habit.'"

"Yes, habit meaning if the gun's going to be useful for self-protection, it has to be loaded. So I left it loaded."

"So even though you were here for days and saw it was a safe place, you left it loaded."

"We're from the city. This is the country. And it's Canada. Wild animals around."

"Like what?"

"Wolves, bears."

"Who told you that?"

"Nobody."

"Have you seen any?"

"No. I just assumed so because it's Canada and wilderness."

"This isn't wilderness. Not at these prices."

"Well I've heard of bears getting into cottages even in the States. So I thought it could happen here."

"If a bear attacked, *your* gun wouldn't help you."

"Still better than nothing. Anyway, I always have the safety off."

"You mean safety on."

"Right."

"Useful not to get them confused."

Chester smiled. Had to agree there.

Zinski said, "Let's talk about your walks. You said you took a walk every day."

"Yes."

"Why?"

"I drive a lot of miles in a truck for work. My back stiffens a lot more than it used to."

"Have you had it looked at by a doctor? Any paper work?"

"No. It's just something I have to stay on top of."

"Where did you take those walks?"

"I either go south, a mile down the road to the waterfalls, rest a few minutes, then come back. Or I go north, along the road and then onto that trail that cuts through the woods and comes out near the golf course. Takes me about an hour either way."

"Would you agree that walking for an hour on a heavily forested cottage road, or through the woods for a mile, would be like walking in the country?"

"Yes."

"Did you have your gun with you?"

Chester saw too late where it was going. "No."

"Well why not, if you're walking in an area crawling with bears and wolves?"

Chester hesitated, and Zinski said, "What's more, why leave your wife and child unprotected back at the cottage during your walks in an area crawling with bears and wolves?"

"Well, after being here for a few days, I saw that it was pretty safe."

"But did you take the gun on the first walk or two?"

"No. I didn't need it always with me. It was a just-in-case sort of thing."

Zinski appeared suddenly changed, suddenly understanding. "I would understand you bringing the gun if you had heard of our serial killer and wanted to protect your family."

A clever question, Chester realized, offering him a palatable answer, a face-saving answer, better than anything he had said so far. It would be so easy to agree. Zinski just wanted him to say, 'Well yes, I had heard, and it was on my mind. I'm sorry I didn't mention that.' But, he realized, that answer would feed him straight to the said wolves. He had already told the news' people on air that he didn't know anything about a serial killer around here. Zinski would pry open that inconsistency so wide you could drive a truck through it. Admitting he had heard of a serial killer here would suddenly give them a very big hammer with which to nail him and his real plan to the wall.

"Yes, but I hadn't heard anything about any serial killer," Chester said.

Zinski leaned in and now his eyes were burning. "You didn't bring that gun on this holiday because of wolves and bears, did you?"

"Detective, having the gun around is habit, and I brought it because this was a place I didn't know, a place in the country. I saw no real harm in it. It gives a little comfort in a strange place. And sometimes…you just never know."

Zinski's look didn't relent, but he did sit back and let out held breath. His look told Chester that although that was the end of the loaded gun thing, it really hadn't passed the smell test, a foul odor still filling the air.

CHAPTER 36

Zinski paced back and forth in the living room in front of Chester for long silent moments. Then he turned to him. "Why did you rent a cottage *here*?"

"Our money goes a lot further here in Canada. People are nice. It was safe, I thought," Chester said.

"But why specifically here?"

"Well, it's a nice area."

"How did you know that?"

"Well", Chester shrugged, "people down our way talking about how nice cottage country in Ontario is. I checked things out on the internet. Liked what I saw around here."

"When did you make the rental arrangements?"

"A month ago. Early June. I was in the Toronto area on a job for a few days and checked out some cottage rentals."

"You booked it without telling your wife."

"Yes. A surprise. I thought she'd like it. She's never been to Canada."

"Describe your activities here from Saturday night until Thursday at 1:00."

"Well, just being around here, a little fishing in the aluminum boat with Amara, playing a lot in the water or on the beach with her, taking the paddleboat out and around, my walks, campfires, wiener roast, barbecues. Just general relaxation. I help with the meals."

"That about it?"

"I think so."

Zinski's eyes fastened upon him. "Didn't leave the place except for your walks?"

"Oh, I had to go to town for some groceries one morning, Monday or Tuesday. Took Amara along for the ride."

Chester saw a momentary change in Zinski's eyes, like something was unhelpful to him, like Amara being along, meaning Chester wasn't having a little meeting with the killer.

"You haven't mentioned Dennis. Why?"

"Oh, Dennis, of course, yes. Just met him Monday. He gave Amara a ride in an inner tube, then after, he invited us to his house for a while to see his place. We invited him over for a marshmallow roast Wednesday evening. That's it."

Zinski was silent, watching Chester, his eyes unmoving, and unblinking. Chester sensed a new attack was about to be launched, Zinski's eyes like a boring tool about to drill a hole right through Chester's honest character.

"Your wife was strongly attracted to Dennis."

"She was just being neighborly."

Zinski's eyes cracked. "If you believe that, Mr. Carter, I don't know what planet you live on. But it isn't earth."

"I know how things looked..."

"Looked? It is OBVIOUS, with capital letters, Mr. Carter. You weren't gone two minutes and she was on the phone to the stud next door. She had even carefully watched you depart, up the road, then invites him over knowing you'll be gone an hour walking three miles as usual, but just to make sure you stay away, she gets you to go buy potato chips. Not five minutes after you're gone, Dennis is in the cottage and she's in the bedroom half naked. And her explanation? She was changing into something decent? Isn't that extraordinary?"

"He was in the bathroom."

"So she says. And big deal anyway."

"Well I believe her entire explanation."

"Every feeble scrap of it?"

"Yes."

"Didn't suspect her of any possible romantic involvement?"

"No."

"Didn't believe it would be *just like her* to have a quick one with the inner-tube friendly neighbor?"

"No. And I don't like you even suggesting that."

"I have found in a long career of intriguing investigations that it's unwise to ever *underestimate the obvious*."

"I believe her."

"You know I questioned your wife at length, about your marriage, Mr. Carter. She was forthcoming. She admitted her behaviors, her inclinations, her proclivities, difficulties between you."

Chester shook his head. He wanted to remain as calm as he could. "Do you have a question, Detective?"

"She said you would have good reason to believe she might leave you. And, of course, that would mean she would take Amara."

"That's still not a question, and I don't know what you're getting at in all this."

"I think you do. I think you're from planet earth like the rest of us."

Zinski was wound up. He motioned with his arm that he wanted Chester to come with him. They stood in the hall, looking down the hall toward the master bedroom door which was open. "You admit you shot and killed the intruder?"

"Yes. I had to. I knew he was going to kill Candace."

"Show me from where it was in the hall that you fired the first two shots at the intruder."

Chester moved along the hall until he was about ten feet from the open bedroom door. "I'd say about here."

"You said a moment ago, just as you told Detective Grant, 'I knew he was going to kill Candace.'"

"That's right."

"How did you know that?"

"Well, from outside I had just heard two gun shots in the cottage."

"So, the intruder was a pretty bad shot, wouldn't you say? Still hadn't hit her. Maybe wasn't going to."

"Well no, those shots, he had just killed a man."

Zinski's eyes lighted up like a fisherman's when the fish has taken the bait. "But how, Mr. Carter, how *at that moment,* from where you were, did you know that? From this far back in the hall, how could you see Dennis's body in the bedroom against the other wall? Can you see around corners I wonder?"

Chester looked a lot like he was wondering, too.

Zinski pressed. "You couldn't know. Unless, of course, you knew that Dennis was in the cottage already, because you had been *hiding outside waiting,*" he said with a hard-edged flourish. "Waiting for the killer. And maybe catch your wife with lover boy."

How could Zinski know about the hiding and waiting? Or was it a bluff? Chester dug deep for the fight ahead and worked at keeping his head. "First of all, I don't know what you're getting at. It sounds like you've cooked up some kooky ideas. Second, I wasn't hiding and waiting. But you're right, of course you're right. I couldn't know at that moment that the shots had killed Dennis because I didn't know Dennis was in there. It was only after that I knew Dennis was in there, but not very long afterward, like seconds maybe, and it got mixed up in my head. A lot of sudden stress right about then, you can imagine. So it wasn't because I knew the intruder had killed Dennis that I knew he was going to kill Candace. No."

Chester felt the needle in his tachometer climbing, but that was good. After all, he was being accused of major shit here, and, innocent as he wanted to appear, he was naturally going to be some ruffled. "It was because here's a guy firing a lethal gun off in my cottage, my daughter's in bed, my wife's on the floor in our bedroom in her underwear, looking terrorized, by which point I know he's not a guy from the rental agency checking on how we're enjoying the cottage so far. And did I mention he was wearing a balaclava?"

Zinski moved a little in his chair like his jacket wasn't straight.

"And then he violently swung his gun around toward me. I didn't see that as a greeting."

Zinski's eyes wavered.

"So when I say I knew he was going to kill Candace, or kill me for that matter, okay, sure, nothing's for absolute certain. But I was staring at a lot of very good clues pointed in that direction. I wasn't about to roll the dice, and with Amara here, too. I sure hope that even in Canada you're allowed to defend yourself to the utmost when you're looking down the barrel of a gun."

Zinski's face looked momentarily resigned. "I will give you that one, Mr. Carter. Or rather, the last part of that one." His face resumed its cunning. "But I'm very bothered by your perfect timing, arriving in here just when you did. 'Miraculous' some might say. I don't believe in miracles. I don't even believe in coincidence. It strikes me as more that you knew it was going to happen, but maybe weren't sure exactly when, so waited."

"You're wrong."

Zinski shook his head and smiled. "No, Mr. Carter."

He led Chester outside to the back yard and Chester was aware that Zinski was watching him closely, ready to note any reaction. "So when you waited, you had to have somewhere that would provide both concealment and a view. I noted that thick set of bushes back there when I first came here. I took a look. Your shoe prints, Mr. Carter. I have evidence that you were standing behind that set of thick bushes back there, hiding. Perfect concealment, yet ample view."

Chester showed the best face of innocence and astonishment he could muster.

Zinski continued. "When Officer Gill and the forensics man brought you here, the forensics man let me know that the shoe prints he took of your shoes this morning matched the shoe prints that were on the ground there."

Chester could almost hear the clunking in his brain, cogs grinding to get purchase on the teeth of some useful wheel. "Well…" Clunk, clunk.

Finally, the heavens answered. "Well…that's where I *was* hiding."

Zinski's eyes were alight with expectation. "Yes?"

"Hiding, like playing hide and seek, with Amara."

Chester saw the light in Zinski's eyes wane a fraction. But

Zinski tried to recover. "But, Mr. Carter, when I asked what you did this week, you didn't mention hide and seek."

"Well come on…"

"I could ask Amara if you were playing hide and seek. And where you were hiding."

Yes, he could. And the problem was they hadn't played hide and seek. "You could, but she's in Ohio." And a damn lucky thing she was. "And, if you know children, a five-year-old's memory isn't exactly precise. She wouldn't be good with a thing like a property's layout."

"But I could still ask her if you were ever hiding in those bushes."

His own young daughter handing them a hanging rope, Chester thought. Clunk, clunk, clunk. Then a slipping cog got purchase. "But, of course, Detective, you must remember, as I say, it was hide and seek. The whole idea is to *hide* so Amara *doesn't* know where I'm hiding. That's the whole point of hide and seek."

Zinski couldn't mask his surprise, like he hadn't seen that particular chess move coming, just as Chester hadn't. Zinski took in a large breath and expanded his chest. "I know what the point of hide and seek is, Mr. Carter."

An important blow blocked. But it wasn't over, Chester knew, in this ever more dangerous life size game of hide and seek with Zinski.

CHAPTER 37

Chester was dropped off by Officer Gill at the cottage parking lot. The ride back had been quiet.

When Chester got to the cottage, he saw Candace sitting on the dock just staring out at the lake, like she was reflecting. Well, he thought, it was a natural reaction to all that had happened, to pull inside, and just think about your life, take some time alone. And maybe think about how good, and safe, life with Chester was.

He went down to the dock and sat beside her, saying nothing, just being there for her, and watching the warm sun sparkling on the wrinkles in the water.

Candace's voice was quiet, like she had been thinking. "They didn't charge you with anything?"

"No."

"But we can't go home yet?"

"No. Zinski wants to see me tomorrow morning at 8:00. He says he's got some new evidence coming in. I also signed some papers allowing him to have my cell phone and our home phone records faxed to him right away. And the same for our banking records. "

"Is there anything to worry about there?"

"No. Why would there be?"

She didn't answer, still looking at the lake. Then she said, still quietly, "How long were you planning this, Chester?" There was no accusation in her voice, no anger, no upset, more a sense of wonder.

When he was a kid, he had once been hit in the head with a swinging baseball bat. It had staggered him a full minute. But her question carried even more impact.

"What 'this'?" he said, a squeak entering his voice.

She continued, ignoring his question, looking only at the lake, her voice still quiet. "Detective Zinski posed a question to me: 'If Chester thought you were going to leave him and take Amara, what lengths would he go to?' I knew he was wrong to ever suggest that you had set up a hit on me. But it got me thinking, all the points he was making. There had to be something else going on."

Chester decided he would be better off to stay silent and see if he could ride this one out.

"As very strange as it is, I figured it all out," she said. "I can tell you, I was some angry with you about an hour ago when I did. But I've thought about it more, and my anger has passed."

Chester wasn't sure what to think. What was her anger about, precisely? When she said 'I figured it out', maybe she didn't mean what it sounded like she meant. Maybe it was something less that she had figured out. He sure didn't want to presume that she had actually figured *it* out, like *the whole thing*.

"What do you mean you 'figured it out?" he asked with innocence.

"All the pieces fit. Your obsession with the weather – if it rained, you couldn't be out for your routine walk, so your plan would have to wait. You brought the gun along on the trip, handy and loaded. Amara almost slept through five gun shots in the next room that would wake the dead, like she'd been drugged. Then I remembered your surprise strawberry milkshake."

Okay, so she had figured *it* out. Chester swallowed. "Just child's cough syrup, Candace. I followed the correct dosage like you always remind me."

Her voice was still even, not accusing. "Good. I'm happy you didn't forget to put her down for the count."

"Who would ever forget a thing like that?" he said.

"Then there was the squeaky cottage door that you were obsessing over and fixed. But I noticed you didn't obsess over the squeak in the bathroom door. I guess you wanted it quiet so I wouldn't hear the killer come in the cottage?"

"And he wouldn't hear me come in moments later."

"Then your miraculous appearance to save me, even though I told Zinski you can be forgetful about something like your wallet. But he said 'no', that you were hiding in wait."

"They got my shoe prints behind some bushes. But I got around that. Told him Amara and I were playing hide and seek back there."

She looked at him. "Except Amara only plays hide and seek when there are at least four people."

"I know. But he doesn't."

She looked back to the lake. "You surprised me with booking the cottage. And it happens to be in an area where a serial killer is on the loose. And do you remember Amara wanting something to make square sand blocks for her sand castle the morning of the ...events?"

"Not really. A lot on my mind."

"Well she did. I remembered seeing an empty shoebox in the closet just after we arrived at the cottage and realized you must have brought it along because it was ours because it was me who bought those shoes for you. The store's price tag was still on the box. At lunch that day, I looked for it so Amara could make square sand blocks – well, rectangle - and it wasn't in the closet. I was going to line it with waxed paper. I forgot to ask you what you did with it. Then right after the…killings, when we had to pack up to go to the motel, I saw the shoebox had miraculously appeared back in the closet, still empty. When the killer was on the other side of the bed, he made a sliding sound, just like a cardboard box moving on a wood floor. Maybe that shoebox? With money in it?"

"Maybe."

"I didn't mention that to anyone, or anything else that I'm saying to you now."

"Damn good thing."

She looked at him. There was both a sort of wonder and a sort of care in her eyes. "Did I drive you to this, Chester?"

A flood of emotion that had been pent up now released in him. Tears came to his eyes. "You drove me some of the way. I drove the rest of the way by myself. I was desperate, Candace. I didn't want to lose you and Amara. What's a guy to do when he thinks his wife's going to leave him and he loves her more than he loves life itself. He hopes she'll reconsider, see him in a new light."

She was still looking at him the same way. She took his hand in both of hers.

"Candace, I was so afraid you'd leave me in search of the light. I thought I could prove that I'm the light, always there for you, your protector, to keep the darkness away. And to prove you're lovable, as deep as love gets from one person to another. You wanted a prince. I was prepared to do anything…"

"I know, Chester. I realized that. Saw that very clearly."

"I had to do something."

"That was something."

"You told me I didn't understand those stories, the prince proving his love. Remember you saying, 'a prince puts his life on the line for her, something no one has ever done. She knows his love is true. She knows she is worthy of true love. For the first time she feels it deeply.'"

"I remember."

"And you agreed, if there's no distress, no prince comes along."

"I remembered your theory. You really latched onto it, that's for sure."

"I had to save you from a dragon."

"A dragon would have been easier."

"Ya, would have been, I can tell you. He was a brute killer, Candace, willing to strangle you to death for cold cash. I've probably saved many innocent lives."

"Good job, I guess. I would have to say, though, that it was ill-conceived."

"Think so?"

"Ya, I think so. But it says a lot about you."

"Like what?"

"Like you were desperate. But none of it was your fault, Chester. You didn't deserve hurt from me. Ever. My world sometimes gets crazy and you just happen to be in it. I don't always see what's happening. I'm sorry."

"You don't need to be sorry, Candace. You didn't deserve what you had to live through, an innocent child. The point is, I'm here for you, always, steady steady. All I want is us to be together."

A tear came to her eye. "I know. Me, too."

"In another way, maybe a stupid kind of way, I thought the experience for you would be like shock therapy, without all the wires. Maybe it would turn on a switch in you that got turned off a long time ago."

"That's not really scientific, Chester."

"No. Just my intuition."

She laughed a little. "You know, Chester, I would never have guessed you had that kind of inventiveness in you."

"I was hoping the police wouldn't think so either."

"You're an odd kind of romantic. In a funny way, I do feel… special. Not that I approve of what you did."

"No. It's not for everyone."

"No. It's not for anyone. No husband of any woman should ever do that. That's what's special."

"That's what I hoped you'd feel."

"Lots of husbands take their wives on a cruise to say I love you. Or buy a diamond. But this was really something. Not that I would recommend it."

"No."

Candace's face shifted and she took a deep breath. "There is, of course, a very big problem here. This Zinski guy digs deep. You could go to jail for a very long time."

"It was always a risk. But I thought my plan was foolproof."

"You just didn't count on another guy being in the cottage at the time, in the bedroom even, handing the police a motive for you wanting me gone."

Chester looked a little forlorn. "No. Wasn't in the plan."

"At least the 'screwed with the money' thing has them confused. Where is the money, anyway?"

"In the woods. They'll never find it. Guaranteed."

"But we're still in a pickle, Chester."

"Only if they're as smart as you. And why *we*?"

She rubbed his hand in hers and looked at the lake long moments, then looked back to him. "I need you, Chester. You took me out of a shit life, gave me a real life, a family, something I never had. You always stood by me when you didn't have to. I see that clearer than ever before, much clearer. I don't want to see you ever go away. I'm going to stand by you every way I can. Get us out of this thing. Get us back home. Together."

CHAPTER 38

Detective Zinski sat at the head of the long maple-wood table in the police station conference room. Down both sides, spread out, were officers Thomas, Gill, forensics officer Spence, and the young rookie, 'cheerful Sid', whom Zinski always just called 'rookie'. He had been doing small jobs for Zinski related to the investigation, a lackey.

"My theory begins with this proposition," Zinski said to them, "that Chester set up the hit on his wife because she was two-timing or was going to leave him and take the daughter, but the thing went sideways with 'Dennis' there. Chester saw his plan as scuppered and he panicked. He's been trying to cover things up ever since."

Zinski looked around at the others like he was waiting for a question.

Officer Thomas obliged. "And where does your theory go from there?"

"Well, of course, I have to go on to explain why Chester was at the cottage at the time of the hit in the first place. I feel confident his miraculous return was not the product of a miracle. But what was his thinking? He realized that if his hired killer came and strangled the wife and left, although we might consider the serial killer was responsible, there would still be no concrete proof. We would have to consider the real possibility that the husband did it; the husband is always the prime suspect."

There were approving nods.

"And as it turned out, fortuitously for us, his motive, which before might not have been obvious, became very obvious with the whole Dennis thing. But even without that, Chester would still have been a prime suspect. So, Chester, to prove that he didn't do it, set up the hit with the plan that he would kill the killer after the killer killed his wife, which explains why he was there near the cottage. But as I say, things went sideways for him."

"So he's at that spot near the cottage in wait," said Thomas, "and hears gunshots and is shocked because, hell, it's all supposed to be a quiet strangling, and his daughter's in there, and something has gone terribly wrong."

"Yes. And Chester runs in with his gun, as he had planned to anyway, but it happens that he has to kill the hired killer before the killer shoots *him*. But unfortunately, it's before the killer has killed the wife."

"His plan is shot, so to speak," said cheerful Sid.

"Yes, rookie."

"His gun loaded and so handy," said cheerful Sid. "Never underestimate the obvious, as you say, Sir."

Zinski nodded sagely. "You may be learning something."

"I suppose," said Thomas, "Chester's original plan of killing the killer also means the killer could never blackmail him later. Might even save some fees, not having to hand over all the contract money."

"And I've been intrigued by the silk-tie," Gill said. "How does a guy from Detroit even know about our serial killer way up here?"

"I've considered that," Zinski said. "Not likely from the Detroit papers. They've got enough crap of their own to care about ours. Maybe on television, an Ontario station. Chester stays over in Ontario on the installs he does."

"Costs money for the killer to come here. And rent a car and a boat, and motel rooms.

More like he was here on prearranged business," Spence said. "On the other hand, he was around for a week, traveling all over the region it seems. That's more like scouting for a random victim than a prearranged hit."

"Yes, yes, of course, all that," said Zinski. "I've already considered everything you've offered here. I acknowledge, however, that there are points that could still be argued against my theory."

He looked at them as if soliciting such points, although they knew that to him their 'offerings' would be but meager, if not redundant. Nevertheless, they began to throw thoughts forward that would argue against Chester being behind it all.

"The 'screwing with the money' thing that the killer said to 'Dennis.'"

"We can't establish any connection between Chester and the hit man, no communications, no suspicious money."

"He has no criminal record whatsoever, no past violence."

"She never talked about separation."

Zinski had been nodding steadily, looking bored. "And she'd make a good witness," he said.

"She asked him to buy chips on his walk. That's why he came back, for the wallet. He had never come back early on a walk before."

"In fact, Candace was counting on him not coming back so she could have a nice visit with lover boy."

"Seems preposterous that Chester would ever set up a hit on the mother with the young daughter right there in the cottage? You'd have to be stupid."

Zinski held up his finger to have them stop. "Which Chester is," he said. "My only question is whether he's very stupid, or merely stupid."

"How about the fact that he killed the killer intruder?" said cheerful Sid. "Doesn't seem likely he's the one who set up the hit if he's the one who kills the hit man."

"You were obviously asleep a minute ago, rookie. I addressed that. Try to stay awake."

"Chester's been fully cooperative," Thomas cut in. "Gave full access to his bank and phone records. Also, not the slightest mention of any violence in the marriage. Candace says he would never hurt her. She's not the least afraid of him, and it's not that she's stupid exactly."

"Correct," said Zinski. "Not stupid like Chester."

"To tell the truth," Spence said, "he even seems like a nice guy. We had a friendly chat yesterday when I was doing his shoe prints. No awkwardness from him or rumblings about anything that would suggest anything suspicious to me."

"Yes," Zinski said. "We have circumstantial evidence only, albeit compelling, but we also have inconvenient conflicting evidence."

"The evidence goes around and around like a dog chasing its own tail," said cheerful Sid.

Ignoring him, Zinski said, "What I really need is to have Chester hang himself, give us something from his own lips. As you know, I've scheduled an interview with him here at the station tomorrow morning at eight. I want him tired. I've told him

I'm waiting on certain forensics' reports, which I'm not. But I want him to sweat about what I may have, to weaken him. Make him edgy and exhausted. Then I'll make him sing like a bird."

He waited a moment for their admiring looks at his colorful language.

"Another possibility is that he'll try to run, which would be a confession of sorts. At least it would give me a good toe hold to work with, break him down. To address that possibility I've arranged for an officer to be in an unmarked car around the clock at the point where the cottage road exits onto the highway. If he moves, I'll know it."

Zinski got up, indicating that the meeting was over. They all rose.

"Good luck with him," Gill said as they filed out of the room, the officers all heading out for the evening, all except Zinski, and cheerful Sid, who had to remain to assist Zinski in any way required.

When the other officers had left, cheerful Sid followed Zinski to the coffee room. "I've been thinking, Sir. I've heard you say several times never to underestimate the obvious."

"Correct, rookie."

"Well, if you take the Dennis guy out of the equation, because presumably he was never in Chester's planning to begin with, and if you look at what you'd be left with, I mean what actually did end up happening, you have Chester coming in, killing the killer, and the wife not getting killed. If we are never to underestimate the obvious, we'd be left to think that what happened was what Chester actually planned to happen, except for the Dennis thing. I mean, hire the killer, killer comes to strangle the wife, and Chester neatly steps in and takes out the killer with the handy loaded gun, and the wife is not killed. That's what actually happened, if you take Dennis out of the equation, Sir."

"What's your point?"

"Well, how is that as a theory?"

"Astonishingly stupid. What possible end would that ever achieve?"

"I don't know exactly, Sir. To impress his wife, maybe? I think my wife would be impressed."

"I can tell you, rookie, that that's the only thinking and theory that anyone's come up with that I didn't think of. And do you know why I didn't think of it? Because it's just plain cuckoo. In this special instance, underestimating the obvious is permitted. In fact, it's mandatory. You are not underestimating the obvious when the obvious produces something as completely and utterly outrageously incredible as that."

"I'm sorry, Sir."

"I hope you don't have your eye on advancement any time soon, rookie. Your ineptitude is remarkable."

"Yes, Sir."

"Think about it. Would you ever want to ask a prosecutor to prosecute a case like that, put that case to a jury with a straight face. "Your Honor, and this esteemed jury, it is the prosecution's case that the accused whom you see before you hired a hit man with the intention of blowing him away with a hand gun while the said hit man was in the act of strangling the wife of the accused, all for the sole purpose of impressing the said wife.""

"It does sound ridiculous, Sir, when you put it plainly."

"Do you expect anyone in their right mind to believe that?"

"No, Sir."

"I assume you have not forgotten, rookie, that the job of the police and the prosecutor is not to offer up to the court any bizarre notions that come to our minds, or to your mind in this case, but is, rather, the very steep job of proving our case beyond a reasonable doubt?"

"I have not forgotten, Sir."

"Well that's good, because good fucking luck with that one."

"Yes, Sir."

"I would suggest you have a strong coffee and wake up."

Zinski thought just how lucky it was that he was the one doing this investigation and not some numbskull.

*

At about nine that evening, having mulled and stewed about the state of the evidence for four hours, Zinski decided that the only sure way to get what he needed was indeed from Chester's own mouth, and that was more likely to come the more edgy and exhausted Chester was for the interview. And the way to make him edgy and exhausted was to make him wait longer, frustrate him.

"Rookie," he called out to the office down the hall.

"Yes, Sir," Sid called back, hurrying to Zinski's office door.

"There is no cell phone service at their cottage, so I want you to make a call on the cottage land line, and make the call right now, informing Chester that the interview tomorrow morning at eight is cancelled because of new very important and suspicious evidence surfacing. Tell him the interview is rescheduled for the day *after* tomorrow. In the afternoon. At 3:00."

"Yes, Sir. That's going to really frustrate them, Sir."

"Yes, rookie. Thanks for that insight."

*

Chester and Candace were sitting at the dock, doing their best to relax, hoping the beautiful glow of the dropping sun and the tranquility of the broad still evening lake would lend a hand.

But then the 'three amigos,' as Candace had called them, materialized again from their lair, three hooting teenagers roaring at high speed on three jet skis, competing to carve the best figure eight into the still, silent water before night descended.

The sound was deafening, and in consequence Chester and Candace didn't hear the cottage phone ringing. And also, when they made their slow way back up to and into the cottage to retire early, both exhausted and edgy, and being unfamiliar with the phone messaging system, they missed noticing the miniscule red light of the phone blinking in its small corner of the living room.

CHAPTER 39

No one likes to be predictable. It makes you appear simple, unimaginative.

He thought about his three kills, striking once per year like clockwork, each victim a younger woman, each death by strangulation, each with a silk-tie, each strike in a warm month, each strike by a lake (well, after all, it was cottage country).

All too predictable. But he knew he was neither simple nor unimaginative, as attested to by the fact that the police still had not a clue who the killer was, had no leads whatsoever, each time more dumbfounded than the last.

Well, not exactly correct, he reflected. The coroner, who had examined all the women, finally had a good theory. What particularly baffled investigators was how none of the healthy young victims had exhibited any external sign of struggle before or during their strangulation.

The coroner determined that a karate-type blow inflicted by a trained hand to the vagus nerve would lead to unconsciousness, or at least incapacity to resist, allowing easy strangulation but leave no bruising mark on the neck. Or if such a blow did produce a mark, it could be concealed by, or blur with, the ring of bruising on the neck produced by the strangulation. So, the coroner speculated, the killer might know karate.

But apart from that development, investigators were still confounded. And no one knew he knew karate, or at least its best rudiments. So, all was well.

Still, though, no one likes to be predictable.

It was July, and he had not killed this year. As much as he felt its seductive summons, he had not killed because he had decided he had to skip a year, to make them wonder. Or if waiting a year would prove too difficult, wait at least a season. Maybe winter.

But then, only days ago, everything changed, the ground shifting and shaking under his feet like an earthquake. She was just too much. He had to kill again. There was no second-guessing. She demanded it.

There was special risk to it, yes, much higher than ever before. But he would never have this opportunity again. And it would feed the escalating need like no one else would.

Just too much, she was, Candace Carter. Beautiful, like his mother had been beautiful. It aroused his wrath, her wanton infidelity, without concern for her young child only a room away. Like his mother with Nick the Serb when he was a boy, driving his father away, killing him.

He slipped the canoe into the calm early morning lake water, the air warm, the sun nicely up. He put the fishing pole and fish bucket into the canoe, then set a short garment bag onto the canoe's bottom. The bag appeared to be half-full. He was wearing only shorts, no shirt. He arranged the black wig neatly on his head before pressing it down under the low baseball cap. He put on sunglasses, not his usual ones.

He shoved off. He had a lake to cross, and not a small one. It was time for Candace to say goodbye.

*

Candace was still asleep so Chester climbed carefully out of bed so not to disturb that precious commodity for her. He was tired, too, but it was already 7:00 and he had to leave by 7:30 to make the appointment with the detective at the station at 8:00.

The detective said he wanted to see only Chester. Candace said she might come along for the ride to get out of the cottage, if she wasn't too exhausted that early in the morning, maybe wait for him in town at a coffee shop. But she also said not to wake her. She would see how she felt, wake herself if she slept ok. But it seemed she didn't feel much like waking or going anywhere.

He really needed a shower. As he lathered and washed, he found himself becoming tense at the thought of more and more pointed questioning at a table across from the unblinking eyes.

He definitely needed a coffee to sharpen his wits, and he remembered the coffee-maker here was slow. But was it slower than him stopping and buying a coffee on the way? The problem was he needed a coffee to properly think about it.

He allowed himself only one more minute in the shower. Wrapping a towel around his waist, he padded into the kitchen and studied the coffee-maker. To study it properly, he first needed an orange from the fruit bowl, a large and very heavy blue-glazed thick-pottery fruit bowl, which he admired.

"Ches…?" Her voice was faint.

He hurried into the bedroom. Her eyes were still closed. She was drowsy awake.

"Morning," he whispered. "Hope I didn't wake you." He touched her arm and lightly kissed her forehead. If she could resume real slumber, he didn't want to waken her more.

"Can't go. Too...sleepy." Her words came out slowly, drearily and wearily, her eyes still closed. "Can you...make coffee?"

With the tension he felt knotting inside, and looking at his poor wife exhausted with the strain that he had brought on, what he had put her through, he felt tears welling up. It was becoming all too much, and he wanted to just collapse onto the bed and cry his bleeding heart out.

"Sure I can," he whispered.

*

The canoe glided without a paddle stroke for the final twenty yards and the bow bumped gently against the bank. He glanced at his watch. 7:30

He set the paddle down as he looked all around and behind, twice. He waited a moment, then moved soundlessly to the front of the canoe, stepping with a lightness onto the bank. With one hand, he lifted the bow just enough to slide the front of the canoe three feet to rest on the hard embankment. The water was a quiet lapping; three feet onto the embankment would give the canoe enough purchase against slipping back, but not enough to leave any real print of its having been there.

He had been on this lake many times before. But late last evening, fishing, he had studied this half mile of shoreline intensely. The fishing wasn't even too bad - a nice three-pound trout.

The shoreline right here was a hundred yard stretch of pristine bush that was centered in a sweeping bay like a half moon. The lake was quiet at this early hour.

To his right, the nearest cottage was a hundred yards away but no one was there; there had been no lights on last night, the owners probably at their home in the city. The cottage beyond that, the last one visible from within the bay, was also not occupied just now. To his left was a cottage about thirty yards, again vacant, and one beyond that, the same thing.

Chester's and Candace's cottage was the third on the left, the last one on this bay. Only its dock was visible from where he stood. But before he announced himself, he had to get properly dressed.

He propped the fishing pole up high against the gunwale to signal the morning's purpose to anyone passing by. He changed the water in the fish bucket once more, swishing the now thawed trout around.

He picked up the garment bag and walked a few yards into the bush to be unseen. He took off the sunglasses, cap, wig, and shorts.

He dressed from the contents of the garment bag: a pair of beige dress pants, a brown leather belt, a light-brown short-sleeved dress shirt, boat shoes, their treads flat to leave no unique signature, a little flip-pad and pen for his shirt-front pocket. And last, but far from least, the dark-brown silk-tie. He fitted it under the collar around his neck and tied it properly, neatly, at the front.

He presented well. It should pass the smell test. Moreover, perfectly in his favor, Candace knew him, or would at least recognize him, had every reason to trust him, would open the door to him. It would be a cakewalk.

He combed his hair then threw the wig and cap and shorts and sunglasses into the garment bag, zipped it up, and glanced out from the bush. Not a soul in sight. He walked out to the canoe and threw the bag in.

He worked his way deep into the bush until he came to the gravel road that gave access to the cottages on this side of the *lake. He checked his watch. 7:40. He followed the road for five minutes until he was near the parking lot that serviced this block of cottages.*

He veered off into the bush and continued in concealment until he could see the lot fully, to check which cars were there. He had to know that Chester was, in fact, gone, that Chester was on his way into town.

*

The policeman in an unmarked car, parked by the highway just at the end of the miles-long gravel cottage road, saw Chester's green Jeep Cherokee exit the road onto the highway, picking up considerable speed very quickly. The policeman checked his watch. 7:50

He followed at a distance while he radioed in for instructions. Chester was exceeding the speed limit - 20 miles an hour over.

The policeman was patched through to Detective Zinski. "It's Sinclair here, Sir. Chester's just come out of the cottage road. Appears to be alone. Heading east in a hurry, doing 20 over."

"Pull him over. Ask him about his speeding, where he's going. Take a look in the car. Check the trunk. Hold him until you talk to me again."

Sinclair picked up his speed, closed the gap, set his lights flashing and touched the siren on and off twice.

Chester's Cherokee pulled over and Sinclair followed in behind. He got out and walked to Chester's window.

"Bit of a hurry, Sir?"

"Actually, I'm on my way to the police station."

"Why in such a hurry?"

"I have an appointment with Detective Zinski at eight o'clock and I'm running late. Slept in a bit. I'm sorry. Wife wasn't feeling well."

Sinclair studied Chester, who looked nervous, but also sincere. Sinclair looked in the back seat. Nothing. "Pop the trunk, please."

"My trunk?"

"Yes."

Sinclair checked. The trunk was empty.

"Okay, Sir, wait here a minute."

Sinclair returned to his car and radioed in again. "He says he has an appointment with you at eight o'clock, Sir. Slept in. Seems on the level. Car's empty."

"That appointment was canceled. We called last night and left a message on the cottage phone saying we were waiting on some new evidence. Maybe he didn't get it. Tell him the appointment's rescheduled for 3:00, *tomorrow*. Apologize for the mix up and any inconvenience. No, forget about the inconvenience. And...don't apologize either."

"Okay. Ticket him?"

"No. But tell him no more free passes."

*

Candace felt she might just drop off into one more doze when she heard the knock, a light rapping at the front door. Or had she dozed and she was dreaming?

She heard it again. Rap rap. Who could that possibly be? Out here?

She was still in her nightgown. She knew the door would be locked because those were her very clear instructions to Chester. The door was also solid.

She pulled herself together and quickly changed the night-gown for shorts and a shirt. She heard the tapping again, insistent. She was getting upset now. Who the hell would be knocking out here at this hour? And what hour was it? She looked at her watch. 7:50.

She left the bedroom and walked down the short hall in bare feet, still buttoning her shirt, and crossed the kitchen to the door. It had a one-square-foot window at eye level. A thin yellow curtain covered that. She drew it back to see.

It took her a moment to register. Oh, okay, yes. She knew him. A nice face. Officer...what was his name? But anyway, why was he here? And so early.

She turned the lock and opened the door.

"I'm sorry," she said, obviously tired, running a hand through her disheveled hair. "I was still in bed."

"I'm terribly sorry," he said, very polite.

He wasn't in uniform, but was neatly dressed, beige dress pants with a brown leather belt, a light-brown short-sleeved dress shirt, a little flip-pad and pen in the shirt-front pocket, and a dark-brown silk-tie.

CHAPTER 40

"Would Chester be in?" Officer Gill said.

"Well no," Candace said. "He's at an appointment with Detective Zinski. I thought you would know that."

"Sometimes they tell us, sometimes they don't."

"Well I'm sorry you've come out all this way."

"Actually, there's another reason I've come. There's concern that Chester may try to make a run for it."

She laughed. Not a great police theory in play. Boy, were they stupid sometimes. "No. That will never happen. You don't know Chester. Don't have to worry about that one." Oh, she almost forgot. "And anyway, he has no reason to run. He's not guilty of anything."

She was still holding the door with her hand, not letting him in. Not that he seemed to be pressing to come in, but she really didn't want to keep standing here talking when she could be sitting down and having a coffee which she needed badly. And alone.

She began to feel irked with this stupid intrusion. "So, officer, what are you saying? You're here to guard him? And you didn't even know he's not here? Not a good start."

"No need to be testy."

"Well look, I'm not getting a lot of sleep, and I, we, would really like to just go home."

The thought also occurred to her that maybe they sent him here looking more casual, out of uniform, appear compassionate to get her to relax, drop her guard, spill something to Officer Nice Face.

"We appreciate your cooperation," he said. "We really do."

Okay, maybe she was being testy. Well, yes, she knew she was. She calmed herself. "Yes, I know. I'm sorry for my tone."

She looked at him, and he at her. But now something in his look, in his eyes, began to make her feel uncomfortable. She wanted to close this off. "Well," she finally said, "maybe you want to go back to the car and radio in and get instructions or something now that Chester's not here like you expected. I can tell you one thing, I'm not running anywhere."

It was like a shadow fell across his face, his eyes changing again, not friendly anymore. "No," he said quietly. "That's for sure."

She didn't know why he said it like that, 'that's for sure'.

"May I come in? Use your phone? The car's out at the lot."

Something seemed wrong. The lot was all of a five-minute walk. "All that way?" She was being sarcastic. Okay, settle down, she told herself. "Sorry. But, really, maybe I shouldn't overhear your private police conversation."

"I'm not too worried about that."

She didn't like his tone now, not at all. "Officer, frankly you're not making yourself clear, about why you're here. Nobody said anything to us, like the detective, about guarding us like we're convicts or something."

Her eyes lowered a moment and she noticed his boat shoes. That's got to be irregular. Police surely don't wear boat shoes on duty, even when out of full uniform. And why was he out of uniform?

Her eyes were still down when one of the boat shoes suddenly jerked to jam the door open. She looked up. His face was mean and angry and two open flat hands punched her powerfully full on the chest, pushing her straight back. She lost her balance and fell backwards onto the kitchen floor.

He was on her in a second, his left hand gripping her hair and pulling her head back. She screamed. His right hand chopped at her neck, but the knife-hand strike was blocked by her arm.

But then came another lightning strike, and she felt herself slipping away.

*

He dragged her into the bedroom and lifted her onto the bed.

He knew the police reports now referred to beds as the serial killer's 'place of death', his modus operandi, at least in kills two and three. Kill one at the cove didn't count, at least not in that particular regard. A bed carried a certain sense of molestation without actually doing anything. He was certainly not impotent, and it kept messing up the profiler who kept positing, is the killer impotent? Bedroom. Bed. No molestation. Yes, the killer's likely an impotent manifesting his impotence, as in, the killer's not a robust policeman. So far, so good.

He unbuttoned the top button of his shirt and lifted the collar and untied the silk tie and pulled it off. Candace, lying there, was certainly attractive. And still well out of it, not coming to. Even if she did, there wasn't anyone around for at least three hundred yards. She could just scream her bloody head off and it wouldn't matter. In her case, he might just make an exception and let her. That would be thrilling. He could let her see and appreciate just what her end was going to be.

But he quickly decided otherwise. Be prudent. Stick with the program. Move this thing along smartly and be safe.

He lifted her head and slid the tie along behind her neck. He rolled her over so he was looking at the back of her head. Stay with the program.

He wrapped an end of the tie around each hand. He crossed his hands and pulled, the tie squeezing into her soft neck. He slowly counted off sixty seconds.

He let his arms and hands relax.

A faint scuff of shoe on gravel. He glanced to the open window but saw nothing. He jumped off the bed and looked out. He saw Chester coming toward the cottage on the gravel walkway, unaware. What the hell was he doing here and not with Zinski?

He had to act fast. He would need a few minutes to neutralize Chester. Candace wouldn't likely come to consciousness by then, if ever. Even if she did, she would be woozy. She was no threat. Chester was the threat.

As he fled the bedroom, he pulled the door closed behind him. He passed through the kitchen and grabbed the first weapon he saw, a thin steak knife, pulling it from a wooden block holder on the counter, tucking it behind him in his belt.

*

When Chester came along the walkway around the side of the cottage, he saw Officer Gill come out the door onto the deck.

Not in uniform, and alone, the door swinging back to close without Candace coming out.

Chester was sixty feet away. He slowed and stopped, his heart racing suddenly. "What are you doing here?" he said.

"Oh, hi, Chester," Gill said, turning toward him, like he was surprised.

To Chester he looked evasive, nervous, his smile false, not surprised. Anyone could have read it.

Chester had only been gone thirty minutes. His first thought was that Gill had been with Candace in some sexual way, or that he had just interrupted something very much like that. But just as quickly, something deeper told him that just wouldn't be true.

"Had to ask her a few more questions," Gill said.

But his voice was off, not authoritative, not take charge. It seemed a lie. And why wasn't he in uniform? If he wanted to ask Candace questions, he would do it at the station, not sneak in here. And so early. And it was Detective Zinski who asked all the questions now.

Unless they wanted to get at Candace alone and catch her tired, make her say something to pleasant looking Officer Gill, something very specific, something in answer to questions carefully crafted and calculated by Zinski to produce some sneaky result.

Maybe. But still, things weren't adding up, so Chester stopped walking, now forty feet away from the deck but now beside the cottage. He felt a mix of fear and adrenaline rushing. While his mind raced, he said, "Did you get all you needed?"

"Yes."

"Not very polite of her not to see you to the door. Where is she?"

He registered that Gill was now more ill at ease. If anyone should be ill at ease, it should be Chester. He sensed Gill was thinking fast, how to get himself out of a corner.

"In the washroom. Said she'll be out in a minute."

Another lie. Chester felt it, and his insides were shaking.

But what could possibly be going on here? He had to know and fast.

Then something occurred to him suddenly, like a three-piece puzzle. "Oh," he said, maintaining outward calm as best he could. He just had to think how best to put the question to set the trap.

It was really so simple. "Where's your car?"

"Up in the lot, of course. Unmarked."

Gill had just stepped into it, both feet.

Chester's mind spun. "Oh, right. Probably that Impala."

"Yes, that's it."

Now Chester was very, very nervous. What the hell was going on? Gill was lying and Chester had him cold. Chester noticed vehicles. He had just parked in the lot and there were only four vehicles besides his own: a much older Honda Civic, a Ram pick-up with a trailer, a Lexus convertible, and a Volkswagen Beetle. None would ever qualify as an unmarked police car. An Impala would, a common unmarked police car, and Gill would know that. But there was no Impala in the parking lot.

Chester could only figure that Gill came in one of those four vehicles, and not on police business. A social visit? And why was he lying?

"Come on," Gill waved, hailing Chester to come, "and we'll go in and talk a minute." He seemed to be in a hurry now.

The only truthful explanation of why Gill was here would come from Candace. And he needed to know that truth from her before Gill left.

"Come on," Gill waved again, more insistent.

Looking at Gill, Chester shouted, "Candace!"

He saw Gill flinch.

The windows of the cottage were all open, just the bug screens there. Candace couldn't fail to hear. And the washroom answer was a lie. That room faced them, the window open, and she would hear everything.

Gill came down the stairs from the deck and began to walk toward Chester.

"Candace!" Chester shouted again.

A man knows when another man is approaching in threat, even a hidden threat.

"Maybe it's better you come with me," Gill said still approaching, "to let your head cool. Or I'll have to place you under arrest for interfering with a police officer in the course of his duty."

"In the course of his duty?" Chester's eyes were alive. "In the course of what duty?"

"Don't resist me."

Gill was twenty feet away and coming, cautious.

Chester didn't move. "My head is cool. I deserve to know why you were with my wife."

"I just said. Questions."

Chester kept worrying why Candace wasn't showing her face. There was no way she wasn't hearing this. And if it was just questions, why wasn't Candace coming out. And more importantly, why wasn't Gill just leaving instead of being confrontational? What was he protecting?

Gill was getting closer, ten feet away. "Just walk with me a minute. Let things settle. Nobody wants trouble."

"What have you done?"

"Relax."

"Tell me!"

"Relax." Gill was putting his left hand out.

"Don't put a hand on me," Chester said.

Gill was shorter than Chester by three inches, but strong looking.

"Don't resist. Let's walk." Keeping his eyes on Chester's, Gill put his left hand out on Chester's right forearm to neutralize the dominant arm. Chester raised his right arm to shake it off.

Gill's rigid right hand flew to the neck, the knife-hand strike.

But Chester's neck wasn't delicate like a 120-pound female's, nor perfectly exposed. But the strike's speed did take Chester by surprise, but only partly. The blow didn't find its target, glancing instead off his jaw. He made a half step back from the blow as Gill moved in, striking again. But Chester was quick, too. He lunged, driving a lightning fist full into Gill's stomach. But Gill's second strike had caught, and both fell to the ground.

Both were quick to their feet again, but now Chester saw a knife in Gill's hand, a steak knife Chester knew was from the cottage, the curved wooden handle.

Something terrible had happened to Candace!

Chester felt a rage like nothing ever before in his life.

He charged full at Gill like a bear, Chester's flying arm blocking a first stab, the knife glancing but slicing arm flesh. They went to the ground. Chester crashed a fist into Gill's face, but the knife struck on the second thrust, plunging into Chester's left shoulder, the knife's thin blade tip snapping off at the bone, leaving the tip buried two inches in.

The broken knife was still in Gill's hand, but Chester got his hand on that knife arm, forcing it down and away, taking close punches from Gill's other hand in doing it.

Chester fought like a man without feeling, pounding his right fist into Gill's face, making it bloodied. Gill was squirming as they wrestled, Chester getting his knees higher up and drove them into Gills' chest and brought both his hands onto Gill's knife arm and smashed it against the gravel until the knife fell away, Chester's face and head still taking close punches from Gill's left hand.

Somehow Gill twisted out from under him and rolled and jumped up. Chester just managed to kick the knife away before Gill could grab it again. It flew off the gravel and into thick shrubs.

Gill quickly swept at Chester with both hands rigid and flying, Chester blocking what he could. At one moment Chester felt a sudden terrible weakness and Gill almost had him, but it quickly passed. Chester threw a bone crunching fist into Gill's face and got in close enough again to neutralize those flying hands, trying to drop Gill again to the ground. His best chance was to keep Gill down on the ground where Chester's superior size could better overpower and check those hands.

His hand gripped Gill's shirt front, tearing it open, buttons flying. The torque Chester got on it made Gill lose his balance and they both went to the ground, close blows flying, rolling and crossing ground.

They both heard it. A coughing. Candace was alive!

Now her voice coming uneven, gasping air, heard faintly through a screen window. "Yes... 911... Please."

Chester didn't see the rock. Gill's hand had found it when he rolled across ground, a good three pounder, and he crashed it onto Chester's head and Chester blacked out.

Gill jumped up, his sole and urgent purpose to get to Candace before she named him on the phone.

CHAPTER 41

Candace struggled to get words out but her voice was weak, hoarse sounding, and the operator couldn't hear her well and kept interrupting. "Send police...... No, it's happening *now*..... I'm Candace Carter......... I *don't know* the address... A cottage..... The *police know* where I am..."

She turned at the sudden sound. Gill was running at her across the living room, his face bloodied and contorted in anger. She could only scream into the phone.

The phone flew out of her hand, crashing against the wall, as she felt herself being flung through the air, too, until she, too, hit a wall and her head suddenly hurt. Now he was grabbing her, lifting her, running with her. She got her breath and screamed again.

They were in the bedroom. He threw her roughly on the bed. She kicked and punched and screamed and saw him grabbing the tie on the bed that had been around her neck when she came to. He quickly got on top of her, his knees digging into her stomach, his strong hands and arms whacking her fighting hands and arms to the side. He brought himself higher on her body. His knees widened out to control her flinging arms until she couldn't move them. Her legs kicked to no effect at all.

*

There was no time to play this nice, delivering a blessed two strikes to her neck to spare her suffering. Moreover, he chose not to. Not with her. She would know her end. A deserving end. A judicial passing. And she would suffer.

Her eyes were wide with terror watching him now. Her screams were irrelevant. He got the ends of the tie around both of his hands and swung it under her head. No rolling her over this time. She would watch, and he would watch, his weight bearing down to hold her firmly in place. He brought the tie once around her neck so he now had leverage.

He pulled tightly and it squeezed into her neck, closing off that offending screaming, reducing her sounds to a strangled gurgle. Her body shook and moved in jerking fits under him.

*

Chester heard something like sounds you hear underwater, sounds that seem far away and indistinct and foreign.

As if rising through water, he surfaced and listened with purpose, the way you listen for a bird's song.

Candace was screaming. It was Candace, screaming!

But now there wasn't any screaming. All was quiet again. Maybe he could sleep now.

But something in his fevered brain reeled to comprehend, and he shook the weakness in his head and the heavy weight of himself lying on the graveled ground like a beached seal.

*

Gill was counting the seconds as the tie squeezed. Twenty-one, and twenty-two, and twenty-three. Candace was still writhing beneath him, but with no air, her struggles were silent.

Twenty-six, and twenty-seven, and twenty-eight.

Through the open window he heard a sudden commotion of shoes scrambling on gravel. Chester was up, damn it!

He shook the ends of the tie loose from around his hands and sprang off the bed. He needed a weapon again, but something better - bigger, heavier, thick-bladed - to kill Chester quickly this time.

He ran out of the bedroom and down the hall toward the kitchen.

*

Chester flung the cottage door open and saw Gill running for the kitchen.

He chased and saw Gill spot the heavy knife rack at the far end of the counter. Gill had his hand on the handle of the biggest - a ten-inch carving knife - when Chester's flying body took him hard into a wall with all his weight. Gill's head hit the wall and bounced off like a ball, his eyes unfocused, but only a moment.

He had somehow held onto the knife handle and the knife was firmly in his clutches. Chester grabbed for it as Gill's head cleared, but Gill slashed at Chester's forearm, slicing the surface. Chester's other fist had been flying at the same moment and caught Gill full on the jaw, staggering him and he lost balance and fell backward.

Chester threw a foot into Gill as Gill scrambled to get up, sending him backwards.

Chester could hear Candace coming down the hall gasping for air like a wild animal bellowing.

Gill was up, the knife firmly in his hand.

The only thing within Chester's reach was the glazed, stone-ware blue pottery fruit bowl he saw this morning, its mouth a foot wide, its base five pounds of hard fired clay like a solid rock. He grabbed it with one hand, sending the oranges flying, gripping its edge, holding it well in front.

Candace was now at the kitchen entrance, staggering, grabbing a rail spindle for balance.

Gill lunged at Chester. Chester blocked the knife strike with the bowl and thrust the bowl at Gill's head. It glanced off, dazing him a moment. He staggered back but his eyes quickly focused.

Gill leaped at Chester again, the thick blade repeatedly thrusting, feinting. Chester backed up with the bowl shielding, but a thrust got past it, piercing Chester's chest a half inch before Chester's swinging arm crashed the rock-heavy bowl into Gill's face with bone crunching force. The side of the bowl broke and the bowl fell from his grip.

Candace was screaming.

Gill staggered and Chester saw one moment of advantage, Gill's knife arm slack from the stunning blow to his face. Chester leaped directly at the knife arm and blocked most of its rise. Both his hands gripped Gill's knife hand and arm.

Chester wheeled Gill's arm over and pounded it against the granite counter's edge, Gill trying to grab the knife with his other hand. But Chester blocked it and kept ramming Gill's hand against the edge.

Gill changed tactics, his left arm wrapping around Chester's neck in a full lock, squeezing off Chester's air. Chester held on, his two-hand strength squeezing at the knife hand, slowly overpowering Gill's grip, slowly working the knife free.

But Chester's air was now limited and he gagged and gasped. He threw his body again and again against Gill smashing him into the counter trying to twist his neck free of Gill's grasp while working the knife free.

Chester finally felt enough of the handle and he jerked it again and again until it came into his hand alone.

With amazing force, Gill threw the heel of his now free right hand under and into Chester's chin like a trained fatal strike. Chester felt sudden blackness as he plunged the knife ten full inches into Gill.

CHAPTER 42

Like the stroke of a soft finger on a cheek, he heard her voice by his ear. "Chester." And again, "Chester."

Boy, he was waking up a lot today. What a day this was.

Her voice again. "You're safe. He's dead."

Someone else dead? Who this time?

He opened his eyes. He was on his back on the floor. Her face was hovering three inches above his face, and there were tears. "You saved my life," she said. "*Twice,* this morning."

His eyes met hers, his voice weak. "… a busy day."

She laughed a little. Her tears were dropping onto his face.

He looked over and saw Gill lying on his side, his face to him, the eyes open and dead.

"He was a damn surprise," Chester mumbled.

"Big time. I thought my number was up, like twice."

"My shoulder," he said, pain registering sharp now, a grimace.

"He stabbed you."

"Part of it's still in there. Is help coming?"

"Yes. Your arm's cut, too. And he stabbed you in the chest. I think I've stopped the bleeding, pressing with a towel."

He saw it was the blue and white striped towel, the signal towel. Funny how things are sometimes.

*

Detective Zinski, Officer Thomas, forensics Officer Spence, and the rookie, cheerful Sid, were standing outside the cottage. They watched the paramedics carry Chester on a stretcher up the slope toward the lot where the ambulance was parked. Candace walked with the paramedics to follow them in to the hospital in the Cherokee. Chester was very weak. He needed to get that knife blade tip out of his shoulder, stitches into his chest and arm, and a blood transfusion.

Zinski and the officers had been at the cottage about twenty minutes already. Five minutes earlier, Candace had unloaded a head of steam at Zinski. 'I came close to being killed *twice* this morning. And so did Chester. One of *your* men came inches from killing us both. Chester has now killed your serial killer. In doing that, he first had to save my life *twice, just this morning.*" As she was saying it, she stomped her foot on the ground twice, sending a primitive communication that Chester had proved Zinski wrong twice, just this morning. "I hope you're able to deduce your deductions, Detective, and realize that Chester never set up a hit on me.'

Now Zinski and the officers went back into the cottage again, gathering in the kitchen again, looking at Gill who was still on the kitchen floor, the knife buried to the hilt. The other ambulance would arrive soon to remove him. Officer Spence had taken all the pictures he needed.

"I guess he was waiting his first opportunity, first day off his shift," cheerful Sid said without the least cheer as he looked at Gill.

"That canoe is Gill's, no question," Thomas said for the third time, still in shock. "I fished with him once and I remember that dark yoke."

"Finger prints will confirm anyway," Zinski said. "I'm confident hair fibers on the inside of the wig will match his DNA. Not that it's critical how he got here. Just to confirm."

"His truck will be parked somewhere around this lake," Thomas said. "Some concealed access point."

Spence said, "What a fucking time of it this morning for Chester and Candace."

Cheerful Sid said, "Candace would have been dead if you hadn't called off this morning's meeting with Chester, Sir. It's a miracle."

Zinski flinched at the word.

"Chester's timing getting back here was damn miraculous, too," Spence said.

Zinski flinched again. Too many miracles for one day. Even for one week.

"If Chester had been just two or three minutes later," Spence continued, "he would have found her dead and our serial killer would be nowhere to be found." He looked at Zinski. "We would have been investigating *Chester* as her killer. Prime suspect and all."

The cottage phone rang. Zinski answered it. "Yes. Yes... good... He did? Good. Okay."

He hung up and turned to the others. "I had them run Gill's shift records. He was on days-off each time one of those three women was killed. Coincidence, perhaps, but more evidence. And something else, I had HQ in Toronto dig out his full original application for the force seven years ago. In the 'personal interests and activities' section, one of the items he referenced was his competing in karate as a teen."

Thomas shook his head. "He never mentioned that to me once in the years I've been working with him," Thomas said. "And even when we all knew the serial killer might know karate, he never once mentioned he knew karate. Now we know why."

*

It was 1:00 when Candace saw Zinski and Officers Thomas and Spence and the young rookie arrive at the hospital. Chester was being discharged, all patched up, thick bandages wrapped around his shoulder, another taped to his chest, another around his forearm. The nurse helped him to get a loose shirt on. He looked desperately tired. No doubt the drugs were working on him, too.

Outside the hospital, the news trucks and journalists had clustered again, impatient for solid information, the rumors having been buzzing and swirling for two hours, that *this time* Chester had killed the *real* serial killer. His killing earlier in the week had only been a practice run.

Candace said to Zinski, "We would appreciate it if you would escort us out of the hospital. Chester's not up to this press scrum stuff again. But before we do, I want to say a few words, Detective."

Zinski nodded.

Candace led them all into a large private room and closed the door. Chester slumped in a chair, his head bowed with fatigue. All the others remained standing.

"I think I made myself pretty clear earlier today," she said to Zinski.

He merely observed her, and not warmly.

She continued. "I thought I would add a few things on top of what I said. Chester told me that you told him never to underestimate the obvious. I suggest you've been doing just that several times over."

Officers Thomas and Spence and cheerful Sid looked on with the keenest of interest.

"First, the 'screwing with the money' thing. If, as you thought, it was Chester, not Dennis, who screwed with the money, and if the hit man was going to know *before* he's going to do the hit on me that the money had been screwed with, why would he ever do the hit? If you were a hit man, Detective, would you go ahead with the hit?"

Zinski just folded his arms.

"No, you wouldn't. So, what would be the *point* of Chester screwing with the money if it meant the hit man wouldn't do the hit on me? *Pointless.* Right, Detective? Unless you just wanted to really upset a hit man. Which again would be *pointless.*"

Zinski's eyes blinked. Once.

"Now, number two, coming back to the neighbor next door, who happens to be, oh right, a *money launderer.* Never underestimate the obvious. But I know what you're going to say because you walked me through your thinking. The killer acted so amateurish. Well, maybe he was an amateur doing a personal revenge thing, not acting for the organization at all. Maybe Dennis ripped him off in some deal. And he's been watching Dennis for a few days, and he brings along a tie to deflect suspicion, and for more deflection, he wants to do Dennis in my cottage, not Dennis's. All you did, Detective, was speculate about how a killer would act, but that requires looking into the mind of a killer. Can you climb into the mind of a killer with confidence? Dicey place I'll bet."

Zinski unfolded his arms, then refolded them, changing which one was on the top. Cheerful Sid had to turn his back to conceal a smile.

"Okay, that was number two. Number three. A five-year-old daughter in the next room. Come on. Who'd ever believe Chester would set up a hit on mom with daughter right there? No, he'd take daughter for a drive into town and spend a couple of hours to be away from the event when it's happening. Ever heard of an alibi, Detective?"

Thomas and Spence turned to join Sid to study the wall behind them for a moment.

"Okay, that was number three. I'm forgetting number four. Oh, ya. And this one's a killer. Well you know what I mean, as far as you overlooking the obvious. Your theory is that Chester had come to hate me, driven by jealousy or whatever, and wanted me killed, because he believed I was two-timing or was going to leave him."

Zinski sucked in a large breath.

"So, not ten minutes after he had left to buy chips as I had asked, Chester finds me in the bedroom, 'half-naked', and finds Dennis in there too, very unexplained, although dead. Now, if seeing that isn't enough to rocket a jealous husband over the edge, I don't know what is, especially a husband who had already arranged to have me killed."

Zinski's gaze turned kind of steely but it didn't slow Candace down.

She continued. "Chester had just killed the killer, who you say was hired by Chester, who you think Chester was going to kill all along. That's a stretch. But here's the thing. If Chester wanted me dead, in his jealousy-on-steroids rage, it would have been just so easy. He just had to use the *killer's* gun to kill me, which pins my death on the killer, the way they do that in books and movies, wiping the gun clean after and then pressing the dead killer's prints all over it. Then Chester would tell the police that when he got to the bedroom and encountered the killer, he shot him, which he did, but sadly it was already too late because I was already dead. And you might say, 'well, Chester shooting his wife takes a lot more nerve than having someone else shoot his wife'. But as I told Detective Grant, and it will be on his little recorder, when I saw Chester coming down the hall, I must have fainted because I was out of things until Chester roused me to consciousness. He was on his knees, hugging me, soothing me, speaking into my ear, comforting me. Don't you see, he had every opportunity to just shoot me! I had fainted! Not too hard for a husband feverishly out of his mind with hate even before he saw me with Dennis in there, a husband who had already planned my murder to have me dead in the first place!"

Thomas and Spence struggled to conceal their enjoyment.

"So when I say you're underestimating the obvious, the obvious is me! I'm still here. Me. Alive! And twice over, this morning."

Zinski finally said, "Only yesterday I told these men that I thought you had smarts. I'm proven right, I see."

"Thank you, Detective. So, anyway, Chester and I have really had it with this vacation. We're going home now. Together."

Thomas and Spence couldn't keep a straight face. And cheerful Sid looked cheerful.

CHAPTER 43

They were on the highway going south to Ohio, going home, Candace driving.

The sky had darkened steadily in the first hour of the trip. They hadn't talked, Chester too tired, dozing off for long periods because of the drugs. But in his half slumber he had sometimes heard the windshield wipers slapping, heard the sound of water slick on the highway.

Now he awakened and saw the sky was clearing, the road drying.

"Sun's going to win out soon," he said.

"Ya, looks like it."

He yawned and looked over at her. "What a week we had, Candace."

"You can say that again. Not a holiday I ever want to repeat."

"Do you think anyone else would do for you what I did?"

She glanced to him. "The whole hit man set up thing?"

"Ya."

"I very seriously doubt it."

Chester nodded. He thought the same. "So, was it really special?"

She looked at him a moment, then back to the road. "Well, I suppose I would say more that it was really *something*. *Really* something. It was definitely that. Okay, special, too. Not that I'd recommend it."

He smiled at that. "No, I guess not. It was a damn lot of hard work, I can tell you. But like people say, you have to do that in relationships sometimes."

"That's hardly what they mean."

"It would have been a damn sight easier if you just liked poetry."

"No kidding."

"Actually, I did work on a poem for you one evening. Something of my own."

"Really?"

"Ya. But I know it's not really your thing."

She looked over at him and he could tell she was more than interested. He said, "What, you want to hear it?"

"Why not? The highway's kind of boring anyway." She smiled. "Just kidding, Chester. Of course, I want to hear it. Say your poem."

"Don't laugh. I've never done this before."

"Well, it's a week of firsts. Go ahead."

"Okay." He took in a breath. "Like the sun beams bright and gives warmth to things…like the rain falls to earth and gives life to things…your shine and your shower give warmth and life to me."

He didn't look at her. She was silent. After a few moments, he looked over. She was watching the road but he saw her eyes were watering.

"Say it again, Chester."

"Okay. Like the sun beams bright and gives warmth to things…like the rain falls to earth and gives life to things… your shine and your shower give warmth and life to me."

He looked and saw her eyes were now full of tears. "Are you okay, Candace?"

She reached and grabbed a tissue from the holder. She was sniffling now. "Sure. Just… nobody's ever done that for me before."

"Well, it's a week of firsts."

She looked over, the tissue still at her nose. "Thank you, Chester. Anyone ever tell you you're a real charmer?"

"Ya, you once."

"Did I?"

"Ya."

She sniffled and reorganized her tissue with one hand, her other hand on the wheel. "Well, it's true, you know. If you really want to know, you're a real charmer, a certified real charmer."

Chester felt like he had swallowed the sun, which was now full, dominating the sky, its light *clasping the earth*.